The Hast
Book 1 of the B

Sarah J. Waldock

©Sarah J. Waldock 2015&2021
All rights reserved, no copying of any portion of this book without permission, contact details under author biography.

ISBN-13 ISBN 978-1508567332

Dedication
Dedicated to my late mother, Margaret, who believed in me.
Thanks to all the people who helped retrieve enough data from the loss of computer and backup and to Kindle for retrieving what was uploaded for me to work on.

Historical notes
Other books by Sarah Waldock
See end of book

Sarah Waldock grew up in Suffolk and still resides there, in charge of a husband, and under the ownership of sundry cats. All Sarah's cats are rescue cats and many of them have special needs. They like to help her write and may be found engaging in such helpful pastimes as turning the screen display upside-down, or typing random messages in kittycode into her computer.

Sarah claims to be an artist who writes. Her degree is in art, and she got her best marks writing essays for it. She writes largely historical novels, in order to retain some hold on sanity in an increasingly insane world. There are some writers who claim to write because they have some control over their fictional worlds, but Sarah admits to being thoroughly bullied by her characters who do their own thing and often refuse to comply with her ideas. It makes life more interesting, and she enjoys the surprises they spring on her. Her characters' surprises are usually less messy [and much less noisy] than the surprises her cats spring.

Sarah has tried most of the crafts and avocations

which she mentions in her books, on the principle that it is easier to write about what you know. She does not ride horses, since the Good Lord in his mercy saw fit to invent Gottleib Daimler to save her from that experience; and she has not tried blacksmithing. She would like to wave cheerily at anyone in any security services who wonder about middle aged women who read up about gunpowder and poisonous plants.

Sarah would like to note that any typos remaining in the text after several betas, an editor and proofreader have been over it are caused by the well-known phenomenon of *cat-induced editing syndrome* from the help engendered by busy little bottoms on the keyboard.
This is her excuse and you are stuck with it.
And yes, there are two more cat bums on the edge of the picture as well as the 4 on her lap/chest

You may find out more about Sarah at her blog site, at:
http://sarahs-history-place.blogspot.co.uk/
Or on Facebook for advance news of writing
https://www.facebook.com/pages/Sarah-J-Waldock-Author/520919511296291
Or participate as a beta reader and get an advanced look at Sarah's work in draft form at
https://mywipwriting.blogspot.com/

Chapter 1

Edward Brandon shut the door with unnecessary vigour, stopping short of actually slamming it.

"She need not think that she can trifle with my affections like that!" he snarled. "I – by Jove, I'll marry the first woman who shows me a kindness without expectation of a reward!"

His groom wisely said nothing as Edward swung himself up into his phaeton and drove away, his bad mood strictly controlled so as not to upset the horses, but his face like thunder.

Miss Amelia Hazelgrove had just made it clear to her erstwhile suitor that she had no interest in a mere 'Mr' who no longer might be considered to have the expectation of inheriting a tidy little barony. He was probably no longer his uncle's heir, since his new aunt-by-marriage was rumoured to be in an interesting condition, his uncle having remarried relatively recently.

Edward, interrupted in the middle of a proposal to Miss Hazelgrove by her refusal, had stared, and upon being informed as to that damsel's reasons had demanded to know whether he meant anything to her but a means of social elevation. The Beauty had tossed her charmingly arranged head of black curls, pouted her exquisite and sultry lips, and informed him that the whole point of marriage was for the participants to be of use to each other. Heartbreak and anger warred in Edward's breast; anger won.

Edward found himself driving out towards Hampstead, and realised that he was going to visit his aunt, the Honourable Letitia Grey. Aunt Letty was always soothing. Edward laughed cynically. He was about to renege on the vow he had made, as he could scarcely marry his aunt. However, the vow had been made, and relatives did not, of course count. He adjusted his muffler against the chill of the March winds, now he had cooled down sufficiently from his anger to notice the surroundings. Edward gave the horses their head as he came out of London and into the country, after passing the toll-house at The Spaniard Inn. It was not far to his aunt's house from here, but he wanted the speed to wash through him, wash away some of the numb anger and agony. He was aware of his groom hanging on grimly and lifted a hand half in apology to him. Spencer was a good man and loyal, and was doubtless already working out that his master had been turned down, as Edward was not generally given to black moods or excessive speed, unless engaged in a race. And Edward preferred those races organised somewhere like a park, with circuits, rather than upon the public highway where one might discommode ordinary travellers or working carters.

He started to slow, preparing to turn off the highway onto the road to his aunt's house, just before Finchley. He slowed his team further with consummate skill just before he turned, as the herd of pigs swept round the bend. The youth in charge of them touched his forelock and as Edward indicated with his whip that he wished to turn off, skilfully shooed his herd to the other side of the road to accommodate Edward's passage. The forelock was fully pulled and a grin adorned the bucolic youth's face as Edward tossed a coin to him, from a selection he kept on the dash. Edward liked to be able to be ready to throw the correct change to tollgate keepers, and to have vails ready in case of need, without fumbling in his pocket, and had had a small box attached to the dash, to stop loose coins being readily thrown off by the motion of the carriage. He drove at a relatively sedate pace up to his aunt's pleasant Queen Anne house, larger than a cottage, but more modest than might be suggested by his aunt's comfortable income from her late husband's skilful investments.

Mrs. Grey's butler admitted him, taking his coat and murmuring that Mrs. Grey was abroad presently, but that there was a fire in the parlour. Edward was about to go through when he heard an exclamation, and noticed that his aunt's quiet young companion had come into the panelled hall, having been arranging flowers in the scullery. She put down the vase filled with ivy and a few windblown narcissi, height given by the white flowers of dogwood, and a few sprays of the yellow dogwood too.

"Why, Mr. Brandon, you look most unwell!" she said. "I will fetch you a nice posset right away; do please go and get warm by the fire, Aunt Letty is out presently, but will return soon."

Edward opened his mouth to say that he would prefer a whisky, but found himself bundled into a chair, and presently provided with a beverage which appeared to be generously endowed with alcohol. He sipped the sweet mixture appreciatively.

"Thank you, Miss, er, Renfield, I am not ill," he said. "Though, by Jove! It would be worth being ill for your posset."

"Gentlemen need building up," said Miss Renfield, demurely. "Excuse me, but you are, or were, quite white, and looked most unlike yourself."

"I had a shock," said Edward; and found himself telling her all about it. Elizabeth Renfield was a good listener; no wonder Aunt Letty found her soothing to have around, thought Edward. As he recalled she was a relative in some degree – which meant she was a distant relative of his too, he supposed – to his mother's family.

Miss Renfield was looking most concerned, which was

very flattering.

"Dear me!" she said. "How very cold blooded Miss Hazelgrove sounds! Of course, I am fortunate to have a good position with Aunt Letty, and she has told me I need not worry about the future, which is generous of her, so I am in a position to look scornfully on mercenary motives, and to marry purely for social advance seems quite as mercenary as marrying for money. And to be honest, if one is content, one is rich indeed, don't you think?"

"Miss Renfield, I confess I've never met anyone content before, so I have no idea," said Edward, "but it's a refreshing way to consider relative wealth. I suspect that in some ways you may be better off than many a duke with a fortune."

"I probably am," said Beth Renfield. "Are you feeling better for having talked about it?"

"Much," said Edward, "and thank you. Though I am still resolved to marry... Miss Renfield!" he said, suddenly struck by a thought, "It occurs to me that you are the first lady I have spoken to who has done me a kindness without considering any reward!"

Beth blushed.

"I suppose I am," she said, "but then, of course, I didn't think of it like that, because you needed someone to take care of you."

"Then, by Jove, you shall take care of me!" said Edward. "Miss Renfield, will you do me the honour of being my wife?"

Beth blushed even darker red.

"Are you sure you mean that?" she said.

"I do mean it," said Edward. "Unless your heart is already engaged by another?"

She shook her head, looking down at her hands. She wished in passing that her hands were not so short and inelegant.

"My heart belongs to nobody else," she said.

Beth, in fact, had been in love with Edward for as

long as she could remember after entering Mrs. Grey's household, straight out of school. This should have been a fairytale ending, and yet, he was only marrying her because that wretched Hazelgrove girl had turned him down, and she was available, and kind to him. Beth wished fervently that she could be unkind to Miss Hazelgrove.

"Then say you will?" said Edward.

"I should refuse such a precipitate offer and beg you to sleep on it," said Beth, who would not tie him to her on such terms.

"I will not change my mind," said Edward.

"Then providing you are still of the same mind in the morning, and delay any notice of engagement until you are quite certain, I agree," said Beth, recklessly. She might regret a marriage to someone she loved to distraction, and who had been no more than ordinarily polite to her up until now and scarcely knew she existed, but she was going to have him!

Edward was feeling extraordinarily light hearted by the time Aunt Letty returned. Beth withdrew tactfully.

"My dear boy! I thought you were on nuptial pursuit bent!" said his aunt, as she permitted him to kiss her in greeting. "I am surprised you have dragged yourself away from the Beauty to see me."

"I am on nuptial bent, and should probably have asked you first, but I purpose to marry Miss Renfield," said Edward.

Leticia Grey blinked as she assimilated this startling piece of information.

"Marry Beth? But you have never shown a partiality before," she said.

"No, well, I never talked to her long enough to realise she is a fine person," said Edward, uncomfortably, and quickly explained about his rash vow.

"And Beth knows it was for that reason you proposed?" asked Aunt Letty.

"Yes, of course," said Edward. "Anything else would be dishonest, would it not?"

Aunt Letty sighed.

"Yes, I suppose it would," she said, "And much more uncomfortable if she accepted and found out later that it was but a vow and not a partiality for her."

"You know, Aunt Letty," said Edward, "Although my heart is broken, of course, I actually *like* Miss Renfield more than I like Amelia. She's more restful, and you know, she's also a rare thing, a contented person. And Amelia's face got quite ugly when she was angry at me for not being an heir any more, whereas I suspect Miss Renfield will always have a beauty of serenity, in never looking a nasty old cat, even if she has no great claim to beauty."

"Her skin is better than Amelia Hazelgrove's, and she has a fine pair of eyes," said Aunt Letty, who had a better idea of the state of Beth's heart than Edward did.

"You are right!" said Edward, struck by this. "Well, a serene woman with fine eyes is a better catch than someone who collects a well-connected husband the way Elgin collected his blasted marbles. And doubtless as much life in her as a statue as well," he added, thoughtfully. Letty did not point out that he was mixing his metaphors here. Young men in a turmoil were not to be argued with; their ability to think logically temporarily left them.

If one might only make sure he got to know Beth well enough before the wedding – if he still planned to go through with it when he had cooled down – he would come to see what a lovely girl she was.

And then the trick would be in getting the clunch to admit to Beth that he loved her for her own sake, when he did, which with idiots and young men, though she repeated herself, was something he would be quite likely to forget to admit to.

Aunt Letty suggested that Edward should stay the night, so that all could think on the matter. If he changed his mind, well, less harm done if he did so quickly. He was man enough to tell Beth honestly. If he still purposed to go through with it, Beth should come out in society and the announcement of the engagement postponed until she had been given some Town Bronze.

Aunt Letty planned to make this announcement after breakfast; but decided to bring her suggestion forward after Beth had asked bluntly, as they met over breakfast,

"Are we still engaged, Mr. Brandon, or are you in a different state of mind this morning?"

"Whether I'm in a different state of mind or not – and I am quite recovered from the shock, thank you – I consider myself betrothed to you, Miss Renfield," said Edward.

"Then you had better call me 'Beth'," said Beth.

"And you had better call me 'Edward' and I shall see about inserting a notice in the *Gazette*," said Edward.

Letty cleared her throat at this point and made her suggestion that Beth should have a Season.

"But I don't need Town Bronze and I don't want a Season!" said Beth.

"It don't signify at all," said Edward. "Point of a Season is to meet people. Miss… Beth and I have met. No need of dancing and all that waste of time."

Letty sighed.

"Edward, have a little kindness for your bride, do," she said.

"Well she don't want a Season," he said. "Well seasoned if you ask me, and knows what to do with cinnamon and nutmeg," he smiled at Beth.

"I do trust that refers to my way with spices and seasoning and not likening me to well aged wine," said Beth, with a note of asperity.

"Jove, no!" said Edward. "I mean, you're out of the schoolroom, ain't you, but not hardly by much." Guessing the age of ladies was something Edward found difficult, so long as they were neither schoolgirls nor ape-leaders, and Beth was by no means old enough to be an ape-leader, he was sure. Her face was not that of a debutante, but she was not old enough for anyone to say she was on the shelf.

"I'm two and twenty," said Beth.

"A good age, I remember it well," said Edward. "At least, I think that was the age I was when I won every race I drove or rode. But Aunt Letty is looking daggers."

"If Beth has some time in Town, meeting people, it puts her less at a disadvantage when she is your lady wife, hosting any engagements you may wish to have, because she will know more people," explained Letty with great patience.

"By Jove, I hadn't thought of that," said Edward.

"Moreover," said Letty, tartly, "If you just send a notice to the paper now, it will seem as though you are marrying her on the rebound, which you are, of course, but there is no reason to be so discourteous to Beth as to say so to all the world."

Edward flushed.

"It was discourteous; I apologise, Beth."

"Do you wish to cry off?" asked Beth, levelly.

"No, by Jove, I do not!" said Edward. "And I can get to know you better whilst I do the pretty, and make it seem we are getting to know each other from the first."

"Quite so," said Letty.

It would also give them time to get to know each other well enough for Edward to find out if he really did not wish to be married to Beth. Letty prided herself on being able to read his moods. She had spent a lot of time watching him grow up, being a child when he was born, and when her beloved sister had died, Letty had been there for the then teenaged Edward. As something of a second mother to him, or perhaps a big sister, she knew him well enough. And Edward was fairly uncomplicated anyway.

Chapter 2

"Aunt Letty, you hate society, we don't have to do anything more than have a few dinners to meet Edward's friends, you know," said Beth.

"Nonsense, my dear; the world – the world which counts itself important, that is the *haut ton* – needs to meet you and see you, so that your betrothal does not seem so strange," said Letty. "And though I may not like society much, as a chaperone with the dowagers, I shall contrive to enjoy it much more than when I was a debutante, because I shall be permitted to make cutting comments if I want to, and I have no axe to grind. I neither need to attract beaux, nor do I need worry if you do or not, as you already have Edward. Of course if you should fall in love with anyone else, he will withdraw the offer, because he is nothing if not a gentleman."

"He is, and how could I meet anyone finer?" said Beth. "Oh Aunt Letty, I can't see you making cutting comments, you usually find something nice to say about most people."

Letty smiled primly, and decided to ignore the second comment. It was too true, though she would undoubtedly enjoy listening to the asides of others, if they were not too spiteful.

"I rather thought you were in love with Edward," said Letty. "However, it won't do him any harm for you to dance with other young men and show him that he might have competition. He needs to think of you as yourself, not an adjunct of mine who has attracted his attention by being there when he needs you this once. He needs to realise that he needs you all the time, and should not take you for granted."

"I should be happy to be his wife and help him, even if he does no more than respect me," said Beth. "I *do* love him, Aunt Letty, and I am happy to do whatever I can to make him happy."

"I daresay you would, but I want you to be happy too. You've been like a daughter to me, the last four years, and helped me cope with losing Grey when I had no children to console me."

"Did you meet Mr. Grey at a ball?" asked Beth. It had been a somehow taboo subject before.

"No, not at all; I was thrown from the curricle of a foolish young blade who was courting me, and whom I had thought to be dashing until he dashed faster than he could cope with, and Mr. Grey leaped from his own carriage, and dragged me away from all the wheels, begged my pardon for his rough handling, and then drove me home. Edward's parents were most dubious about it, mostly because he was fifteen years older than me, as well as his birth; but Grey, bless him, was quite unrepentant about having no *ton* at all, but he had friends in the diplomatic service, and a respectable fortune, so he was permitted to call on me. I had had enough of dashing young fools by then, and did not mind the age gap at all," she sighed. "I miss him still, but at least his fortune means we can cut a dash, as they say, and be quite fashionable. I must get some fashion magazines and employ a dressmaker. Last time I was fashionable the idea of the high waist and thin muslin was something quite new and the profile of the figure quite different to what it is now. A shame feathers never went out of fashion, though," she added. "They make me sneeze. Still, we shall manage well enough, and there are other confections for the head that do not involve feathers, if you will indulge me in that, my dear."

"Of course, Aunt Letty!" said Beth, warmly. "Feathers look better on birds anyway. Though thinking about fine fabrics is not something with which I have hitherto indulged myself, I confess the idea is not without some excitement," she added. "I have very little figure, though, and I fear I will look foolish."

"That's the point of picking only the fashions that suit, and not the ones that will emphasise any defects," said Letty. "We shall not dress you in a gown with a contrasting bodice, as it will show you up as short-waisted; a single colour all the way through will be more flattering. They are going out of fashion anyway I believe, not that I follow such things, but the *Morning Chronicle* does describe the fashions shown in *Ackermann's Repository*. Your arms are well shaped so we shall remove the attention from your hands, which hidden with gloves will seem longer anyway, with short or elbow length sleeves and puffs at the top, or ruches. And a high neckline also increases the length of body and adds an air of modest mystery. It will have to be low for a ballgown, but need not be as low as some wear, which will give you a better line. Especially if your corset fits properly."

"I am a little careless with remembering to tighten it when the ties stretch," confessed Beth. "And I never wear the busk in it at all; I need to bend."

"Well, there you are. We can get a maid to do it for you," said Letty, "And perhaps you can wear the busk for dancing. It does help the posture, you know."

"I do not need a maid," protested Beth. "It's not right that you should spend so much on me; I am only your mother's cousin's step-niece and plain into the bargain."

"And I'm fond of you, and I'm fond of Edward, and it's for him too," said Letty, gruffly. "And you are not plain. You have a most characterful face; lovely eyes, clear skin, and a direct gaze, for you are no simpering idiot. You are no beauty, but you will look very well indeed when your hair is not tortured back into that practical but most unflattering knot, and when you are dressed in colours that flatter you. And it is a good excuse for me to get you out of those depressing mourning clothes, and you will permit me to do so as you do not want to show me up in public, do you?"

"Aunt Letty, you are bullying me, but I would like pretty clothes," said Beth "It just seemed profligate when the mourning for Papa was still perfectly serviceable."

"Sometimes serviceable is a notion to be dispensed with," said Letty. "Black does you no favours; it makes you look washed out. Once we have you in blues, lavenders and even, I think, lemons we shall see your colour come out very well."

Beth heaved a happy sigh. It was foolishness, but foolishness could be fun.

The next few days passed in a whirl for Beth. Letty whisked her off to London, where they stayed in a hotel, which was, Letty said, more convenient than driving back and forth for several days running, and kinder to John Coachman and the bay mare. Beth was impressed by the grandeur of the hotel, and stayed very close to Letty, who was more than equal to acting *la grande dame* if she needed to. Beth was much impressed that someone who was capable of darning her own stockings could sound like the sort of person who left such mundane issues to the seventeenth under-maid or some such. She said so.

Letty laughed.

"Oh, Mama was a marquis' daughter, and we grew up not only capable of being starchy at need, but also capable of running a household. Mama was of the old school that believes that a lady cannot run a household if she is not capable of every task she may be called on to oversee, so I had a very thorough training, which my dear sister Emma continued. I can buy new stockings without counting the cost, but Mama had very strict ideas about profligacy, and so I darn once before throwing them away. Edward learned similar ideas at my sister's knee, and is a very good manager of his estates in Suffolk. You need not worry that he is profligate, or that he is incapable of soliciting attention from waiters and jarveys. Nothing so irritating as a man who cannot procure one a cab in the rain."

"No, indeed, I should think not," said Beth.

The first thing that Letty arranged was for a hairdresser to visit, to tut over Beth's straight brown hair.

"Perhaps Miss might consider a little darkening dye to her hair, to make it more fashionably dark?" suggested the hairdresser.

"No," said Beth. "It is the colour that it is, and if I once start acting a lie with it, I should be obliged to continue forever, though I see no point in doing to anyway."

"Miss should be aware that brunettes are held to be more beautiful than blondes at the moment, and certainly more so than any non-descript colour," said the hairdresser, severely.

"And you should be aware that I will not feel at all attractive if my hair is the wrong colour for me," said Beth, stubbornly. "And it won't curl. I've tried curling it in rags and it falls out within a couple of hours. It goes frizzy with a hot poker, but curls it will not do."

"That is unbelievable!" said the hairdresser.

"Nevertheless, it is a fact," said Beth. "Anything you can do with my hair must be done without expectation of curl."

"I had hoped to curl a fringe and set side ringlets, and a cluster of ringlets at the back," said the hairdresser.

"I'm afraid it isn't going to work," said Beth.

"Perhaps a wig or switches…" suggested the hairdresser.

"No," said Beth.

"When I was a girl, there was a fashion for some to cut their hair like the poor queen, Marie Antoinette, very short," said Letty. "It would soften your face,

Beth, to have short wisps, doing the same thing that ringlets do, in making the line less severe. What if Madame Lefevre were to do the front, and you can see if you would like the rest shortened?"

Beth regarded the hairdresser without trust.

"Why don't we cut it all off and see if it grows back curly like some people who have had a fever?" she said, brightly. The hairdresser threw up her hands in horror.

"*Quelle horreur*!" she cried, recalling that her horror should be expressed in French. The tones of Bermondsley were apparent.

"No sense of humour," said Beth. "Letty, if I brush some forward and make narrow plaits, and coil them back under a comb, and plait narrow plaits at the side, and draw them back loosely, it will still soften my face, without any, er, barber-osity to it."

"Beth, you have a wicked sense of humour," said Letty, reflecting that Beth had taken against Madame Lefevre.

"I am sorry, but I cannot help a touch of levity to improve my spirits," said Beth. "My hair may be of an unremarkable colour and incurably straight, but it is fine and long and it gleams when I bother to brush it enough, and I think that hair with highlights in it is more interesting than a flat dark brown, or common blonde."

"Well, well, it is your hair, and though it will grow again, I can see your desire not to lose it," said Letty. "I am sorry, Mme. Lefevre, to have brought you on a journey for nothing."

The hairdresser sniffed. The young lady was missish, and could not possibly know anything about her own hair!

Beth took more interest in a visit to haberdashers in Bond Street, where any and all kinds of cloth on bolts might be found; and permitted herself to be talked into the purchases of a selection of muslins, plain and embroidered, some cotton printed cloths for walking dresses, and sarsenets and lustring for undergowns to be made for ball gowns.

"I shan't need all these fabrics, surely?" Beth protested.

"You cannot be seen in the same costume twice," said Letty, firmly, "and we can be clever with what we have here to make over several gowns to appear quite different, by the use of different overgowns, different sleeves and different trim. With the addition of Vandyke d trim about the hem one day and scallops down the centre front another, and different collars, we shall contrive very nicely to make things different. And we shall get some nice warm Merino to make you spencers, all matching so that the colour is not broken at your waist. Then we may start with covered buttons, and braid, and then put military style frogging on, for with Bonaparte on the run, you may guarantee that military touches will be in favour."

"I bow to your superior knowledge, Aunt Letty," said Beth.

"Well, I'd worry if I thought you were permitting me to dictate to you, but I hear the laugh in your voice and take your acquiescence with a pinch of salt," said Letty. "You can make some silk flowers to alter the trim, too; your fingers are deft enough."

"Ridiculous, is it not," said Beth, half amused and half regretful, "That they be nimble without looking like it."

"Yes, well, that Beauty that Edward was sighing over looks fair on the outside and is rotten within, like an apple full of worms," said Letty. "I know a perfectly good seamstress who can make these up for you and we can return home while my man of business finds us a small house to rent. I have no plans to give great balls! A few musicales and rout parties will introduce you to the right people, and I know enough people in town to get you introduced to balls other people are prepared to give. Why should we go to the effort when others are ready and happy to do so?"

Beth laughed.

"You are certain we shall be invited," she said.

"Oh we shall be invited," said Letty. "Grey had a lot of contacts, and I have kept in touch with most of them. Many of them owed him a favour or two as well, and it would be a fine thing if they did not repay that with a small favour like an invitation. Of course the other guests are likely to be the serious side of the *ton*, being diplomats and the like, and doubtless a lot of diploming or whatever they call it with That Man on the run and retreating for Paris, but we can pretend not to understand what they are talking about."

"Why would we do that?" asked Beth.

"Oh, my dear, men never like women to understand politics," said Letty. "Edward fortunately is an exception, you can discuss what you please with him. He's not a half-baked widgeon like so many young men. My belief is that they don't like women discussing politics because they are afraid we might be better politicians than they are if permitted the chance."

Beth laughed.

"I should have thought there is very little difference, save in scale, between budgeting for a household and budgeting for the country, after all," she said.

"Precisely," said Letty. "And now, I do not know about you, my dear, but I am happy to return to the hotel for a cup of tea and a doze."

"I think I may forego the doze, but a cup of tea sounds heavenly," said Beth.

Chapter 3

Edward meanwhile had taken himself to visit his uncle. Adam Brandon, Lord Darsham, was the older brother of Edward's father, and had been a widower for more than twenty years, after his adored wife had died in childbed. Edward had very little recollection of his Aunt Lucy, but he remembered having to wear black for her death, and being told by Uncle Adam that he was his heir and would need to learn about the estates.

Edward did not resent not being the heir; he was glad his uncle had found love again, though he did wonder what Uncle Adam saw in Tiffany Pelham. Edward thought her a silly shallow piece, and had not been one of her suitors when she had emerged upon the *ton* a few years before.

"Ah, my boy!" said Adam, genially. "I hope you don't mind being cut out of the succession, I presume you have heard the rumours."

"Yes I have, and no, I don't," said Edward. "Happy to help the sprout in any way I can. Congratulations."

"Well, that is a little premature," said Adam, cautiously. "But thank you, anyway. Tiff doesn't come down for her meals, she feels very unwieldy, so I shall have to carry your best to her by proxy, as you might say."

Edward felt his eyebrows raise. It was scarcely seven months since the wedding.

"Quick work, Uncle Adam," he murmured.

"Yes," said Adam. "Now don't you go asking if I was premature with Tiff like Letty did."

"Letty has no tact," said Edward.

"No, and besides she was off the mark there," said Adam. "Behaved with perfect propriety towards Tiff."

"Naturally," said Edward.

Well, it was none of his business.

Actually, if Adam had not been previous in his relations with his wife, it might be Edward's business, but if Adam was happy with the baby, Edward felt that no questions need be asked, and with luck it might be a girl, and a second child have no question as to its parentage. Adam was as hale as a man half his age and might sire a quiverful of children on Tiffany, if she permitted it.

Somehow Edward did not see Tiffany permitting anything that ruined her figure.

As it happened, Tiffany was plainly curious enough to come down to see who was visiting; or else, as Edward thought cynically, was more likely, the servants had told her who had come and she wanted to gloat over cutting him out of the succession. Women were such odd creatures. Some of them seemed to take a positive delight in scoring points in some obscure game of their own devising, even over people who weren't playing, and it had been something he had observed in Tiffany before.

Adam was plainly besotted, and fussed round his lovely wife to get her seated comfortably at the table, thanking her for taking the effort for family. Tiffany fluttered her eyelashes winsomely at him, and Edward hoped he could eat dinner without wanting to be sick if she billed and coo'd quite so flagrantly throughout.

"Poor Edward, I'm afraid that your hopes of a barony are quite dashed," murmured Tiffany.

"Much I care; I'll help the little nipper all I can, but I'd as soon stick by my own lands," said Edward, cheerfully.

"Oh, you are good to put a brave face on it," said Tiffany.

"Not a bit of it," said Edward. "Ready to do m'duty for Uncle Adam, but just as happy not to have to. After all, you chose him over Lord Finchbury, didn't you?"

A flash of anger was startled into Tiffany's eyes.

"No, the Marquis and I would not have suited," she said.

Edward said nothing, but he smiled at her. Uncle Adam would not be upset by such a good-humoured expression, but Tiffany knew as if he had said out loud that Edward was reflecting that the Marquis had plainly failed to come up to scratch. Tiffany had been seen much with Evelyn, Lord Finchbury, despite warnings to her mother from other chaperones that the man had a nasty reputation as a rake.

"Well, well," said Edward, "I have to say I applaud your choice. Uncle Adam is, in my opinion, a better-looking specimen than Finchbury. Finchbury may be hardly any older than I am, but he looks much older than Uncle Adam. All that dissipation, I suppose. And though some people admire swart piratical men, dark hair does go grey quicker, and darker skins rapidly look coarse. We Brandons are all as blonde as butter and wear very well."

"I have no idea how well he might wear," snapped Tiffany. "I have no interest in Finchbury."

"No, very wise," said Edward. "A toast to your golden beauty, Lady Darsham, and to the next generation of Brandons!"

He could apologise with a handsome christening gift if the baby was as blond as any Brandon.

Adam happily joined the toast, and as Tiffany, looking unnerved, lapsed into silence, the conversation over the rest of the meal revolved around farming. Adam took Edward's advice and considered opinion seriously, and they bickered amicably about under-draining.

"I shall retire upstairs, so you gentlemen can linger as long as you wish over your brandy," said Tiffany, at the end of the meal.

"Are you all right, my petal?" asked Adam.

"A little tired, nothing serious" said

Tiffany.

"Well, well, my dear, I shan't linger long, and Edward don't stand on ceremony, and won't mind going off home so I can join you," said Adam.

Edward's jaw tightened as he surprised an expression of boredom on Tiffany's face at Adam's promise.

If only Adam was not so besotted with the wretched girl! He was going to get hurt, and that angered Edward.

Well, there was nothing he could do about it. Not at the moment, anyway. But if the baby was dark... well, he did not want to hurt Adam, if Adam accepted the child, but if Adam was in the least bit concerned, then he, Edward, would fight for a crim.con. suit. Not because he wanted the Darsham barony, but because he did not want a cuckoo in the nest to supplant a true Brandon; and because he did not want Tiffany to make a fool of the uncle he loved and respected.

As he rode to his own small manor house Edward reflected that Tiffany was as mercenary as Amelia. She wanted a title, and had settled for a baron when a marquis did not come up to scratch. It would probably help her to accept with equanimity that Uncle Adam was rather better blunted than Finchbury, whose pockets were always famously to let through gambling debts. Finchbury was after an heiress, and the modest thousand a year that was Tiffany's portion was not sufficient for his needs. Adam need not fear, however, that she would be left in penury if the wretched woman had married him as soon as she knew she was in the family way. And perhaps Adam knew. Edward reflected that it was a Brandon feature that honesty was likely to win their hearts, and if Tiffany had had the sense to throw herself on Adam's mercy and explain her predicament, he would likely have married her out of compassion.

Somehow, however, Edward doubted that Tiffany had either the sense or the honesty to do so.

He was glad of an almost full moon as he rode home, though it was often enough covered by scudding cloud, and a thin drizzle that was almost sleet started. Edward shivered. He hoped that Beth would not be too overcome by fashion to wear thin muslin sheer enough to leave the wearer's figure only too apparent. The risks of catching cold were considerable, in a cold spring following what many were saying was the coldest winter in living memory. He wondered if he should suggest a small house party at his manor instead, with Letty as the hostess. Still, it should be warmer in London; it always was. The proximity of so many people and their houses, all with fires burning, could not but have an effect on the surrounding atmosphere. And if it led to sooty fogs, well, that was the price to be paid. Beth and Letty were both practical people; they would not get carried away by any foolishness just to be fashionable.

Letty and Beth were in fact perusing fashion magazines and discussing this very matter.

"Morning gowns and promenade gowns seem to show high necks, and layers too, with full overgowns, even if in a matching jaconet muslin to the gown," said Letty. "The evening gown in the February issue there has a contrasting bodice and short sleeves, but who goes to balls in February? Well except maybe in Bath, where they have a welter of Little Seasons all year round, so far as I can gather."

"I expect they are also anticipating the Season beginning around Easter, and some people being in town a little earlier," said Beth. "And one must anticipate warmth in Spring, though it seems precious unlikely at the moment."

"I think we should plan for both warm and cold," said Letty. "As you are wearing high necks, you can wear a quilted petticoat with impunity, for it can be less padded above the waist so as not to spoil the line of the bodice. And as we are planning on several sleeves for each half-dress gown in any case, we might also plan on heavier, lined sleeves, and a selection of what they describe as a 'loose robe pelisse' and I would call a wrapper, but no matter what it is called, it is another layer. And if we make a lining as well, that can be quickly sewn in, or left out as seems appropriate. You will want short sleeves at balls, my dear, the vigour of the exercise will leave you too hot not to want to wear as little as possible whilst dancing, and a Norfolk silk shawl between dances."

"And a good heavy pelisse to come home in," said Beth.

"Indeed, and maybe a Russian cape over a pelisse too," said Letty. "We shall contrive to make you fashionable whilst keeping warm. And as we shall not be likely to finish all the sewing we need in time, we can always put some out to a seamstress."

"Thank you, Aunt Letty," said Beth, impulsively kissing the older woman on the cheek.

"I am wondering whether custom will finally dissolve this year for full dress," said Letty, "if it is indeed going to continue so cold into the Season."

"What custom is that?" asked Beth.

"Full dress has been short sleeved ever since we moved out of panniers," said Letty, "and though you will be glad enough of that for a ball gown, it might be uncomfortable for any other evening wear, visiting the opera, musicales or rout-parties for example, where you may be expected to sit still, and bare arms, even the small gap between sleeve and glove, would be intolerably cold. We shall have to find out whether any hostess objects to long sleeves beforehand, and then we may baste on whatever sleeve is appropriate."

"I did not know it was the custom not to have long sleeves; I am glad that you know how the *ton* goes on,

Aunt Letty; I might have made a horrible *faux pas* otherwise!"

"I shan't let you make any *faux pas*, my dear!" said Letty. "I was a wild, headstrong piece when I came out, so I know all the pitfalls. I'm sure you will not permit foolish young men to take you driving without a maid or groom, nor walk down Bond St with no male escort, nor run out at night into the street to look and see if the carriage of your escort has yet arrived, and find that you need to apply the end of your fan viciously in a place that deters most men."

Beth giggled.

"Aunt Letty, did that happen to you?"

"It did indeed," said Letty. "London is now installing gas lighting, which I am sure will soon spread to all the better streets, since Westminster Bridge was illuminated at the end of the year, which will make it safer than the oil lamps, for giving more light, though it still leaves many regions of shadow. Of course with oil lamps, anyone might be lurking, and this fellow took me for a lightskirt who had been ejected from some bawdy party, or so I now surmise, and decided to offer me his dubious protection. I left him emptying the last few brandies into the Area, which had me cursed to perdition, no doubt, by whoever had to clear it up in the morning. And that was why I turned down the beau I was waiting for."

"For being late?" asked Beth.

"Well, that did not endear him to me," admitted Letty, "but more because he arrived as I was using my fan and stood there wringing his hands saying 'oh dear, oh dear.' Bellamy – Edward's father – came out, and rang a peal over me for going out in the first place, and handed me my cloak, and told my escort to try not to lose me, which I thought a trifle unkind. And when the clunch tried to propose within minutes of having shown himself to be as much use as a sugar umbrella, I'm afraid I laughed at him. It is never polite to laugh at the fools who propose to you, however funny they may be," she added.

"No, ma'am," said Beth, not suppressing her own gurgle of mirth at the images conjured by Letty's tale! "I shall also endeavour not to make a target of myself by straying far from your side!"

"You're more sensible than I was," said Letty. "I learned sense, and Grey, bless him, said he liked me remaining just a little bit silly, for it made him feel protective. So I learned to be just silly enough for him," she sighed. "I am grown accustomed to being sensible, but I do sometimes miss being silly on purpose, just for my Grey."

Beth embraced her again. Letty was so dear!

Chapter 4

The house Letty's agent had found was rather on the edge of the fashionable part of London, being in Red Lion Square in Holborn. The neighbourhood had once been fashionable, but was declining. The buildings were not as elegant as some, but were well-built, and if a rather squat and ugly obelisk in the centre of the garden in the square marred its appearance, it was not too obtrusive. The square itself was longer in one aspect than the other, and was served by streets entering it on three sides, and footpaths at every corner. The stone watch houses at each corner were a comforting feature too, to discourage any lawless elements from disturbing the peace of the square.

"I am told by my agent that three regicides are supposed to be buried here, Oliver Cromwell, Ireton and Bradshaw, and that their ghosts walk," said Letty, gaily. "I told him that any spirits that walked were more likely to have come out of the decanters lately emptied by anyone who had seen them."

"I thought Cromwell was supposed to be buried in Westminster Abbey," said Beth.

"Of course he is, my dear; but since when has that stopped people making up Gothic stories for their own amusement and to scare others?" said Letty. "Somebody thought it a good story, and thus the story became legend."

"And sometimes good stories would be better for being forgotten, perhaps," said Beth. "Well, I am sure I shall not expect to meet Oliver Cromwell wafting insubstantially about the place; even if the story of his body being buried here were true, I am sure that so devout a man has better things to do in the afterlife than to trouble good Christians. And if he does, we must hold a musicale on a Sunday, and invite young men to sing some of the livelier songs they know to scare him away."

"Beth dear! Sometimes your levity gets the better of you!" Letty reproved. "Though I wager Edward would find it funny."

"I'll tell him when I see him next, then," said Beth. "I should like to cheer him up after his disappointment over Miss Hazelgrove."

"In my opinion he's well shut of her," said Letty.

The house was comfortable, and as well as furnishings it came with servants, which meant that apart from John Coachman, Letty's servants might be left undisturbed, to the great relief of the married couple and the cook who saw to most of her needs, even if the tween-floors maid regretted the excitement of the city. It may be recorded that she received a dressing down from the cook for daring to be such a little fool. Letty's angular and cynical dresser came of course, and unbent enough to offer her services to Beth until Beth might find a maid of her own. Beth was used to shifting for herself, but thanked Sowerby politely. With balls and routs and such to go to, having help with her clothes, and especially with her hair, would be useful. Brushing took such a time, and plaiting the little plaits. However, as the effect was quite as pretty as any ringlets, and more unusual, the time spent was worth it!.

The seamstress Letty had employed, one who made up her own gowns, had wrought wonders, and by the time they were settled into the narrow little house, deliveries were being made of promenade dresses and a rose-coloured velvet pelisse that brought out the slight colour in Beth's cheeks and looked very well over the white and lilac muslins she had chosen.

"There now, we must get some muslin in rose, or rose pink, and pale pink!" said Letty. "It suits you very well; I was not entirely sure how well it would do, but I confess myself satisfied, and though a shawl or Russian cloak over it would look very fine, it needs no such embellishment to knock back the colour. My dear, you have a very fortunate complexion."

"I suppose that makes up for my nondescript hair," said Beth, with irony.

She and Letty caught each other's eye and they both giggled.

"Mme. Lefevre came highly recommended," said Letty. "She may be a fake Frenchwoman, but I have heard she is reckoned to be very good with hair."

"She can be very good with the hair of those people who like to live a lie," said Beth. "Why, in the days of wigs, and all kinds of strange adjuncts to clothing, perhaps it was natural to be other than what nature intended, but in these enlightened days, even our corsets are only there to provide aid to posture, and to make the clothes lie flat. We do not need artificiality."

Letty smiled. Beth was still quite naïve.

And Edward would like her better that way.

Beth liked to believe herself to be cynical enough, but as yet had no idea how many of the people she would meet might be wearing hair pieces, or buckram assistance to various parts of their bodies, males more than females, but enhancement of bosoms could occur to some extent, so long as gowns were not worn too low cut. Make-up was not considered proper for debutantes but that did not mean it was not employed judiciously, and Cumberland corsets helped the waistline of those gentlemen who had rather more 'too, too solid flesh' than Hamlet had ever envisioned. With luck, Beth would not have to spend enough time in town for the subterfuges of those seeking marriage to become 'weary, stale, flat, and unprofitable' as the soliloquy said later.

The first event that was to be attended was an informal rout given by the Medlicott family.

"They're Cits, but very wealthy, and second generation so have a veneer of gentility," explained Letty. "Grey had some business dealings with Mr. Medlicott, so now that they are bringing out their daughter, they are happy to make acquaintance of someone who might introduce her to a better class of people than they might meet without the connections I have. I hope Miss Medlicott – her name is Elizabeth, too
– proves to be a convivial girl."

"So do I," said Beth. "But I shall be quite civil to her, even if I do not like her, or perhaps more because of it to cover any dislike. It is good of her parents to be ready to receive an unknown like me, on your recommendation."

The gossip on the lips of all of those at the rout was how Napoleon Bonaparte was besieged in Paris, and likely to surrender at any moment. Beth had been following the news in the Morning Chronicle, and was able to discourse intelligently on the subject. The effective hostess of the rout, Elizabeth Medlicott, said very little on the subject, and appeared quite unaffected by the news, but Beth surprised a look in her eyes that showed that she was following the debate keenly. The little flicker of contempt for the breathy woman who declared that it was all *too* thrilling and that she *just loved* military men in uniform was also interesting.

"I believe many of the military men were more interested throughout the campaign with having enough to eat and avoiding disease as well as bullets to take much notice of their uniforms," said a girl who had been speaking quite knowledgeably, her name, Beth recalled, was Abigail Meynell.

"Oh! Let us not speak of such horrid things!"

fluttered the breathy woman. Beth had not caught her name and had no desire to know her anyway. "The Militia look so much more splendid and gallant than some of the miserable looking creatures with ragged clothes who returned after the Peninsular campaign."

"Perhaps because the Militia don't do anything much to get dirty," said Beth. "They serve their country in guarding military places, but they are not the ones preventing Bonaparte from having ambitions to invade Britain and grind us under his heel as he has done to so many countries."

"Quite so!" said Miss Meynell.

"Well said, ladies," said the tall man in slightly faded regimentals. His arm was in a sling. "We don't complain about the hardships, because it is no more than duty, but we do like to be appreciated for our efforts."

"M.,,may I introduce Major the H…Honourable Charles Whittall," said Miss Medlicott. "M…Miss R…Renfield, Miss M..Meynell and M…Miss Tancred."

Beth smiled at Miss Medlicott warmly. A stutter would be enough to make anyone wish to avoid being ridiculed in public, and it must be galling to feel excluded from conversation thus.

Major Whittall bowed. He was a man in his late thirties, Beth thought, and well built, with an arrogant carriage of his head.

"Delighted," he said. "Whilst one does not, of course, expect ladies to understand the intricacies of military matters, which like politics is of course quite beyond your pretty heads, it is gratifying to know that some of you have minds above the set of the uniform."

Beth found herself sharing a look with Miss Medlicott of some derision over the Major's assumption that they could not understand politics, and was then startled that Miss Medlicott then looked suddenly stricken.

Miss Meynell seemed happy to engage the Major in conversation, so Beth slipped an arm into that of Miss Medlicott.

"What's wrong?" she asked.

"Oh, Miss Renfield, I...I am wondering if it is that you understand politics," she asked.

"As well as most men, I suspect and better than most women," said Beth. "Which is not to say that I claim to understand politics. And that is simply because I am not sufficiently interested to bother to learn more. Were I to wed a diplomat or a politician I should feel it behoved me to learn more. Aunt Letty's late husband was not a diplomat but he was on friendly terms with many who were, and I believe was quite an expert on politics, so she has taught me much."

"Oh, she was lucky to have a h...h....husband who did not mind," said Miss Medlicott. "I...I am t...taking such pains to make sure n...nobody finds out I am a bluestocking, b...but you seem not to m...mind!"

"I rather admire bluestockings, actually," said Beth, "though I cannot claim to be one. When I was small I had a rather muddled and discursive sort of education from my governess, and though I try to read widely, it is not the same as having been given a good broad education to begin with, for one does not know what to learn or where to start. And Letty had much the same kind of education. You have sensible and indulgent parents, Miss Medlicott."

"Oh p,,,please call me Elizabeth!" said Miss Medlicott. "You are Elizabeth too, are you not?"

"I answer to Beth, so we may be told easily apart," said Beth.

"Oh, th....that is splendid!" said Elizabeth. "My parents provided me with a m...most excellent governess, and I have so enjoyed learning! And st...still do, but you see, I am t...told that men do not like it, so I m...must hide my learning."

Beth sniffed.

31

"I can't think of anything worse than being married to a man who can't appreciate your talents," she said. "If I were you, I'd make no secret of it. You are, I collect, wealthy enough not to need to marry, so you can afford to wait until the right man who will enjoy your talents comes along."

Elizabeth brightened.

"D...do you think so? Th...then I will, and Miss Percy m...may go to perdition!"

"Miss Percy?"

"M...my parents hired her to help me make my come-out by telling me how to go on, because she is a lady, if impoverished, and I can't stand her," admitted Elizabeth. "She's arch, and very acidulated and treats me as though I am an idiot child, and totally beneath her."

"Well, if you ask me, you seem to know how to go on perfectly well, and if you have any queries, you may ask your friends," said Beth. "We are going to be friends, aren't we? Aunt Letty will always advise you, and she's the daughter of a Baronet and has an honourable to her name, if she cares to use it, so I think she ought to know anything that needs to be known. I am sorry this Miss Percy needs to seek employment, but she ought to be a little more careful in her manner. If she treats you as though you are beneath her, she's not got the instincts of a lady," said Beth. "I suggest you ask your parents to dispense with her services."

"I will!" said Elizabeth. "And I cannot see I can do better than copy you or Abigail – Miss Meynell! She is a friend of mine too. She was left enough for a season by her godmother, you see, as she is the eldest child of a long family, and she hopes to marry well enough to help with the younger ones, the cost of the season being an investment."

Beth nodded.

"Yes, one can only stretch a legacy so far, if it is just enough for a season," she said.

"Abigail is clever, though I do not find her an entirely kindred spirit," confessed Elizabeth. "I want to promote her chances of course! But she has been careful to read the right books to be able to enter into conversation, rather than because she has chosen them for enjoyment."

"Dear me!" said Beth. "It sounds quite calculating, but then if I had a host of younger siblings, I suspect I should be prepared to be quite calculating to see them provided for. Is she then an orphan?"

"Oh, no! She is the daughter of the manse in our home village, and she is coming out with me, which is all the favour her father would permit, my mother's chaperonage, though I can give her the odd gown claiming to have bought it and then not liked it."

"That is clever and kind," said Beth. "If you don't mind me mentioning it, you don't stutter when you are relaxed."

Elizabeth gave a wry smile.

"No, I don't," she said, "But society s...scares me."

"You should not let it!" said Beth. "Why, you are one of the luckiest girls alive; you have two parents living, who love you, and you have enough money not to have to worry about being anyone's governess, or companion or anything, and you have an education that allows you to enjoy reading anything you choose. You are also extremely pretty and very stylish, and if you weren't such a nice girl, I'd have to hate you a little bit for having so much that's enviable."

Elizabeth laughed, for Beth had put it in a droll manner, and there was no offence in her words.

"Well, I will try to think of how l...lucky I am when I f...feel nervous," she said. "And when I get to know people, I do not stutter at all when talking to them!"

"Why, then, you should remember that there are no such things as strangers, only friends you have not met yet!" said Beth, gaily.

The rout being informal there were no calls for anyone to perform musically, nor any dancing. The gentlemen and dowagers were accommodated with a card room, and the rest of the company might chat, or play such childish games as Lottery Tickets that might take their fancy, to break the ice; and Beth persuaded Elizabeth to join a game with her.

They had a lot of fun, and Beth declared the evening 'most enjoyable' as she drove home with Letty.

She had made her first entry into the *ton*.

Chapter 5

Edward came to call before any further social engagements, and Beth entertained him with her suggestions of how to rout Oliver Cromwell's ghost should it come calling. Edward roared with laughter.

"I think that would shock him into gobbling incoherence, if not drive him back to his grave," he said. "But what do you know of lively songs, Beth?"

"Nothing beyond the hearsay that they exist, I'm afraid," said Beth. "And that only because I once heard you upbraid John Coachman for singing something that ladies in the house should not hear. I had not caught the words in any case, but it was a jolly tune."

Edward blushed.

"As well you did not catch the words!" he said. "And I fear that such songs do often have rather lively tunes too, and a shame that the catches and glees suitable for ladies to sing or listen to at musicales so often sound as though they are dirges."

"I cannot really pass judgement, not having heard any yet," said Beth, "though I fancy some of the effect may be caused by an excess of sensibility and an unwillingness to be too gay in front of everyone. I am not, myself, sufficiently accomplished to play and sing, though I am a sufficiently competent pianist to play accompaniments, I think."

"Thank goodness!" said Edward, with heartfelt relief. "Of course, I'd listen and applaud, but there's nothing much more tedious than having to pretend to enjoy the efforts of young ladies whose mamas think them far more accomplished than they are, and encourage their daughters to think so too!"

Beth laughed.

"You will not need to practise hypocrisy with me, Edward," she said. "And I will not bore you with recitals."

"No, waste of time when we could be discussing things like silly ghost stories," said Edward. "There's a lot of daft folklore to be found if you go looking. Most of which, I swear, has been made up as a hum by someone, the same as we did at school."

"Oh do tell!" said Beth.

Edward chuckled.

"Three of us managed to convince the wife of the new senior master that the school was haunted, and we even fixed up an apparition of a tall figure, taller than any of the boys, filmy and white, that whisked round a corner and disappeared."

"How did you manage that?"

"I put a sheet over a broom which I held over my head, and round the corner I shoved the broom out of the window onto the conservatory roof, poked the sheet behind the curtains, climbed out of the window, and shinned up a drainpipe. Nobody thinks of looking *up,*" he added.

"You were naughty!" giggled Beth. "I hope the poor woman wasn't too frightened?"

"We didn't care much; she was mean," said Edward. "Lud, how we all laughed! And we never got found out, so as far as I know, the story of the doleful lady is still circulating."

"I wish I knew if it was," said Beth. "Ah well! Perhaps your sons will tell you."

"Our sons," said Edward. Beth flushed. "Will you like more than one?" he added.

"You and I are both only children," said Beth. "I think that it would have been jolly to have had siblings, don't you?"

"Yes, rather!" said Edward. "Having Letty just ten years older than me was almost like having a big sister, but it would have been nice to have had someone closer in age. And I apologise for putting you to the blush."

"Oh, please do not regard it," said Beth. "I am not

entirely cognizant with the process of that side of marriage, but one does not live in the countryside without making a few shrewd guesses, which means it is my indelicate prurience which caused my blushes, not you."

"What a splendidly honest girl you are, Beth, without even saying anything improper!" said Edward. "And now I am blushing also."

"I am sorry to put you to the blush, Edward," said Beth.

"Well, I think it is a subject we should not be discussing," said Edward. "Lud, how did we get onto it?"

"Asking your non-existent sons about ghost stories," said Beth.

"Oh yes, of course!" said Edward. "I say, may I escort you to the musicale tonight? Letty said you had invitations, and that your friend Miss Medlicott is also going. Doesn't sound like the name of someone quite of the gentry to me, but then, times change."

"Miss Medlicott's grandfather made a fortune importing Indian fabrics and saw when the time was right to set up a cotton factory," said Beth, who had been told this by Elizabeth. "Elizabeth – Miss Medlicott – is a perfectly ladylike girl, and oh, Edward, I know you will be nice to her, for the poor girl stutters in company!"

"Deuced awkward," said Edward. "One of my friends at school stuttered, and some of the chaps would rag him, until we doused his worst tormentor in ice water in mid winter, so he was duddering with cold, and couldn't form a sentence without shivering, and asked him how he liked stuttering. No more problems."

"Ah, Edward, that was a clever way to help your friend!" said Beth. "Did he get over it?"

"Yes, we made him declaim poetry and Shakespeare until he could do it without a pause. He went on to fund several troupes of players, and to take part in amateur dramatics," said Edward. "Clever chap, his hobby was ballooning, even when we were young. Burned a hole in the floor when his vitriol burned through the bottom of the kettle he'd put it in with iron filings to make hydrogen gas to fill a balloon. We were well whacked for that, for of course we wouldn't let him take the blame on his own."

"It sounds very dangerous," said Beth.

"Well, less so if it's done in a safer vessel than an old kettle," said Edward. "He's made several ascents, without too much mishap."

Beth laughed.

"I like the way you say 'without *too* much mishap," she said. "Presumably he has suffered some problems?"

"Well, the hydrogen went on fire once, when he passed over a factory, and some stray spark set it off; but fortunately he was sufficiently close to the ground, and there was a lake too, and he dived out of the basket as the burning of the gas brought the balloon closer to ground level, and suffered nothing worse than a wetting," said Edward. "Then there was the time he was in a hot air balloon and some idiot of a drunken parson shot the balloon, thinking it was the devil, and he fetched up in a gorse bush. Nothing serious, you see."

"Oh, no indeed," said Beth, manfully managing not to laugh.

"Well, enough of my clever, idiot friend," said Edward, "I'll be picking you up tonight, and don't you go bringing Mr. Cromwell."

Beth laughed.

"I somehow doubt he'd enjoy it," she said.

"Well, I tell you what," said Edward, "maybe I can persuade one of my other aunts to hold a fancy dress ball, and I'll come as Cromwell if you come as Queen Henrietta Maria."

Beth laughed.

"That might be fun," she said. "But I'll not start devising any costume unless such a ball occurs!"

"My daughter Madelaine is of course very accomplished, and will be delighted to play the pianoforte," said the large and overpowering woman to the hostess of the Musicale, Juliana, Countess of Eversleigh. The Countess was launching her own daughter, the Lady Cressida Stonhouse. It seemed that the Earl had been a close friend of Mr. Grey, hence the invitations to both Beth and her less well-connected friends Elizabeth and Abigail.

The Countess gave the pushy mother a look of disapprobation.

"If Madelaine wishes to perform, of course she shall do so, Mrs. Vardy," she said.

"Oh please, mother, must I?" the tall, gawkly girl looked horrified.

"Of course you must!" said Mrs. Vardy, sharply. "You do wish to show off your accomplishments, don't you? If you do not, I shall wonder why we paid to have you taught to play."

"I did not ask for lessons," muttered the girl. She was more than a girl, not, Beth thought, as old as she, but not straight out of the schoolroom as Elizabeth was. Abigail was older too, and so was Lady Cressida.

"The Vardys are distantly related to the Stonhouse family," Edward murmured to Beth. "And how it galls Lady Juliana that the Stonhouse family are severely penny-pinched, and the Vardys are wealthy and yet really rather vulgar. Mrs. Vardy's father was in trade, and Vardy was strongly attracted to her dowry, though by all accounts she was attractive when she was young."

"Madelaine would be quite pretty if she didn't look so miserable," said Beth. "Poor girl! I suppose her mother is hoping to find her a titled husband."

"Undoubtedly," said Edward. "Lady Cressida just wants a wealthy one, who also meets her criteria of what is suitable; and that's why at twenty she's still unwed. Those who are gentleman enough to please her are generally poor, and those who are wealthy generally fail to please her. I doubt the Earl can afford to give her another Season after this one; it's her third."

Beth looked curiously at Lady Cressida; the girl had attractive, even features, thick, dark brown hair that may have owed the curls of its ringlets to art, but which at least looked natural, and pansy brown eyes. She would have been quite lovely were not her eyebrows just a little heavy for beauty, and set in what was almost a scowl. It could not be easy, thought Beth, to have to be the sacrificial lamb, to be sold into marriage to bring the family fortunes about.

"Beth, I've been asked for an introduction to you by two young men," said Letty, coming over. "Miss Renfield; allow me to introduce Mr. Archibald Dansey, and Mr. Brook Chetwode."

The two young gentlemen could not look more different.

Beth blinked in surprise to see Mr. Dansey, who looked as though he should be on display made of marble. He had the features of a young Greek god, with curly golden hair and perfect proportions. The only thing that gave such apparent perfection a note of reality and humanity was the pugnacious set to his chin, and a twinkle in his eye to offset the air of determination. His evening coat was just a little worn at the elbows and cuffs, but he wore it with an air of defiance. Mr. Chetwode, on the other hand, was pleasantly ugly, tall, loose-limbed and though his clothing was of impeccable taste and quality, it seemed to be in danger of wrinkling. His brown hair was unruly, his nose too big for his face, and a nasty case of acne, but his eyes smiled happily on the world.

"Delighted to make your acquaintance," said Mr.

Chetwode, in an unexpectedly soft voice.

"Likewise," said Mr. Dansey, as though he half expected to have to fight someone for enjoying the introduction.

"I am pleased to meet you both," said Beth. "Will either of you be performing any musical feats for our delectation?"

Both young men went rather red.

"Absolutely not!" said Mr. Dansey.

"Only if anyone finds out that I have learned to play the piano, and I'm sure I can trust you to stay silent on the subject, ma'am!" said Mr. Chetwode. "Unless you play, and are looking for someone to perform a duet with," he added, hastily.

"I only play well enough to accompany others or for dancing," said Beth. "My musical talents are indifferent to say the least."

"How nice to hear, a lady who is not so fond of herself that she puts herself forward," said Mr. Dansey.

"And I am fortunate that I am not pushed, either, like poor Miss Vardy," said Beth.

Mr. Dansey rolled his eyes.

"Her mother is a harridan!" he said. "I am fortunate to be no catch at all, being penniless, so I am not one of her targets, unlike poor Brook, here!"

"Poor Miss Vardy," said Brook Chetwode.

A tinkling bell announced that the Countess wished to address all present.

"We shall open with a pianoforte recital by Miss Vardy," she said. "Please take your places!"

Poor Miss Vardy, looking stricken, clutched her music and stumbled forwards towards the grand piano, catching her foot in the over-long flounce of her gown as she did so, and falling, breaking her fall on the piano stool as the sound of ripping announced that she had torn the gown.

"Oh poor girl," said Beth, as Miss Vardy managed to get to her feet, red faced as most of those present tittered, and fleeing for the door. Beth turned urgently to Edward. "Do stop her mother from coming out! I'll go and see if I can help her!"

Edward nodded, and moved smoothly to intercept the furious Mrs. Vardy.

Beth followed the girl to the cloakroom.

"I have my sewing kit in my reticule, Miss Vardy, may I help you mend your gown?" she said.

Miss Vardy sobbed.

"Oh, Mother will be so angry with me!" she said. "But I am so nervous in front of people, and I don't know where my hands and feet are at all!"

"Oh, but how lucky you are to be so tall, and if you will only learn to enjoy your height, not bend forward and try to hide it, you will not fall over so much!" said Beth, getting out her huswife and threading a needle rapidly.

"Mother says I am too tall, and what a shame it is," said Miss Vardy, dolefully.

"You're no taller than she is," said Beth, tartly. "You must not let yourself be cast down by criticism, for there is nothing so lowering as having only faults shown! You need someone to tell you what's right with you, and I would love to have your inches and slender figure, my dear girl, because I don't need anyone to tell me I'm short and a bit dumpy."

"Oh, but what lovely kind eyes you have!" said Miss Vardy. "I wish I was short, I could hide better! And I might not lose track of where my feet are, too."

Beth wished she could give Mrs. Vardy a piece of her mind, but it would not do at all. And that bustling female came in at that moment, Edward presumably unable to delay her any longer.

"Madelaine! You naughty girl!" she began, and caught sight of Beth, kneeling on the floor sewing up the flounce. "You, girl, get out," she said.

Beth turned, and raked her with a look from head to foot, copying as best she might Letty being a *grande dame*, anger alone giving her the courage to do so.

"I beg your pardon, were you by any chance addressing *me* in so rude a tone?" she asked, icily.

Mrs. Vardy had the grace to flush.

"I ... I beg your pardon. I assumed you were a servant, assisting my daughter," she said, assessing Beth's evening garb.

"Indeed?" said Beth. "Such things should be matters for friends, not servants. Madelaine, I am sure you will want to compose yourself, I will send a servant in with a glass of wine."

"Thank you.... Beth," said Madelaine as Beth mouthed her name to her.

A servant interrupting would prevent her mother from ringing quite such a peal over her; how kind this Beth was!

Beth arose, dropped a slight curtsey to Mrs. Vardy, who failed to notice the ironic way in which she did it, and swept out.

Beth was as good as her word in finding a servant to take a glass of wine to Madelaine Vardy, and then slipped back into the music room where Lady Cressida was providing a very accomplished performance of something that sounded very complicated. She found Elizabeth and Abigail sitting together and went to them. As the applause started, she said,

"I wish the two of you, one at a time, will find an excuse to go to the dressing room so that awful Vardy woman cannot conveniently upbraid her poor daughter!"

"C...certainly!" said Elizabeth. "Oh h... how I f...felt for her! B...but I saw you go, so I knew she would be in g...good hands!"

"I will go now, for I am to play after Lady Cressida's encore on harp, and it can be accounted nerves," said Abigail Meynell. "Dear me, what a dragon that woman is!"

She slipped out, and Beth heaved a sigh of relief. It

would not stop poor Madelaine from being bullied at home, but at least she would know she had support. And it was nice to be able to sit down and listen to Lady Cressida, who really was very good.

Chapter 6

Abigail was called upon next, and gave a creditable performance of some airs by Haydn on the harp-lute. It was a pretty sound, but Beth thought it a waste of time to learn an instrument which might only be played in public by a lady who was unwed; if Abigail did attract the wealthy husband she hoped for, she would not be able to play at any gatherings she hosted, even for dancing, for the etiquette of the instrument was very strict. It was accounted far too romantic and appealing an instrument for any woman to play in mixed company once she was married, for it would be tantamount to flirting! However, Beth applauded, for Abigail was plainly quite skilled on the instrument. Elizabeth slid out after listening to her friend, to see how the unfortunate Madelaine Vardy was doing, and managed to firmly take her by the arm and lead her back into the music room.

"Rescued from durance vile!" laughed Beth. "Sit with us, Madelaine, and if you wish to play, one of us will let Lady Juliana know, and if you do not, your mother cannot make you if you sit in the middle."

"Why are you all so kind to me?" asked Madelaine.

"B…because I s…st…stutter," said Elizabeth.

"Because my mother is a sweet person who would hate to upset any of us," said Abigail.

"Because I feel a little lost in society too," said Beth. "And I have been so lucky in having someone lovely like Aunt Letty to live with, who loves me, and that makes me wish for other people to be happy too!"

"My mother does love me, but she finds me so very exasperating," said Madelaine. "She has waited as long as she thought reasonable before bringing me out, in the hopes that I might have outgrown being clumsy and awkward, but I am still just as bad as ever, or worse!" her eyes filled with tears.

"It is the s...same as m...my stutter!" said Elizabeth. "The m...more I th...think about it, the w...worse it is!"

"I will teach you the language of the fan, if you like," said Abigail. "I learned it in case I needed it, and it means you can have a fan in your hands and send silly messages by playing with it, which will stop you worrying where your hands and feet are. I did that when I had a growing spurt, not playing with a fan, but I took up knitting, so I had my needles everywhere with me, but that will not answer at a ball."

Madelaine managed a chuckle at that.

Somebody, meanwhile, had evidently let out the secret that Mr. Chetwode knew how to play, and the Countess called upon him to perform in a tone that brooked no refusal, hushing the chatter between performances. Mr. Chetwode made a comic face to his friend, and shambled up to the pianoforte, looking rather like a spider running along the wainscoting. Lady Cressida stared in some disgust as the loose-limbed, untidy young man sat himself down.

Lady Cressida's stance and face changed within moments of Mr. Chetwode's opening bars, as it became apparent that he was really very good. Indeed his skill surpassed any but Lady Cressida herself, and he played too with great feeling. Beth watched Cressida's face with as much enjoyment as she listened to the music, as expressions of pleasure, then a war between amusement and horror, crept over her face as Mr. Chetwode, who was playing without music, ran smoothly for several bars from a piece by Handel to Gay's 'Beggar's Opera' and back again. The smoothness of the transition meant that very few people even realised the impudent insertion!

Cressida went over to talk to Mr. Chetwode when he had finished, and he gave her the most impudent smile when she appeared to be scolding him. Mr. Dansey approached the girls.

"Brook is in trouble with Her Icicleship I see," he said cheerfully.

"What else might he expect for inserting several stanzas of 'Fill every glass' into the 'Arrival of the Queen of Sheba'? said Beth.

Mr. Dansey chuckled.

"I bet him nobody would notice," he said. "Well, I've lost the bet, but worth it to see Lady Frosty sit up and take notice."

"Poor Lady Cressida, she is so plainly truly musical," said Abigail, "and to sit through the performances of those of us who are less so must be acutely painful. Her mother has no musical feeling at all, she sits tapping her foot not quite in time to the music, with an expression on her face that is meant to be rapt enjoyment and looks more as though she... forgot what I was going to say," she added in a hurry.

"Abigail!" said Elizabeth.

"It comes of having younger brothers," said Abigail, blushing.

"Lady Cressida would know about that," said Madelaine. "I wonder if poor Lucien will be brought out to make a harp recital?"

"Oh, how old is he?" asked Abigail.

"Sixteen," said Madelaine. "Mother would like me to marry him, to rejoin our families together; she is certain that Uncle James and Aunt Juliana would leap at the chance to keep our family money in the family, but I doubt Uncle James would think much of his son marrying someone four years older than himself."

"No, indeed, from that age it is, I fear, positively ancient," said Abigail. "I am almost twenty myself, and my brother Daniel thinks me quite middle aged. He is sixteen, too. But he is at university at the moment, of course."

"Oh, I think Lucien is not going up until next year, though I am not sure," said Madelaine. "Our families are not close! But Uncle James, who is really a cousin, is civil to my father, and kind enough to insist that as connections, mother and I must attend any functions here."

A slender youth who had an odd gleam in his eye, and firm set to his mouth, was being brought into the room by a man who was unmistakeably his tutor. Introduced by the Countess as her son, Lucien, the youth sat down at the harp. The strings sounded the introduction of a familiar nursery rhyme, 'There was an old woman lived under a hill' and the youth began to sing in a pure angelic voice.

The words were, apart from the first line, however, entirely unfamiliar and as the old woman and her daughter sold beer, and gave lodgings to a soldier and his nag, looked to be anything but as angelic as the young voice.

The song was cut short by the tutor who boxed the young musician's ears hard.

"Go to your room," that worthy said, and bowed to the room. "My apologies, ladies and gentlemen," he said, in fury. The gentlemen, for the most part were laughing, and the ladies looked, on the whole, quite bewildered, including the Countess.

"Mr. Abingdon, what is wrong?" she asked. "I thought Lucien was playing particularly well, and he was on fine voice."

"Yes, my lady, and his clear voice would have continued with lyrics *not* suitable for the ears of ladies," said Mr. Abingdon. "I do apologise. I knew the devil was in him when he was so docile about coming to play.
I will make sure he recognises the error of his ways."

"Oh!" said Lady Juliana, blankly.

"Is it very bad?" Beth asked Edward who had come to join her knot of friends.

"*Worse* than bad," Edward assured her.

"Dear me, I do hope he does not get punished too harshly for rebelling so," said Beth.

"I have no doubt he will take whatever is given with philosophy for making sure he is never asked to play again," said Edward. "Young limb!"

"Daniel would do something similar, I am sure," said Abigail. "Dear me, boys will be boys!"

Lady Cressida had gone over to the harp to play the sad ballad 'the Grenadier and his lady' to fill in the awkward silence. Her singing voice was pretty enough if a little weak, and she was applauded as much in relief as in pleasure at her excellent playing.

The incident was mostly forgotten as other performers gave more, or often, less, virtuoso performances.

"Do we have someone who would be prepared to accompany 'The Banks of Doon'?" asked the Countess.

Beth pulled a face to herself, and stood.

"I know it, My Lady," she said. "I am no great pianist, but I can accompany."

The gentleman who was to sing was an older man, perhaps in his forties, who bowed as Lady Juliana introduced him.

"Lord Leomer Bysby," she said. "Miss, er, Renfield, thank you."

Beth curtseyed.

"My pleasure," she said.

Lord Leomer was a handsome man, in what Beth thought was a slightly rakish sort of way, and reflected how hard it was to define that. He had a devil-may-care look in his eyes, and she had seen him laughing freely over the choice of song of Lord Lucien. She hoped he would stick to the original words of 'The Banks of Doon', which albeit in quite incomprehensible Scots were at least a love song and nothing questionable.

Lord Leomer had a pleasant, rich baritone voice, and the song was much applauded. Beth went to sit down, only to find that Mrs. Vardy had taken her seat, and was hissing to poor Madelaine that if only she had volunteered to accompany him, she might have had a chance to wed the younger son of a marquis.

"But he's *old*," said Madelaine. "Why would I want to marry someone as old as that?"

"He is not old!" said Mrs. Vardy. "Why, he is younger than I am!"

"Excuse me," said Beth, coldly, "I believe that is my seat."

Mrs. Vardy flushed, and eased herself up.

"Come, Madelaine, and sit with me," she said.

Madelaine cast a miserable look at the other girls and obediently followed her mother.

"We are all very lucky," said Abigail, soberly.

"St…stutters and all," agreed Elizabeth.

Fortunately supper was announced at this point, and Beth found herself being taken in to supper by Edward. Elizabeth was on the arm of Mr. Dansey, and Abigail with Mr. Chetwode. Lady Cressida went in to supper with Lord Leomer, being the man who took the highest social precedence at the gathering next to the Earl and Countess.

After supper, the evening was largely over, a few musical spirits choosing to strum informally at pianoforte or harp, and Edward frowned as a hearty 'push him in by the head, pull him out by the tail' erupted from a group of young gentlemen who evidently knew more of the words of the song Lucien was not permitted to sing.

"Excuse me," he said, and strode over to give them a piece of his mind.

The young enthusiasts subsided.

"Edward, what is so improper in it?" asked Beth, on the way home.

"Dear me!" said Edward. "It is all in metaphors, but it is… quite carnal, you know!"

"Too carnal to sing to us, Edward?" asked Letty, chuckling.

"Most certainly!" said Edward.

"Perhaps you can explain when we are married, and then I may pass it on to Aunt Letty to spare your blushes," said Beth. "And describe the metaphors."

Edward made a strangled noise beside her in the carriage.

"I am glad it is dark in here to preserve my countenance," he said. The idea of demonstrating the metaphors to a girl who would not shriek in horror was really rather too much for his equanimity! "You must not say anything like that in public!" he admonished.

"Why of course not, Edward!" said Beth, "but we are both quite comfortable with you, and feel that we can say quite anything!"

"So long as you don't forget and say quite anything when there are others listening," said Edward.

Beth chuckled.

"I shall try not to," she said.

Edward was glad when the carriage reached Red Lion Square, and he was able to hand the ladies down and see them into their hired house, still much under the cover of darkness. Then he might be alone with his own thoughts, and the surprising concept that being married to Beth might be more than just comfortable, it might actually be quite entertaining! If, of course, Beth did not find someone she preferred. Those two young men had been quite attentive to the group of ladies, and Lord Leomer had seemed admiring too. Edward scowled. It really wasn't fair to Beth not to let her have a choice, after having rather bludgeoned her into accepting his proposal. He must stand back.

Chapter 7

Letty and Beth continued to eagerly follow the progress of the war in France in the newspapers, marvelling that Napoleon Bonaparte had made his own people so sickened by war that no hindrance was placed in the way of the advancing armies of Wellington, Blucher and Prince Schwarzenberg.

"Listen to this," said Letty, " The paper says, *'The Plymouth Telegraph announced yesterday the following important intelligence, which we immediately communicated to the public, though of course it could not be in the whole of our impression: 'The South of France is in Insurrection against Buonoparte, and in favour of the Bourbons. Two Gentlemen arrived as Deputies from the Royalists, on the road to London.*"

"Does it say who they are?" asked Beth.

"No, alas, no more was known when the paper went to press," said Letty, "but I wager the war may be over by the end of March, God willing. It says many towns are raising the white cockade for the Bourbons, so this terrible bloodthirsty country may soon return to normal."

"I hope so," said Beth. "Whilst it is said that the French aristocracy was quite despotic and cruel, the Reign of Terror was more so, and the Monster Bonaparte was not to be satisfied until he ruled all the world, quite like the tales of Jengiz Khan!"

"And here is a report from the Dutch Papers," said Letty. "It seems that Bonaparte's men have been putting about reports that the French army, far from being in retreat, is winning, and there is an appeal to the soldiers of France, from Marshal Blucher, to disregard such lies, and save life by surrendering."

"Too cruel!" said Beth. "Why, if such lies are believed, it will lead to unnecessary deaths on both sides."

"Yes, and the negotiations for peace have broken down too," said Letty. "The Monster is determined to drag it out for as long as he might."

"Oh it is too bad; no wonder his own people have lost faith in him," said Beth. "Is there anything more?"

"Only the usual idiotic letters from men who have never even been in the militia, suggesting how Lord Liverpool should direct Lord Wellington," said Letty, dryly.

"Dear me, and doubtless it was people like those who managed to seize power during the Terror, and went mad with power," said Beth. "I cannot say that rule by the people will ever work unless there are people chosen who are educated solely to rule, in the way that a monarch has his sons trained to rule, from birth. Since the education of the great schools is aimed towards leadership, one might assume our own government to have been so trained but I'm not sure of that."

"Some better than others," said Letty, dryly.

"True; but an infinitely preferable system to any that the French have managed so far," said Beth.

"I cannot argue with that!" said Letty. "Oh! Listen to this tragedy; there has been an action between the packet, 'The Duchess of Montrose' and the sloop of war 'Primrose', each thinking the other to be the enemy, but how good it is to know our mails are well defended, for the packet made the sloop back off! Eight men killed and twenty-eight wounded in all."

"How terrible! How could they mistake the colours of England for those of the enemy?" asked Beth.

"Who can say!" said Letty.

Edward called after breakfast, to take the ladies for a drive.

"And wrap up warmly," he said, "it has been a hard frost, and the wind is chill."

"I believe I may wrap a shawl around my head

under my bonnet, if you do not mind, Edward," said Beth.

"I think the better of you for having so much good sense," said Edward. "If you choose a light one you may breathe through, you can also pull it over your face if the wind in your face makes breathing painful."

"How thoughtful you are, Edward!" said Beth. "It is good to know that you are so sensible. I hope the officers in France are as sensible, and will keep their poor men as warm as possible. It cannot be easy for them, camped outside Paris."

"No, indeed," said Edward, "Though for all we know, they may be billeted within Paris by now; the news we get is always several days old, and I believe the last report was from the twenty-fourth."

"Indeed, it is hard to wait for news, but of course infinitely harder for those who have husbands and sweethearts fighting," said Beth.

"You are such a kind and thoughtful girl," said Edward.

"Past my girlhood, I fear," said Beth.

"Oh, you are a green girl from where I am looking," said Edward.

"I am not sure whether to take that as a compliment or not," said Beth.

"Oh, it is a compliment," said Edward, and hurriedly changed the subject. "Have you heard of the great hoax?"

"No, what great hoax?" asked Beth.

"Why, it was put about on the twenty-first that Napoleon was certainly defeated, and it was all with the intent of raising the price of certain stocks to sell at profit!" said Edward. "Some fellow representing himself as the aide-de-camp of Lord Cathcart, newly come from France spread false intelligence!"

"My goodness, how bold!" said Beth. "We were moving on the twenty-first, if you recall, Edward, and must have missed the whole announcement. Though surely it only pre-empts the truth by a matter of a few weeks, so can it really be harmful?"

"Yes, because the lie manipulates the stock market falsely, and is therefore tantamount to stealing," said Edward, "and it also throws doubt on true news, and leaves those who have relatives abroad left in a state of doubt and uncertainty, unsure what news to believe."

"Oh! How dreadful for them, of course it must do," said Beth. "Though I must say, the way stocks fluctuate in value seems very silly to me; for surely the price of things should be based merely on the labour it costs to produce them."

"No, there are more things than that," said Edward. "For example, with the coldest winter in living memory behind us, and spring not really advanced, it means the crops sown this year may not do as well, unless we have a hot summer, but with reasonable rainfall, to make up for late planting, and fruit trees unable to flower for the cold. That means food prices will rise, for not having as much to sell, including meat, whose winter fodder ran out for some farmers. And I believe many lambs have been lost too, to the cold."

"Dear me, I had not considered that," said Beth. "You are right; I am green."

Edward laughed kindly.

"But you are clever, withal, and ready to learn, ready to listen, and you immediately understand a point when it is put to you," he said.

"So how did thinking the war was over raise the price of stocks?" asked Beth.

"The stocks involved were in the public funds; so if the war was over, less would have to be paid out by the government, so more could be invested of the funds, so that their dividends would be likely to rise," said Edward.

"Ah; now I understand perfectly," said Beth. "And people would wish to invest to make sure of an income from the funds, and thus would enrich those selling their stocks. Though it is still only a matter of being premature, and unkind to those hoping to see loved ones home, but not really stealing, is it? Because the funds will go up when Bonaparte is defeated."

"It's underhand and lying," said Edward, "because those who did it could not know for certain that Bonaparte was going to be defeated, and even now, on the last day of March, we cannot be sure. The negotiations might have only been a bluff on the part of that wily creature, and he may have some other army hidden, waiting to fall on our troops."

"Surely Lord Bathurst would know?" put in Letty. "Mr. Wickham reports to him, and he knows everything that goes on."

"More than likely, but it's more than he's telling the rest of us," said Edward. "Ah, and of course, Grayling Grey was a friend of his, I had forgotten."

"Grey was a friend of a great number of people," said Letty, demurely.

"Was he a spy?" asked Beth, interested.

"Now, that is not a question I ever asked him," said Letty. "I would not have wanted him to feel he could not answer. He was a good man and a good husband, and the thing that interested me most was that he did not have affaires when he was on a business trip abroad."

"Sorry," muttered Beth, burning red.

"You let your tongue run ahead of your good sense, sometimes, my dear," said Letty.

"And I was too nosy not to see if you would answer, Aunt Letty," said Edward.

"You are an impudent boy," said Letty.

Edward chuckled.

"You noticed!"

Few other people had braved the cold to drive or

ride in the park; Major Whittal was one of them, and he rode up to doff his hat and bow gracefully from the saddle, no mean feat to perform at all with one arm in a sling, and an adroit act to perform with grace and aplomb.

"Ladies! I see you are quite hardy!" he declared.

"Oh, we are country ladies, Major, and inured to inclement weather," said Letty. "Tell us, as a military man, do you think that Blucher is in Paris by now?"

"Oh I am certain of it," said the Major. "The French were on the run when I was sent home with despatches, and I cannot think of anything that would delay the advance into Paris. I heard a rumour that Bonaparte had received a mortal wound, but the man has as many lives as a cat, so I doubt its veracity. No such luck! But you ladies will have a chance to buy fashions in Paris before long, I make no doubt!" he bowed again and rode off.

"Do you like that fellow?" asked Edward.

"He is all that is amiable," said Letty.

"He puts my teeth on edge," said Beth.

Edward brightened.

"It's not just me that wants to shake him to see if his air of perfection falls off then?" he said.

Beth laughed.

"He is very patronising to the ladies and our 'pretty little heads'," she said, "and I cannot for one moment see him explaining why the hoax was so wrong, because he wouldn't expect a woman to be able to understand stocks at all."

"You don't, but at least you try," said Edward. "And if you want to know more, you'll need to ask a downier fellow than me; because I understand enough to know I can't explain them."

"It's a wise man who knows his limitations," said Beth, "and to be honest, I'm not that interested. If I want to know more, I'll ask Elizabeth; she's very clever."

"Didn't exchange more than a word or two with her to find out," said Edward. "Wise of her not to mention it too freely though; being too clever frightens men off."

"I told her to be frank about it," said Beth. "That way she might meet a man who appreciates her for herself."

"Hmmm," said Edward, "There's something in that. Not as though she has to marry, after all; her father's as warm as Croesus. Huh, there's that fellow Byseby that you played for at the musicale."

"Yes, he is quite nice," said Beth. "Rather put me in mind of the old gaffers who sit outside the Black Boar and pass comments on the ankles of girls who pass by and chuck the pretty ones under the chin if they come within reach."

Edward started laughing, and was still fighting with his mirth as Lord Leomer Byesby rode up and raised his curly brimmed beaver.

"Are you quite all right, Brandon?" he asked.

Edward got himself under control.

"Perfectly, thank you, Byesby," he said. "Something Miss Renfield was telling me, about some village worthies, which struck me as more hilarious than I think she intended. I didn't look for you to be abroad in this chill weather."

"Oh, I like to blow away the fug of the gambling dens from time to time," said Lord Leomer. "Wanted to pay my respects to Mrs. Grey; I knew Grey quite well, you see," he added. "And of course the lovely pianist, Miss Renfield!" he bowed again.

"I am sorry I never met you when he was alive," said Letty. "He had so many friends though."

"And some of us appreciated him for himself as well as his generosity," said Lord Leomer. "I wasn't in debt to him when he died. Not like some I could mention."

"There was nothing in his papers of that," said

Letty.

"No; Grey kept all he loaned in his head," said Lord Leomer. "And I believe I can repay the debt of friendship that he extended by making sure that others remember that they should recall what they owe."

"There is no need, my lord; Grey left me very comfortably off," said Letty.

"Oh, it will be a pleasure," said Lord Leomer. "One of those who conveniently forgot is a close personal enemy of mine."

"You're an odd sort of fellow, Byesby," said Edward.

"Devilishly so," agreed Lord Leomer. "Your servant!" and he raised his hat again and rode off.

"Dear me!" said Letty. "What an uncomfortably attractive man, to be sure!"

"I would have strongly advised Beth against forming a *tendre* for him had she not described him in the way she did," said Edward. "He is still an attractive man, even though he is in his forties; which is not so old."

"Oh, it was not precisely his age," said Beth, "Though I confess it would not occur to me to look at a man of his years in the light of being a beau! It was more that the gaffers would run a mile if any of the bold milkmaids offered them more than a screech and a playful smack when they importune them, and it strikes me that Lord Leomer is particularly good at Spanish coin to the ladies, and has no intention of being actually cornered by any of them."

"He has a reputation as a rake," said Edward. "Also as a gambler. I should worry if he became an intimate of the family, Aunt Letty."

"Oh, I daresay Grey bankrolled him because he had a good fund of stories," said Letty. "He seems to be the sort of man who can make himself tolerably agreeable; and Grey loved to be gregarious. He would have looked upon a loan to a man who entertained him as fair exchange for the pleasure of his company, even if it was never paid back."

"I suppose it is a measure of him that he wishes you to know that he is not indebted to Grey," said Edward, reluctantly. "Can't make him out! And by the way, shall we go home? My prads don't like this wind much."

"By all means!" said Beth, smiling at him. "It would not do to let them take cold!"

Chapter 8

Elizabeth's parents were hosting an April Fool's Ball, which, said the invitation, was an excuse to wear silly masks and a domino, and only those people personally known to them to be invited, so there was no risk involved. There would be prizes for the most decorative mask, the most humorous, and the most grotesque and those invited were asked to decorate their own.

This was great fun, and Letty and Beth had much fun discussing what to do.

"Of course the Venetian masks of earlier times were quite fantastical," said Beth, "and what fun it would have been, were feathers not such a bane to me, to have gone as a chicken!"

"That would surely have carried the prize for the most humorous," said Beth. "I believe I might have a pink domino, and put a pig's snout on my mask, for the only other think I can think of is to make the mask into a cat's face, and that is so ordinary. Or – wait, I know, I have seen some most entertaining gargoyles on some of the London churches, I shall be a gargoyle, and wear a grey domino. We hire them, do we not?"

"Some will purchase them, but I see no point for a single night, and you might wear it over a lavender gown which will go well enough with the grey," said Letty. "We may have to settle for plain black ones, which are most common, but it does not matter. Masks and dominos are to be laid aside before supper. An excellent idea, it prevents too much rowdiness building up before the unmasking, young men being young men; and moreover means they have no chance to slip away and hide any overly high spirits in anonymity. Anyone missing for supper at a private masquerade would be noticeable by their absence, and anyone would then know if that individual and his mask had been at all inappropriate in behaviour. I am glad that Mrs. Medlicott specifies dominos not fancy dress too. Hats are permitted, I see, so that will be a means by which one might also express a character. Dear me! I fancy most people will choose characters from the classics or the *comedia del' arte* and I shall go as the notorious medieval witch and prophet, Mother Shipton. I will fashion a huge nose and have a hairpiece of straggling black hair, which will be quite sufficient with a black domino. We had better get to work! Mrs. Medlicott plainly expects all her guests to make their own masks on a basic loo mask, for there is no time to have one made, and I am glad, otherwise it would be the wealthiest who would show the best masks. She is a very sensitive woman."

"I expect that she recalls a time before she was so plump in the pocket," said Beth.

"Indeed, I am sure you have the right of it, for she was, I believe, the daughter of a minor squire in straitened circumstance when Medlicott married her, and if it was an arranged marriage, it has turned out most fortuitously," said Letty. "For she and Medlicott are plainly very fond of each other."

"And such kind parents without being doting," said Beth. "I am glad, though, that they listened to Elizabeth and got rid of that awful woman who was grinding her down; she stutters less now."

"Which is good," said Letty.

A masked ball was exciting, and just a little scary; and Beth hoped that she would be able to guess who everyone was. Letty insisted that Edward go on his own, as they had John Coachman to drive them, so that they had to guess him too. Beth wondered if he would come as Oliver Cromwell after their discussion the other day; but it seemed unlikely without consultation with her, and moreover this was not full fancy dress, it being an impromptu affair.

The dominos were largely black, a few red, some blue, some white, and one person wearing one each of red, white and blue, tacked together to make one domino, with a bicorn hat and a fair caricature of Napoleon Bonaparte on vellum cut as a mask, and a pair of devil horns out of the front of the hat. The wearer struck postures such as Bonaparte was portrayed striking. Beth thought it likely to be one of the very young men, like Mr. Dansey or Mr. Chetwode, but probably Mr. Dansey, as the figure was not as tall as she recalled Mr. Chetwode to be.

"The enemy of mankind!" she declared, cheerfully, "or so say the papers; I think I know you."

Napoleon the devil bowed.

"Oh, fair gargoyle, I believe I know that voice," he said. It was Mr. Dansey. "May I claim you for the first dance?"

"I should be delighted," said Beth.

"Alas! I had hoped I might claim the first dance," said a black domino, whose mask was flesh coloured velvet with an eyepatch. He also wore a bicorn hat on which were pinned a paper skull and crossbones. The voice, Beth thought, belonged to Edward.

"And would you be any particular pirate, sir, whom I think I know, or just a pirate without a name?" she asked. It was part of the etiquette of the masque to use a phrase like 'do I know you?' or 'I think I know you' when holding a conversation with a masked member of the opposite sex.

"Alas, I am but a pirate without a name, since I could not recall the particulars or look of any real pirate," said Edward. "As I am certain that I know you, I shall claim the second dance, and the supper dance."

Beth solemnly inscribed 'A nameless pirate' on her dance card for those two dances, and 'Napoleon Bonaparte' on the first. She was relieved that none of the dances were waltzes in the modern fashion, and thought again how thoughtful Mrs. Medlicott was to make sure that no possible impropriety might occur. It would be too easy, in concealing dominos, for bold behaviour to occur during a dance in which the gentleman's hands familiarly held one.

Beth took the opportunity to look around and see who she might recognise. There were a lot of masks just decorated with beads, sequins, feathers and ribbons, a few men with masks painted like Grimaldi the clown, and one who was easy to identify as Major Whittal, who had made a virtue of his disabled arm, coming with a flesh coloured mask with an eyepatch, a bicorn hat with gold braid, and quite obviously meant to be the late Admiral Lord Nelson.

The beautiful and fantastical bird almost had to be Elizabeth, Beth recognised her upright and graceful carriage, and that had to be Abigail beside her, using her fan with aplomb, with her mask decorated as a butterfly. Who was the tall, elegant lady dressed in a white domino, with a white mask, powdered hair, and a hat that suggested that she was a multi-layered cake with icing? Could it really be Madelaine Vardy, able to stand tall when no-one knew who she was? Why it had to be! How much more confident she managed to be when she felt herself to be anonymous!

"Fair gargoyle!" a voice she did not know. "I do not know you, for I have not been presented, I think, but might I take advantage to make myself know to you? I am as you may guess Julius Caesar."

The mask was painted in the semblance of a carved stone statue, and the man wore a laurel wreath, and he wore a grey domino.

"What, are you weeny, weedy and weaky?" laughed Beth. "Which is the extent of my knowledge of Latin, I fear."

"Ah, Veni, Vedi, Vici," said Julius Caesar. "I came, I saw, I conquered. I wonder if I do conquer well enough, Madam La Grotesque, to claim a dance?"

"Most certainly, Mighty Caesar," said Beth. "I'm a

gargoyle."

"Ah, a specific kind of ecclesiastical grotesque," said Julius Caesar. "Only a woman of perfect serenity could bear a mask that is a mockery of the human form, and I salute you. Pray tell me, is the pirate your brother, that he looks on me with such enmity?"

"Why no, I have no brothers," said Beth. "He is a distant connection of mine, and an old family friend."

"Then he looks to your protection from an unknown piece of statuary," said Julius Caesar. "Shall I tell him that my antecedents are impeccable and that I am a man of honour?"

"If he cannot guess that, from Mrs. Medlicott making assurance that only persons known to her would attend, then his wits have gone begging," said Beth, recklessly, hoping that Edward was jealous.

"Oh, Amabel – Mrs. Medlicott – is my cousin," said Julius Caesar. "I shall be doing duty as an honorary brother to Elizabeth, though it seems odd to think of little Lizzy all grown up and beautiful! Last time I saw her, I'm afraid I tied her to a tree by her plaits."

"Unkind!" declared Beth.

"It was at least half her fault; she was boasting about how long they were," said Julius Caesar. "And I was only eighteen and felt that a fourteen-year-old cousin was a bit of a pest."

"Well, if Elizabeth has forgiven you, it is all that matters," said Beth.

"She appears to have done," said Julius Caesar, "however if, when I go to bed, I find a jug of water balanced on the door, or an apple-pie bed or something, I shall preserve a dignified silence on the same, and hold her to be well avenged."

"I shall go and suggest it to her," said Beth brightly.

"Fair unkind!" cried Julius Caesar with a dramatic gesture that almost whacked a gentleman with a large nosed mask and a cavalier's hat, who almost had to be Cyrano de Bergerac.

"OY!" said the voice of Mr. Chetwode.

"Oh, Mr. Ch...er, I mean, I seem to know you, M. de Bergerac," said Beth, "would you escort me to Elizabeth, so I might tell her that she owes her cousin a practical joke?"

"Right willingly, Miss, er, statue," said Mr. Chetwode.

"Gargoyle," said Beth.

"Oh, yes, couldn't remember what they were called," said Mr. Chetwode.

Elizabeth embraced Beth.

"You and Mrs. Grey are very brave to come with such hideous masks!" she said. "I wish I were so self-confident!"

Beth laughed. "Oh, I want to win the prize for the most grotesque," she said. "I have been talking to your cousin."

"Philip is a lot nicer than I remember him," said Elizabeth.

"Yes, so I gathered," said Beth. "And he said he would preserve a dignified silence if you played him a practical joke like an apple-pie bed, whatever that may be, or balanced a jug of water on the door."

"Don't think it hasn't crossed my mind," said Elizabeth. "An apple-pie bed is when you take the top sheet and put it under the pillow like a bottom sheet, and fold the bottom of it up to look like a top sheet, and the blankets and counterpane all over as normal. You put your feet into bed, and can only get them down half way. He made one for me, years ago, and I ripped the sheet, not knowing what it was. Boys learn things like that at school. But I, too, shall preserve my dignity by *not* lowering myself to play a joke on him. Only, I pray you, do not tell him so!"

"I shall not," said Beth. "Isn't Madelaine looking splendid, not feeling a need to hide her height?"

"Yes, and we must tell her so," said Elizabeth. "Oh,

the first dance is about to begin; have you engaged to dance with anyone yet?"

"Yes, I am dancing with Mr. Dansey, I mean the Monster of France," said Beth. "I hope he can control that outsize domino and not trip in it."

"Not he," said Elizabeth. "Not that I'll answer for anyone else not standing on it!"

Beth enjoyed dancing; and though her dance with Mr. Dansey was curtailed by Mr. Chetwode falling headlong as he did an allemande the wrong way into the outrageous domino, it was still fun.

She was claimed next by Edward.

"Who is that Julius Caesar fellow?" he demanded.

"What, Oh, Pirate, did you wish to challenge the Imperial trireme on the high seas?" asked Beth, merrily.

"I do like to know who people are," said Edward. "You are a green girl, and you stand in danger of silver-tongued rogues."

"Why, I did not think that Mrs. Medlicott would invite silver-tongued rogues!" said Beth. "He is a cousin of hers, and Elizabeth refers to him as Philip; he is some four years older than her, so a year older than I. Does that satisfy your curiosity?"

"Ah, yes, the Honourable Philip Devereaux," said Edward. "Well, he is held to be an eligible bachelor and welcome anywhere."

Beth wondered whether to tease Edward that he did not sound at all pleased about Philip Devereaux's eligibility, but decided that there were times to speak, and times to hold one's tongue.

She danced with Mr. Devereaux as promised and laughingly told him that she must be honour bound to withhold Elizabeth's plans for vengeance. Mr. Chetwode claimed a dance, and so did several other young men whom Beth thought she had met at Elizabeth's rout party. It was all very exciting!

One of the masks was an outrageous beak, the head-dress of the young man wearing it the red poll of the greater spotted woodpecker; and Beth managed to slide away sideways as he bore down on her, having noticed that he liked to use his beak to 'peck' at his dancing partners. She ran into Major Whittall.

"Oh, Major, I mean, Admiral!" she said. "May I sit the next dance out with you?"

"I'd be delighted, Miss Renfield," said the Major, who considered pretence to be rather foolish. "And by the next ball, I hope to have my arm back in action, to be able to dance, for surely all will be at peace very soon!"

Consequently, Beth was able to drop a polite curtsey to the woodpecker and declare that she was claimed for this dance; and fortunately Major Whittal was too fond of his own consequence to be hurt by any suspicion that he had been used.

The supper dance with Edward was perhaps the best of all, for they had much time to chat, and compare notes about their guesses as to who was whom. And then it was the unmasking before supper, and Madelaine Vardy noticeably wilted and hunched her shoulders even as she took her mask off.

"And the prize for the most decorative mask goes to Miss Meynell for her butterfly," announced Amabel Medlicott, "The most humorous to Mr. Blacknell" – a man Beth knew only by sight – "for his outrageous woodpecker, and the most grotesque to Miss Renfield, whose gargoyle looked quite ready to spill water onto passers-by!"

There was applause, and Beth thanked Mrs. Medlicott for the beautifully-tooled leather-bound notebook which was her prize. It was a lovely thing, with gilding in the tooling and gilded edges to the pages, which had been already carefully cut apart to use. Beth personally thought that Mr. Blacknell might have been a more amusing person to get to know, had not his games with his beak been rather too boisterous; but perhaps he would grow out of such things. However, it had been a most enjoyable ball, and was another first for her, both her first ball and her first masquerade!

Chapter 9

"Oh, my dear Beth, we have been invited to a ball at Arvendish House!" said Letty. "Lord and Lady Arven are quite leaders of society, and of course they are friendly with Lord and Lady Everleigh."

"Who are Lord and Lady Everleigh?" asked Beth.

"Oh Beth! The parents of Lady Cressida Stonhouse!" said Letty.

"I do wish that these aristocrats would not have such very different names that they use!" said Beth.

"Well, of course, they have a family name which may be the same as their title if they had the title from the very beginning of it, or acquired other titles subsequently. That young limb who played the questionable song is Viscount Stonhouse as well as having the surname Stonhouse."

"I see, I think," said Beth. "So the family were given an earldom as well as the viscountcy for some signal service like procuring girls for Edward IV, supporting Henry VIII in his divorce plans or lending money to any random Stuart?"

"Cynicism aside, yes," said Letty. "Dear me, now you have come out of yourself, my dear, in chattering with other young things your age, I declare you are quite as bad as Grey!"

Beth chuckled.

"Well, as you were very fond of your husband, I shall look upon that as a compliment," she said. "Anything in the papers this morning?"

"There's a report of Lord Wellington taking a wound," said Letty, "a spent musket ball in the thigh, but not serious enough to make him quit the field of battle. That's the action of the twenty-seventh of March. Oh, and there's an announcement that one must expect soon a proclamation regarding a cessation in hostilities, but nothing definite said; mere speculation, along with the assumption that now Princess Charlotte may be expected to marry the Prince of Orange."

"Is he the stupid one who looks like a frog?" asked Beth, "for if so, she's wasted on him."

"He may have hidden talents; and besides, it's a dynastic marriage," said Letty.

"I'd have thought someone who was not a ruling prince would be better for the only child and heir of the Regent of England," said Beth.

"Well, I have no doubt the Princess will manage to make her feelings clear if it is not her choice; she is quite good at doing so," said Letty dryly. "As to the rest, it is just the same old thing about negotiations having broken down, and reprinting reports that are ten or twelve days old. I thought we might go shopping, and make sure your ball gown for this ball is truly memorable."

"Letty, I have ball gowns, and as I wore a domino, I can wear the one I wore last night," said Beth.

"No, we want a proper gown for you to make a debut in what is the highest society to which you might normally aspire," said Letty. "And a petticoat of silver tissue, with sheer satin-striped muslin over it, and adorned with pink roses is what I have in mind."

"It sounds monstrously extravagant," said Beth. "But I confess, I would like to wear such an extravagant confection."

"Well, then, we shall go shopping," said Letty. "The ball is on the sixth; plenty of time."

This shopping trip had more purpose to it than the previous one, where the ladies had been purchasing a selection of cloths that might be made up, though Beth was delighted to bump into Madelaine Vardy.

"Madelaine! I loved your costume as a multi-layered cake, and how elegant you looked, walking tall inside it!" she said.

Madelaine gave a slightly hysterical giggle.

"Oh, Beth!" she said, "I was never meant to be a

cake, Mother said I should dress as the leaning tower of Pisa as I drooped so, only I forgot to droop at all!"

"How unkind of her!" Beth's eyes sparkled in anger.

"Do you think so? Oh Beth, is it totally evil of me to dislike my mother?"

"Well, I dislike your mother, and I don't even know her as well as you do," said Beth. "She is quite unkind to you, and maybe she does not mean to be, but you would think by now she would realise that the more she bullies you, the more you droop and the clumsier you get."

"I think she thinks I merely lack will-power," said Madelaine, gloomily. "For two pins I'd run away and…and become a governess!"

"Do you have the education to become a governess?" asked Beth.

"Oh! Yes. I have had a very expensive education and enjoyed learning," said Madelaine. "I could teach quite happily."

"You may be a bit too pretty for a household with a teen-aged son, or an errant father, but if you do decide to run away, I will certainly help you," said Beth. "I see your mother returning from the haberdashery counter with the triumph of Blucher at the gates of Paris."

"They found her the ribbon she wanted, then," said Madelaine. "Even if they had to send a girl to purchase some from elsewhere and make no profit. Mother always gets what she wants. Mother, you recall Miss Renfield, do you not?"

Mrs. Vardy looked at Beth with dislike.

"Yes," she said.

"*So* clever to dress Madelaine as a tall cake with icing, to give her the courage to stand tall when wearing a mask," enthused Beth. "I was tremendously impressed."

"Hmmph! Yes, well, we are purchasing something

for her for the ball at Arvendish House, on Wednesday next," said Mrs. Vardy, her eyes glittering in triumph. "Madelaine received an invitation to attend."

"Yes, it will be my first big ball," said Beth. "Exciting, is it not?"

Mrs. Vardy's face froze, and the chagrin she felt that the dumpy little nobody would be going as well was plain upon her face. Beth smiled at her with real happiness at having managed to spoil a piece of spite and gloating. Madelaine was hiding how pleased she felt. Doubtless the wretched woman would spend the whole journey home, and after, wondering out loud how come Miss Renfield should also have been invited; and complaining about it.

Edward was waiting when Letty and Beth got back to their house, pacing up and down outside.

"Your fool footman won't let me in to wait, and it's perishing cold out here," he said, greeting Letty with a peck on the cheek.

"I am very sorry, Edward, he is a London footman and very proper," said Letty. "I shall tell him that in the future you may be admitted when I am absent, since you are my nephew. Ah, Simpson, Mr. Brandon is always to be admitted, he is my nephew, and since he is now a very cold nephew, the urn and tea caddy if you please, in the blue parlour," she added as the footman opened the door.

"Very good, Madam," said the footman.

"Now, have you news for us, Edward?" asked Letty.

"Yes, but I have no intention of sharing it until that supercilious fellow has served tea and taken himself off," said Edward. "I know it's a deuced unfashionable time to come calling, but I've some news I must share with you, before you hear a garbled version from someone else, or read it in the newspapers."

"It sounds ominous," said Letty. "Ah, Simpson,

73

thank you, that will be all."

Letty unlocked the tea caddy and mixed the tea the way she knew Edward liked it, which being the way her sister had served it was a mix she liked herself, and that Beth had learned to like as well as any other mix she had tried. The urn was hot, and Letty raised and lowered the tea pot a few times to steep the tea before pouring. Edward helped himself to sugar, looking a little apologetic for taking three good sized lumps.

"I can't claim it was a shock, but though I was not surprised, it was still unpleasant," he said.

"You're making a mull of it," said Beth. "Start at the beginning."

Edward smiled, briefly.

"That would go back to before the time Uncle Adam got married, at which point Tiffany, his wife, had been seen much with Evelyn, Lord Finchbury. But the budget of news that I wish to impart really begins with Tiffany having given birth overnight to a baby girl. And that baby girl has a tuft of dark hair, and ears with slight points on them. Both Uncle Adam and Tiffany are blonde, and the only person I know with slight points to the ears is Finchbury. Add to that a bouncing baby of seven and a half pounds at what is supposed to be seven months, and even Uncle Adam had conniptions."

"Oh, poor Adam," said Letty. "He just about worshipped that ridiculous girl."

"I know," sighed Edward. "And she admitted it, and screeched at him that she would not have married a boring old fool like him if it had not been necessary. And of course, he could try to get a son on her as soon as possible and say as little as possible about this girl, but he didn't marry her for a son, he married her because he was so besotted. And she has fallen from her pedestal with a crash. I was prepared to push, but I didn't have to. She jumped."

"Wouldn't it have been unkind to your uncle to

have pushed?" said Beth.

"Possibly, but it would depend on whether she took a lover and foisted another cuckoo into his nest," said Edward, "because I surprised a look on her face last time I was there, and it made me angry on Adam's behalf, and chary that she might go seeking diversion elsewhere. So there is to be a Crim. Con. case against her, because she wants to divorce Uncle Adam. At least, she does at the moment; and as there were witnesses to her admissions, she is going to get her wish even if she changes her mind later and wants it hushed up. That her maid was also induced to admit to meetings with Finchbury in a place of assignation means it should at least be quick and easy. Adam is devastated, but quite devoted to baby Lydia already; Tiffany wants nothing to do with her. He told her that he would provide for the baby, and arrange that all she brought to the wedding is restored to her, for she had a handsome jointure."

"Generous," said Letty. "Especially when one considers how expensive it is to proceed to a private bill to obtain a divorce. And I doubt he'll get much out of Finchbury, whatever damages are set."

"He would not wish to hold on to anything that was hers, I wager," said Beth, "save the helpless baby which caused all the trouble, but unwittingly, that she is also betraying by not wanting her. I expect he feels fellow feeling with the poor little scrap."

"Indeed," said Edward. "Anyway, I thought it best to make you aware, before someone asks you about it."

"Dear me, yes," said Letty. "Tongues will wag, however quietly it is done. After all, it will be necessary to make sure that it is known that the poor baby is not in any way going to inherit titles or anything else of right, otherwise she would be the Lady Lydia. Oh, Edward! That means that you are Adam's heir again!"

Edward shrugged.

75

"At least it's a role I am prepared for," he said. "Beth, will you mind being a baroness if Uncle Adam does not remarry for a second time?"

"Edward, do you mind having a secret betrothal to someone of no land or fortune, who cannot add to the barony in any way?" said Beth.

Edward shrugged.

"Oh, I'm sure you will bring calm good common sense to the lands, and be an admirable baroness," he said. "We know each other tolerably well, now, do we not? And that makes for a good partnership."

"How unromantic you are, Edward," said Letty.

"I'm not a very romantic person," said Edward. "But do you mind, Beth?"

"Not if you think me suitable," said Beth. "I am sure I can learn to be a baroness. If I can learn this pesky waltz that Aunt Letty wants me to have the chance to dance, running a barony will be relative child's play."

Edward laughed.

"Phlegmatic and practical as always," he said. "And that is more likely to stand you in good stead as a baroness than a title or two, and all the tea in China."

He finished his tea, and took his leave.

"*Well!*" said Letty.

"Or indeed, not well," said Beth. "It will be most embarrassing for all those most nearly concerned, of course. Let us hope that a victory is announced soon, and that it chases all other news right to the back of all the papers, so the whole business may be got over quickly and quietly. If Bonaparte is found to have a fatal wound, as was suggested, it will be much more likely to take up
half the papers in speculation."

Letty laughed.

"I doubt that the war will arrange itself to the convenience of Edward and his uncle," she said. "What a silly piece Tiffany Pelham was, to be sure! Fancy permitting a rake like Finchbury to sweet-talk her into his bed! But then, the Pelhams have never been noted for their brains. It will doubtless be the talk of the ball, but may with luck be a nine-day wonder and will blow over."

Letty did not add that it was not improbable that Amelia Hazelgrove was likely to turn on her not inconsiderable charms towards Edward again, once she thought him heir to a barony once again; it would only serve to worry Beth.

Beth wondered if The Beauty would try to get her hooks into Edward again, and whether he would be fool enough to fall for her wiles; and swore quietly to herself that Amelia Hazelgrove would not have him. She said nothing, however, of this to Letty, for fear of upsetting her.

Chapter 10

Whispers of a possible impending Crim. Con. proceeding were abroad almost as soon as the notice of the birth of a daughter to Tiffany Brandon, Lady Darsham, née Pelham, with no mention of her husband Lord Darsham in the notice. Gossip centred around whether Lord Darsham would merely quietly separate from his wife, or be satisfied with the church's solution, a *divortium a mensa et thoro*, in which the divorce was legal but remarriage was not, or whether civil proceedings against somebody would go ahead, and the full weight of a Criminal Conversation action be brought, to be followed by the private Bill in Parliament to finalise the divorce.

"Aunt Letty, why do you think Lord Darsham is not just settling for a separation or a church divorce?" asked Beth, on hearing the speculation.

"Because Adam is a fool, a loveable fool, but a fool nonetheless," said Letty. "He will be determined to give Tiffany her freedom so that she might remarry. Whether she will wish to or not is a moot point; and though her reputation will be in shreds, divorced women have remarried. But Finchbury certainly can't afford her, especially if he has to pay thousands of pounds in damages, as is common in such cases. Which he won't be able to, of course, and Adam is sure to let him off, if he only takes Tiffany off his hands. Not that she can marry him anyway, legally. At least, I say so, because a divorced woman may not marry the man with whom she committed adultery, but I wonder if this will be tried as a fraud case, that she was with child before marriage? have no idea if it counts or not."

"Is it not expensive to have to have Parliament sit in judgement too?" asked Beth.

"Indeed; as much as five thousand pounds," said Letty. "But then, you should consider that there are gentlemen who will lose that much in a night, gambling; Adam has no vices, he can afford it, and to ask for negligible damages."

"How insulting to Lady Darsham, though, to have a nominal fee set on her fidelity!" said Beth.

"Perhaps that is where Adam plans to take his revenge on being fooled," said Letty, dryly.

The ringing of all the bells in every church in London, and the town criers shouting glad news was a relief from hearing speculation about Adam and Tiffany.

"Oyez! Oyez! The war with France is over! Allied sovereigns entered Paris on the thirty-first ultimo!"

"Well, it's only taken five days for the news to get here," said Beth. "You'd have thought the allies could have used the French telegraph to send the news to Calais, a few hours to cross the channel, and the telegraph to London from the coast. But what do I know? I'm only a woman."

"I suppose they only wanted official news to get out, which means despatches," said Letty. "But you would think that they could have sent a courier at least with news by word of mouth, someone known to the Home Office or at Horse Guards. Still! At least we do know, now."

Letty insisted that Beth should rest on the day of the ball. It would be a long affair, probably not breaking up until well into the small hours, and Beth thought that she would be glad to have been given such instructions. She got dressed excitedly, shivering in the thin gauze and muslin of her pretty ballgown, pulling her long gloves over the goosebumps on her arms. It would be hot enough, dancing with the press of people, and the heat from all the candles, but here in the little house in Red Lion Square it was cold! Beth swathed herself in a shawl on top of a white velvet spencer, and ran downstairs, as soon as Sowerby had dressed her hair for her, and fastened pink and white silk roses into the comb that held the hair off her face.

"You look a picture, Miss," ventured Sowerby. As Sowerby was not given to compliment, Beth permitted herself to feel that she looked quite presentable. Had she known it, the thought that she might dance that fast and wicked dance, the waltz, with Edward had given her more countenance than usual, and she was very much in looks. She donned a pelisse and a cloak, and the fur-lined overshoes that would mean she was less likely to get chilblains, and they set off. Letty too looked quite fine, in a deep ruby velvet gown, with black lace over it, and she had written to ask if chaperones might be permitted long sleeves, for Letty had no intention of dancing. On receiving the intelligence that long sleeves were considered quite acceptable for full dress in this inclement spring, Letty had been much relieved. The heat from the crowd and the candles would help, but those people who were not dancing but sitting all evening would be likely to become chilled down.

Arvendish House glowed with light. Not only were the lights inside spilling out onto the pavement, but lanterns were set outside, some to give light, and some with coloured glass to make a gay patchwork of colour thrown onto the pavement. Inside, the grand hallway had a most wonderful mosaic floor which copied the design of the painted ceiling above it, an extravagant gesture that quite took Beth's breath away. Footmen took wraps and coats, and stood ready to take overshoes as they were removed, and maids carried them upstairs to the rooms set aside as dressing rooms, so that the ladies might not be overheated once they were within the house. The dressing rooms were two in number, an outer room where the outside garments were laid, and where maids might wait in case of any need to mend garments; and an inner room was discreetly outfitted with a number of screens, behind which the usual offices might be found, put there for the comfort of the ladies during the evening. It was a relief that one would not have to make one's way to an outside closet in the cold!

Letty guided Beth back down stairs, where footmen waited, and one showed them to the ballroom, and announced them. It was all very grand! The ballroom was a double-cube room, of perfect proportions, and the wonderfully painted ceiling that was in here, too, was echoed by the chalked floor. Beth had heard that some grand balls had chalked designs on the floor, but she had never seen it before, and had chalked her slippers, as had everyone else, at Elizabeth's masked ball. The extravagant riot of colours of classical figures must have taken an age to execute! And yet in a short time, it would all be danced to a mix of colours! It seemed a shame, in a way, and yet, no more so, perhaps, than eating a marvellously contrived confection. So far, almost everyone was treading around the outside of the main pattern to preserve it for as long as possible until the dancing started, so that later arrivals might appreciate it too. The candelabra threw myriad twinkling lights from their cut glass ornamentation, and the light and the colour was breathtakingly exciting!

Introduced to her host and hostess, Beth curtseyed deeply, and murmured her thanks for the invitation.

"Well, well, nice to meet you," said the Duke.

"Juliana said what a nice-mannered girl you are, and how you did not make sheep's eyes at Lord Byesby," said the Duchess.

"Why, he is too old to make sheep's eyes at, even if I found him handsome!" said Beth.

Lord Arven roared with laughter.

"Poor Byesby, too old and not handsome," he said. "The vicissitudes of an ageing rake."

"I, however, find Lord Byesby disturbingly

attractive, and therefore treat him warily," said Letty, as she, too, was introduced, "but he was a friend of my late husband."

"Ah, Grayling Grey had many friends, most of whom were as true to him as he was to all men," said Lord Arven. "You are welcome, Mrs. Grey."

They moved on into the room as others were arriving to be greeted, and Beth froze momentarily to hear announced,

"Miss Amelia Hazelgrove."

"You know she is much in society," said Letty, quietly. "It would be almost wonderful if she were not here."

"I suppose so," said Beth. "I wish to turn round casually so I may see the beauty over whom Edward has made such a cake of himself."

She turned to look around, and saw the perfect figure and curling black ringlets of the Beauty, her skin fashionably pale, and her lips pinker than anyone might reasonably expect without some artifice. Their famous pouting bow made the artifice a little more obvious than if she had left them to their natural devices, and Beth was a little chagrined to find herself spitefully pleased about that. The pale skin was not so flawless as her own, and the eyes were a little small, and a pale blue-grey, Beth thought. She suppressed a sigh, however, for Miss Hazelgrove had a figure like a Greek statue, and was dressed to enhance it, her snowy bosoms thrust up on a pillow of blonde lace. Miss Hazelgrove wore her white muslin over a gold gown with a gold bodice and gold ribbons on her ruched sleeves.

"Doesn't do anything for her complexion, gold," said Letty, in satisfaction. "I daresay it looked quite fetching in daylight, but she forgot the candles. Always dress with candles in mind; they enhance any yellow, and that girl has a yellow cast to her skin tone."

"So she has," said Beth, happily.

At that moment, Edward arrived, and was announced. Amelia Hazelgrove spread her fan and flirted it at him as he finished greeting his host and hostess.

"La, Edward! How nice to find that you are attending the ball! I declare, the only thing that could change it from a tedious squeeze into something quite entertaining!" she said.

"Tedious? A ball by Lord and Lady Arven? Hardly!" said Edward.

"How rude!" said Beth to Letty. "I would not invite back someone who was so rude about any entertainment I put on, surely the Arvens have heard!"

"It is fashionable to be endowed with *ennui* over the Season," said Letty, "and to have one's entertainment described as a squeeze is, in fact, a compliment."

"Indeed? It seems discourteous to me," said Beth. "And Edward has said her nay, and he is the soul of courtesy!"

The Beauty had pouted. Beth thought it made her look like some of the more ill-natured putti one saw on engravings of the Italian Masters.

"How you do take one up, Edward! I merely meant that any event would be flat without your presence to make it interesting!"

"How strange!" said Edward. "And I thought that you found my interests in country life and farming quite boring. At least, as I recall, you were always yawning when I spoke of them."

The Beauty gave a little titter.

"Oh, but you do not usually make such lapses of taste!" she said. "You have also been wont to tell me what excellent looks I am in, and to discuss fashion with me!"

"I have never discussed fashion with you, Miss Hazelgrove," said Edward, "I have listened to you discussing fashion, however, and it appears I have managed better to mask my total lack of interest from you."

"Why so formal, Edward?" said Amelia, coyly flirting her fan across her face. "You were used to call me by my name!"

"Well, that was when I was anticipating you accepting an offer from me," said Edward. "I could hardly do so when we parted with angry words."

Amelia laughed. It was a much-practised, low, breathy laugh.

"As if I considered that anything but a lover's tiff!" she said. "I do hope we might soon be upon the same footing we were before?"

"I doubt that, Miss Hazelgrove," said Edward. "You explained how you felt, and I came away. That is an end to it."

"Oh, but Edward! All is changed now it seems likely that your uncle is entirely without an heir again, save you!" said Amelia.

"All may be changed in that respect, but I prefer not to court a woman whose motives are all too clear," said Edward.

"What can you mean?" said Amelia.

"He said he doesn't much wish to be with a woman who sells herself on a long term lease for a barony any more than one who charges a shilling an hour in Covent Garden," said Letty.

Edward winced.

"I had not intended to put it so baldly, Aunt Letty," he said. "Miss Hazelgrove, my aunt, the Honourable Leticia Grey; her ward, Miss Renfield."

Beth curtseyed prettily.

"Pleased to meet you, Miss Hazelgrove," she said. "You will want, I think, to retire to the ladies' dressing room and repair the damage to your lip-rouge, it has smudged when you pouted."

Amelia gave a little squeal, and retreated, her fan over her mouth.

"She wears lip-rouge?" said Edward.

"You great fool, of course she does," said Letty. "She's so vain about her big lips she wants to draw even more attention to them."

"Oh!" said Edward.

Beth half considered saying something pitying about how it was the only way she might draw attention from her imperfect skin, and decided she would not descend to such tricks. She smiled at Edward.

"And were you planning on filling in some places on my dance card?" she said.

"Yes, indeed!" said Edward. "The waltz is danced in Arvendish House, though many think it fast; and if you will save me the supper dance, too, I should like that. If you are happy to waltz? One has the undivided attention of one's partner to chat, which can be interrupted in a country dance."

It might have been nice to have had Edward's attention on the scary and exciting closeness during the waltz, but wanting to talk was the next best thing.

Edward approached Lady Arven, and with a bow, asked her permission to waltz with Beth.

"She seems a nicely-behaved girl; I have no objection," said Lady Arven. "Do you know how to waltz, Miss Renfield?"

"I hope so, My Lady," said Beth, dropping a little curtsey. "I have studied the instructions, that Aunt Letty obtained from Vienna, quite assiduously, and we had a dancing master in the other day. I am sure that Mr. Brandon will put me right if I go wrong, though, in his usual tactful and kindly way."

"I'll steer, and you row," said Edward, cheerfully.

Lady Arven smiled upon them. She was pleased to see Edward Brandon with a nicer-seeming girl than the spoilt Beauty. Edward was popular at any soirée or ball, as he might be guaranteed to be kindly and polite even to the shyest and most unprepossessing debutantes!

Beth smiled shyly, and inscribed Edward's name on her dance card next to the waltz. There was a second waltz, but he must not stand up with her more than twice, and only for one waltz, or she would be labelled as 'fast'. And so long as he did not waltz with Amelia Hazelgrove, Beth did not mind in the least!

Chapter 11

Beth's dance card was rapidly filled; she was by no means the prettiest girl at the ball, not the most elegant, but her air of genuine enjoyment made her a more approachable figure for tongue-tied young men than the more fashionable, and often younger, girls who carefully assumed expressions of boredom. She danced two dances with young men of more enthusiasm than skill, and when the third confessed to two left feet, asked if he would sit the dance out with her, so long as he could procure her some lemonade. Mr. Grindlay, which was his name, managed this with alacrity, and a plate of macaroons and rout cakes.

"It's been a long time since dinner," he said with naïve honesty.

"It has, hasn't it?" said Beth, never loath to nibble a macaroon. Mr. Grindlay gave his heart to a charming young woman who did not make him dance and who understood and condoned hunger pangs.

"Are you enjoying yourself, Miss Renfield?" asked Lady Arven. Beth arose to curtsey.

"Yes, thank you, your ladyship," she said. "It is a beautiful house, and a lovely ball! I only regret that the chalking must be destroyed as we dance on it."

"It was a very creditable job the chalkers made of it," said Lady Arven, sounding pleased. "It is refreshing to see true enjoyment."

"I don't think I like fashionable *ennui*," said Beth. "It seems so discourteous to someone who has gone to as much trouble as you have. Oh, have I made a social gaffe in saying so?" she asked.

Lady Arven smiled.

"Probably, my dear, but I don't heed it. I am delighted that you have noticed, and are enjoying the result. And your view of courtesy is quite charming!" she smiled and moved off, circulating amongst those presently sitting out.

"Her Ladyship terrifies me," confided Mr. Grindlay.

"I think she seems a lovely woman," said Beth.

"Yes, but you ain't in her bad books," said Mr. Grindlay. "I don't dance very well, and I can't remember what to say when I'm supposed to make small talk, and I know nothing about fashion or *on dits* or anything like that, I don't find crim. cons in the least bit interesting, and I don't even find the turn of the dice very thrilling. Card games are moderately interesting, but only games of skill."

"What things do interest you, Mr. Grindlay?" asked Beth.

"Engineering projects," said Mr. Grindlay.

"Then I know just the lady you should meet," said Beth. "She's much cleverer than I am, and if you explain all about how it works, I should think she'd be able to discuss engineering with you. Miss Medlicott is immensely well read."

"She didn't seem to have anything to say when I danced with her earlier," said Mr. Grindlay.

"Well that's because she's even shyer than you are, and stutters at social gatherings," said Beth. "Talk to her about bridges and steam engines."

"I say! Really?" said Mr. Grindlay, interested.

"Indeed! Miss Medlicott is a bluestocking and is looking for friends who share her interests," said Beth. "Ah, the dance is coming to an end, let me beckon her over…. Elizabeth, Mr. Grindlay is interested in engineering and is consequently not the boring fellow you doubtless took him for whilst he was pretending not to be clever. Have you a dance free for him?"

Elizabeth blinked slightly at this forthright speech.

"I've been to see the Iron Bridge in Coalbrookdale, to see how it is constructed," said Mr. Grindlay, "and it is most ingenious."

"I believe my next dance is free, Mr. Grindlay, why

do we not sit it out, and you can tell me all about it?" said Elizabeth. "I have studied some mathematics, and would like to learn more about engineering, and perhaps with your help I will be able to follow your description."

Mr. Grindlay lost his heart for a second time that evening, especially when he discovered that Elizabeth was no more averse to light refreshments than Beth had been. It may be noted that Mr. Grindlay was almost called out to fight a duel as Elizabeth forgot that she was engaged for the next dance and had to be discovered by her partner behind the potted palms discussing such subjects as reciprocating motion and pressure differentials.

Beth danced with Mr. Dansey, and with Mr. Chetwode, though in the case of the latter, they were of more danger to the other two couples in the set than not, Mr. Chetwode being uncoordinated in the extreme when not seated at an instrument, and much taller than Beth. Fortunately one of the people stood next to them was Lady Cressida, who was tolerant, it seemed, of Mr. Chetwode, and on the other side, Mr. Dansey had led out Abigail Meynell.

"You big oaf," said Lady Cressida, without rancour, as she re-fastened the feather that Mr. Chetwode had managed to knock out of her headdress, after the dance.

"Sorry, ma'am," said Mr. Chetwode. "I rather bent that. Buy you another. Buy you a dozen!"

Lady Cressida laughed.

"No real harm done," she said.

Beth was waylaid by Major Whitall.

"May I ask for your hand in the waltz?" he asked. His arm was now out of its sling. "It is all the rage in France, you know."

"I am sorry, Major, but I am already promised for the waltz," said Beth. "Lady Arven gave her approval."

"Oh. Who are you dancing with?" asked the Major,

with more chagrin than grammar.

"I will be dancing with Mr. Edward Brandon," said Beth, demurely. "And I am engaged to sit out for the second waltz with Mr. Philip Devereux."

Philip Devereux had also asked permission to waltz and had asked Beth's hand in order to wheedle her, he said, into gaining Elizabeth's better graces than mere polite acceptance of a relationship. Elizabeth had declined to waltz with someone she did not know well, but suggested sitting the dance out instead.

"I don't know this Devereux; sounds like a Frenchie," said the Major.

"He's a cousin of Elizabeth Medlicott and quite as English as you are," said Beth.

"Hmmph. I hope you ain't hoping to catch Brandon now it seems likely he's heir to a barony again?" said the Major. "Heard the Baroness laid a cuckoo in the nest of the Baron, but it ain't any good pursuing Brandon, he's dotty over the Beauty, Miss Hazelgrove."

"My second cousin Edward is indifferent to titles," said Beth, coldly. "I have heard it said that soldiers gossip like old women, but I had never hitherto credited it; pardon me, my partner is looking for me."

She walked into Edward's arms for the waltz almost shaking with anger.

"That poltroon has put you in a pother," said Edward. "Want to talk about it?"

"No, I want to call him out," said Beth. "But as I cannot, I shall contrive to forget his foolishness. He was warning me off Mr. Devereux because he sounds French, and off you because you are enamoured of Miss Hazelgrove."

"So he made a wrong guess on both counts," said Edward. "You are right; the best thing to do is to put such foolishness out of your mind. What were you talking about so assiduously with Mr, er, Grindlay?"

"He is interested in engineering, so I was

persuading him that he and Elizabeth would get on tolerably well," said Beth. "Did Miss Hazelgrove wish you to cry off the supper dance with me, in order to dance with her?"

"Yes, but I told her I was better brought up than to do something like that," said Edward. "Beth, do you know what, she is most dreadfully shallow."

"I fear that her parents have made much of her looks, and not encouraged her to broaden her mind," said Beth. "Not that mine exactly encouraged me to do so, but I never had a pretty face to dwell upon, to take my mind off reading and wondering about the wonders of the world."

"And your face reflects your delight in the world," said Edward. "You are quite wasted as a woman, Beth, I'm sure you'd have made an excellent farmer."

"Oh, more than likely," said Beth. "But I am what I am, and I am content in my lot, you know!"

"It's just as well," said Edward. "Will you miss all this, when we are married? I like to live quietly in the country for the most part."

"Not in the least," said Beth. "I am enjoying it no end, it is a great novelty, but to be honest, I suspect that it would eventually pall, and I would long for my days to start early and finish early, as I am accustomed, instead of the other way about."

"What a nice girl you are!" said Edward.

"And you are a most agreeable and thoughtful man," said Beth. "I am surprised you did not get married years ago."

Edward laughed.

"Oh, too buried in the country at first, and then enamoured of Amelia, and blind to everything about her that is the antithesis of what I really wish for in a bride," he said. "Really, I cannot see what I saw in her. She is pretty, but I do not think it will last for she frowns and pouts too much, and that makes her look like a dyspeptic codfish."

Beth laughed.

"I expect somebody told her that her lips are sensuous and she tries so hard to draw attention to them that she has no idea that the attention drawn has become negative."

"Well, perhaps that is so. Do you think I should point it out to her, in the spirit of having once been close?"

"I fancy she would take it in bad part," said Beth, dryly, "and would be likely to take it as an insult not a friendly gesture."

Edward considered.

"I believe you may be correct," he said.

Beth smiled at him.

"I do not want to stop you doing what you think is right, but I cannot see Miss Hazelgrove taking kindly to what she would perceive as criticism," she said. She wanted to say something, to make sure there was no void of silence in which she might enjoy too much the sensation of Edwards's arm about her shoulder whilst hers encircled his and their other hands were clasped together, in the proper manner according to the rough sketches of the dance that had been in the instructions Letty had acquired. It was all very exciting, and at times their bodies came close to touching as they rotated through the dance's evolutions.

Many young ladies were not waltzing; it was considered by some to be quite immoral, even if sanctioned by society leaders like the Duke and Duchess of Arven. Beth knew that this meant that there would be some sticklers who would never invite her to attend any ball they threw because of it, but she did not care. Being propelled around the floor by Edward was a heady sensation. Miss Hazelgrove was not one of those who eschewed the waltz, and Beth caught her looking over at her and Edward with a brief flash of anger, presumably that Edward was not languishing over not waltzing with her.

It was over too soon, and Beth retired to sit quietly beside Letty, fanning her hot face which was not red purely from the heat of the ballroom, and to recover from a giddiness that was not altogether to be explained by the circular motion of the dance.

Beth danced another dance with Mr. Chetwode, who had likewise danced two dances with Lady Cressida. Lady Cressida did not waltz, but then, the image Beth conjured in her mind of Mr. Chetwode waltzing was more comedic than in any wise romantic. It was, after all, quite plain that Lady Cressida was much less of an ice maiden with the uncoordinated but very musical Mr. Chetwode; or so Beth thought!

The supper dance left Mr. Grindlay and Elizabeth to the right of Edward and Beth, and Edward said,

"I hear you are interested in engineering, Grindlay, have you looked much into drainage?"

"I can't say I have," said Mr. Grindlay, "Though I can see it's a necessary subject to study."

"Even the principles of under-draining, which are simple enough require some necessities of engineering, though they may be summed up in two simple rules, which sound comedic and are yet profound," said Edward.

"What are those?" asked Mr. Grindlay.

"Water flows downhill; and it ain't all water," said Edward. "You have to make sure there's somewhere for the runoff to go and to pass it through sand before it goes back into drinking water to clean it."

"It is as profound as it sounds simple," said Mr. Grindlay. "I say, do the ladies mind us talking about drains?"

"For my part, I am glad that there are gentlemen who talk about drains, so that I may enjoy the comforts of their engineering," said Beth.

"And I echo that s…sentiment," said Elizabeth.

The conversation turned to bridges, after the

couples had been involved in the exigencies of dancing, hampered by the inability of one gentleman ahead of them to keep time at all, and the flat footed shuffling of another, who was half of the couple who followed. This discussion went on into the supper room. Fortuitously, Mr. Grindlay and Elizabeth were placed opposite Edward and Beth. The conversation, to Beth's unholy glee, sent Amelia Hazelgrove, on Edward's other side, almost apoplectic.

The repast was grand, and Edward piled Beth's plate high with delicious looking food. It was not ladylike, of course, to eat too much in public, but since the gentleman on Beth's other side was Mr. Chetwode, whose musical conversation with Lady Cressida was quite as deep and technical as that between Edward and Mr. Grindlay, Beth felt at ease to enjoy the food, and to listen and learn from the discussion on bridge building.

Whether it was the food, the warmth, or the exercise, but Beth felt almost too tired to dance after supper. She was glad to be sitting out the waltz with Philip Devereux, and to watch how elegantly Edward performed with his hostess. And she fell asleep in the carriage on the way home, despite the cold, in contrast to the heat in the ballroom! Letty had to shake her awake, and Beth almost fell into bed, uncertain quite how Sowerby had helped her undress and get into her night rail and night cap.

It had been a most delightful evening, and Beth waltzed all night in Edward's arms in her dreams.

Chapter 12

"This is a very select gathering, Miss Hazelgrove, I understood your mother was inviting a number of people to dinner," said Edward, looking around with some disapproval at the dozen dinner guests, few of whom he knew well, and less of whom he liked at all.

Amelia laughed.

"Why, if it was too large a gathering, we should hardly exchange more than a dozen words, we were very hampered at the ball, were we not? And that tedious man going on about drains and demanding your attention, *where* the Arvens found him, I do not know; such a guy of a figure, and so pushy, quite a mushroom!"

"Hardly a mushroom, Miss Hazelgrove, the Grindlays may be found anywhere," said Edward. "A perfectly respectable family, even if Mr. Grindlay prefers his mathematics in the building of bridges, not the set of his neck-cloth. I found his conversation absorbing and informative."

Amelia pouted.

"It was taking your attention from *me*," she said. "And I thought I told you to call me Amelia?"

"My partner for the supper dance did not complain," said Edward.

Amelia gave a tinkling laugh.

"Oh, I know she is a distant connection of yours and you have to do your duty, but Edward! What a little squab of a creature, so dumpy, and the amount she ate! Why, she knows herself to be of no account, and therefore does not dare complain about being ignored for such tedious subjects. I assure you, if I had been your partner, I would have made my feelings clear."

"Oh, if Beth had objected, she would have said," said Edward. "Lucky girl; can eat what she likes

95

without putting on an ounce. She'll still be as slender as she is now when all the rest of the girls her age are forty and fat, I make no doubt."

"Edward, surely you do not mean to imply that I will be forty and fat?" said Amelia, dangerously.

"Well, assuming nothing happens to you first, Miss Hazelgrove, I fear that one day, being forty is quite inevitable," said Edward, reflecting that as she already had a tendency to plumpness, nature would doubtless take its inexorable course. He added cheerfully, "Being fat and forty comes to all of us in time, save those who are blessed with the ability to eat like a horse without effect."

"How dare you!" Amelia's voice rose to a shriek.

"Excuse me, how dare I what? It would be unrealistic to deny the passage of time," said Edward. "Surely you hope that your beaux accept that time will pass? Otherwise it would be a miserable sort of marriage. I know I shall be decidedly portly by the time I am forty, and probably with a myriad of lines on a weather-beaten face, from spending time outside."

"I do not find this kind of banter amusing," said Amelia, coldly. "When we are married, you will, of course, hire a steward and will not waste your time playing at being a farmer."

"Well, as we are not getting married, your wishes to stop all my pleasures are by the by, are they not?" said Edward, pleasantly. "I am not going to ask you again, because I have become aware of how we should not suit at all. You do not enter into any of my interests, and I do not enter into any of yours."

This was the point at which Amelia began a full-blown temper-tantrum which would not, Edward commented, have been considered appropriate by the children of the oldest of his married cousins, one of whom was almost three. As Amelia cared nothing for Edward's young relatives, this did nothing to abate the storm. Edward arose, and made his bow to his host and hostess.

"I appear to be indigestible," he said. "Thank you for the invitation. Perhaps I should avoid your daughter if I see her at any other functions."

"By Jove!" said Mr. Hazelgrove, "I'll see you for breach of promise!"

Edward raised an eyebrow.

"And what promise is that, sir?" he asked.

"Why, my daughter considers herself as good as engaged to you!" said Mr. Hazelgrove.

"Well, she could consider herself as good as engage to the Duke of Clarence, but it would not make him available for a breach of promise suit any more than it does me," said Edward. "Her imagination must be greater than I realised."

"But dear Edward, you came to propose to her early last month!" said Mrs. Hazelgrove.

"And she refused me, as I am sure you know," said Edward. "And she was quite right to do so; we should not suit at all, and I have been trying to explain this to her. I would never marry a woman whose expressed intent was to make me give up all my pleasures in life, after announcing she is only interested in what my social position can do for her, and who pouts like a baby when things do not go her way. Miss Hazelgrove is not, I think, mature enough for marriage; and I am glad to have realised it. She did me a favour when she refused my suit. I am sorry for her, because she will leave a bad impression of herself on the *ton* for future Seasons, but doubtless I shall have secured a wife by next Season, who, if we come to town, can help her overcome that bad impression."

Mr. and Mrs. Hazelgrove exchanged glances. Amelia had been enjoying herself in the little Season, and now in the main Season, breaking hearts, and there had been those people from whom they had expected invitations, and whence none had been forthcoming. Edward Brandon could not be accused of being diplomatically tactful, but perhaps his words were as true as they were forthright.

"You will always be welcome, here, Edward," said Mrs. Hazelgrove, who had scolded Amelia for refusing Edward, just because he appeared to be out of the succession. The Brandon family, after all, was quite prestigious enough even for those without a title.

Edward bowed.

"Thank you, ma'am, but I think it would be uncomfortable," he said. "I apologise for breaking up the company, but it will be better if I leave now."

"Perhaps so," said Mr. Hazelgrove. He longed to slap Amelia for showing herself up like this and for letting a prize like Edward slip through her fingers. If Edward were gone, Amelia might at least behave herself.

Edward left, feeling quite aggrieved that he had been lured to the dinner party through false pretences, as the invitation had had a note appended, that had said that it would be a moderate-sized gathering, consisting of people well-known to Edward. And yet all of the gentlemen were fops and idiots, some of whom were also claimants to Amelia's hand, and the ladies were all quite insipid. He might have dined quietly with Letty and Beth, and had decent conversation!

Edward took himself to his club, where he immersed himself in the newspapers.

Edward might have had his eyes opened about Amelia, but Amelia had not given up the idea of marrying someone who would be a baron one day. Whatever was causing Edward to behave so differently must be the fault of his horrid aunt and that wretched ward of hers. Amelia determined to watch them narrowly and look for an opening to separate Edward from his family.

Beth and Letty had spent a far more entertaining

evening, at the final performance at the Theatre-Royal in Covent Garden, seeing the breathtaking spectacle of the Olympic Circus. The thrilling horsemanship of men vaulting on and off the backs of running horses, with and without stirrups had Beth applauding; and the men also performed such feats of acrobatics as the Egyptian pyramid, those at the base supporting those who balanced upon them, feats on the slack wire, including the amazing Mr. Cunningham, who danced, Beth declared, better on the slack wire than she could manage on the unyielding ground! Of less interest was the interlude with the clown, but the feats of strength and balance were enough to keep both ladies gasping! The first part of the program was rounded up by the feats of riding of a single horseman, whose control of his mount was quite incredible. To leap from his horse's back while it cantered over obstacles to land perfectly on its back again was something Beth could never have believed possible, had she not seen it with her own eyes!

"I can see that this is a marvellous way of drawing the attention to the lessons they give to ladies and gentlemen whom they instruct scientifically in the art of riding," said Beth, looking at her program. "Though so far as I can see, the melodrama to follow, 'Alphonso the Brave, or the captive princess' is just an excuse for more feats of horsemanship, loosely held together with a plot."

"Oh, almost certainly, my dear," said Letty, "But it should still be entertaining."

It was indeed entertaining, and the escape from the tyrant's burning castle was most ingeniously arranged. Beth clapped until her hands tingled.

"I am glad we came to see this," she said. "Tomorrow will be all solemn, being Good Friday, but tonight has been delightful."

"It's a shame Edward couldn't come, but before I could ask him, he said he would be dining out and could not really cry off," said Letty.

"Oh well, I hope he had some stimulating conversation," said Beth. "One cannot expect him to dance attendance upon us every day."

They went out of the theatre, and Beth drew her cloak around her more closely in the chill of the night air, and as she did so, felt a tentative hand reaching for her reticule. Beth gave a shout of surprise, and grabbed the hand, her wrists strong enough for digging Letty's garden, which was one of the chores she enjoyed.

Her captive was a girl of about fourteen or fifteen, with a white, peaked face, shadows under her eyes and a look of terror in them.

"You are not a skilled thief," said Beth.

The girl hunched into herself.

"It be the first time I tried it, though you won't believe that, missus," she said.

"I might. Why are you trying to steal from me?"

"Because I'm so hungry, missus. I ain't had anything to eat, 'cept a wrinkled old apple I found, since I escaped."

"The child is quite blue with cold," said Letty. "If you were planning on taking her home, I suggest asking the rest of her tale when she has got warm and had something to eat. You were planning on taking her home, I presume?"

Beth chuckled ruefully.

"I was," she said. "What's your name?"

"Molly. Molly Burford," said the girl.

"If you had a position, would you swear not to steal again?"

"Wouldn't I just! My ma'd have the skin o' me backside black and blue if she knew!" said Molly.

"Well, you had better come along with us, then," said Beth.

Molly hung back.

"I ain't going to no more knocking house," she said.

"Molly, if that is what I surmise it to be, do you

think we'd be dressed as we are?" said Letty, crisply. Molly regarded them.

"No," she said. "You're dressed classy, swell morts, not flash morts. I ... I'll trust you."

"Good girl," said Beth. "Here's our carriage; hop in."

Letty would permit no more questioning of Molly until the girl had been taken home and sent with Simpson, the footman, to be fed in the kitchen. Letty regarded with disfavour the supercilious look the footman gave the girl.

"Molly is wearing tawdry finery of a whore because she has been kidnapped," she said, firmly. "She is a good girl, and Mrs. Simpson is to find her clothes more appropriate to her situation, which is as a maid. You will instruct her to do so, and to arrange for Molly to have a bath, to help her get that awful make-up off her, and to put her into a night-rail and wrapper to come to us in the parlour when she has eaten her fill and bathed. And a bed is to be warmed for her; you can put her in the dressing room next to Miss Renfield. And if you say even one quarter of what you are thinking you may kiss goodbye to any honorarium I might have considered giving you for your services."

"Yes, madam," said Simpson in a colourless tone.

"So I should think," said Letty.

Molly, clad in a night-rail several sizes too big, and a wrapper that had once been the banyan of a former resident of the house, appeared in the parlour. She was clean, and looked more salubrious by far.

"I know you are probably sleepy after your sufferings," said Beth, kindly, "but tell us what happened; did Mrs. Grey guess the main part of it, that you were kidnapped?"

"Well, yes an' no, missus," said Molly. "I come up to London to look for work, and this woman says to me she's looking for a maid, and so I went with her, and

101

she took all my clothes and said I'd do nicely for a client who likes virgins, and I said, what did she mean, and she told me I was a whore now. And I went for her, so she beat me, and then she told me to put on them clothes as you saw me in, and made my face up, and locked me in to wait. Well I weren't about to lose my thing, so I climbed out of the window and down the drain pipe, account o' how I know how to climb, and it weren't no harder than going up after magpie's nests to see what they been stealing, to get rewards. And then I thought, best place to hide is amongst other whores at Covent Garden, which even in the country we have heard of, account o' how she'd look for me to try to run right away, see?"

"That was well thought out and clever," said Beth.

Molly looked pleased.

"Well, then I thought, I have to eat, so… so I picked you to steal off of. And you know the rest."

"Resourceful girl!" said Beth. "Would you like to be my lady's maid and learn to be my dresser?"

"I'd think I was in heaven," said Molly.

"Good," said Beth. "That's settled then! Now run along to bed, and Sowerby will train you and show you what to do. She's kinder than she sounds, I promise you!"

"Thank you, missus!" said Molly, dropping a clumsy, country curtsey and running off.

"And now we hope that our instincts are right and she is not a born thief," said Letty.

"Not one who's that inept," said Beth.

Chapter 13

Many of the *ton* went to St George's, Hanover Square for Easter, or to St Paul's; Letty and Beth went to the nearest church to Red Lion Square, rather than be involved with the *beau monde* and their ulterior motives to be seen to be celebrating Easter properly. Beth suspected that they enjoyed the service more, being taken simply and movingly by the local vicar, than by some celebrated orator. The church they frequented was St James', Holborn, an ancient church rebuilt by Sir Christopher Wren, with a magnificent marble-clad tower. The magnificent interior was light and airy, and though the congregation was large, consisting largely of the lawyers employed in the nearby Inns of Court, it did not feel oppressive.

The rest of the day was spent soberly, though with the necessary business of sorting out clothes for Molly. Sowerby had loaned her a gown to be able to go to church, and Molly would do just about anything for Sowerby, never having expected to be able to worship as she would have done in her own village. St James' magnificence was something of an object of awe to Molly, used to a quite plain medieval church with no real decoration, and she begged Sowerby to help her by writing down what it was like, for the vicar to read to her family. Sowerby had been quite stiff and starchy at first, but unbent enough to tell Molly that her own mother had warned her about these women, and she had been able to avoid being taken into a bawdy house herself, when she came to London seeking her fortune. Molly thought Sowerby tremendously clever, and Sowerby allowed that Molly had displayed resource and sagacity in managing to escape. And the first thing Sowerby turned her efforts to was breaking Molly of calling Mrs. Grey and Miss Renfield 'missus'. Beth suggested using some of the fabrics they had bought to at least make sure that Molly had respectable underclothes, and to see what Mrs. Simpson might be able to find to alter for the girl.

"Sowerby will get some suitable fabrics to make up for you, to dress as befits a lady's maid," said Beth.

"Thank you, mis... Miss Renfield," said Molly. "Oh I am glad I fell in with you!"

"Well, I think I am lucky to have a maid who knows how to use her brains and keeps calm in a crisis," said Beth. "You never know when having someone who can think quickly may prove very useful. Even if it's only in thinking of clever ways to effect a repair to clothes torn at a ball."

"Oooh Miss Renfield, I am good at sewing," said Molly. "I've always sewed for all the little ones at home, and I took in some sewing too, but there ain't enough at home to make enough to help out. Please, Miss Renfield, what will my wages be? So I can send some home to my mother."

"I thought we might start at nine pounds a year, while you are being trained, rising to fifteen guineas over the next two or three years, and after that, we'll see," said Beth.

"Oh, Miss Renfield! Thank you!" said Molly.

"If you would like, I will arrange to have such monies as you wish to send to your mother sent to her directly every month," said Letty. "I know enough people who travel frequently who are trustworthy."

"Oh Mrs. Grey, how kind you are!" said Molly. "All I need is a shilling a week for myself, that's two pounds twelve shillings off of it, that'll make a heap of difference to ma having two-and-fivepence extra every week."

"You are a good girl," said Beth. Her pin money from Letty for being her companion would easily cover paying for a lady's maid, and it would make Sowerby's life easier. And if Edward did marry her, she could easily afford the increased wages a dresser would require.

The weekend passed quietly until the joyous Easter Sunday service, to which Edward accompanied the ladies, raising a brief interrogative eyebrow at Beth's acquisition of a maid. The organ playing of one John Grosvenor was sublime, and the swelling chords of Handel's 'Messiah' filled Beth with joy. She explained Molly to Edward as they walked quietly in the extensive church gardens after the service.

Edward nodded.

"Yes, I can see that you felt you had no choice," he said, gravely. "And even if she had been stealing for a while, I believe that if it was from necessity, she would have quickly stopped such a felonious habit once given trust and a good position. I have been minded at times to try the rehabilitation of those released from jail, or to offer surety for the very young who might abandon crime if given another course to pursue. Obviously I would not consider anything like that without the say-so of my wife; would you be agreeable?"

"Certainly," said Beth. "People are often only dishonest because they despair. And obviously one must be scrupulous not to place temptation in their way."

"Quite so," said Edward. "I am glad you are agreeable. If I am to inherit the title, I shall have to take my place in the House of Lords, and really it behoves me then to have some reforms in mind. My own lands are in good heart, so I can afford to spend time considering other unfortunates."

"You are a good man, Edward," said Beth.

"Just practical," said Edward. "It must surely cost the country less to expect some wealthy men to give second chances to those who have paid for their crimes, or for those who are not fully embarked upon a life of crime, like your Molly, than to transport them."

"One would think so," said Beth, smiling to herself

that Edward must needs be self-deprecating about his kindliness, as though it would somehow unman him. "I suppose too many would fear that they would be quite recidivist in their nature, however, and would betray the trust."

"You can never know until you give trust," said Edward, "and a man will not be trustworthy unless he *is* given trust, for it is in giving trust that one receives it in return, like loyalty."

Beth nodded. His words made sense.

Easter being a contemplative time of year, without social engagements, Amelia Hazelgrove had also been contemplating.

Edward Brandon was a handsome man, easy-going on the whole, though it appeared that he had a temper and could have a quite cutting tongue at times. This was a side of him Amelia had never seen before, but if he was cutting with his tongue, she reasoned, he was not likely to be violent. And that was always an advantage in a man. She must marry; women must, unless they were so wealthy that they could eschew convention and live alone, and she could not conceive of being a governess, or companion, the two feasible occupations for an unmarried woman without support. Her portion would be a comfortable competence, and indeed, Amelia could afford to live unwed, but this was unthinkable to her. She examined her reflection in the mirror with complacency, pouting her lips and noting that they were made to be kissed, and her face was made to be worshipped by men. And preferably a man who was sufficiently wealthy to continue to indulge her every whim as her parents had always indulged her every whim. No traces remained of the illness that had almost carried her off in her childhood, she was pleased to note, but sickly as she had been for so long, her parents had been glad to give in to her will and give her all she wanted. They knew she deserved it, reflected Amelia, and her tears at their unkindness over being upset at the dinner party had soon shown them how wrong they were to act as if she had been in the wrong. It was Edward who was in the wrong! He should recognise that it was a woman's prerogative to change her mind, and proceed to adore her as he had before; after all, it was plain that a Beauty like herself could not marry someone who would remain a mere 'mister' all his life. He was preoccupied by his aunt and her ward, and they must be persuaded somehow to leave him alone. Perhaps it would be wise to get to know them better. Yes, that would be it, and then Edward would see how nice she could be to his tedious and plain relatives, and he would be grateful to her. Amelia preened gently, seeing herself as a bountiful and beneficent baroness, dispensing largesse beyond what was deserving to Edward's poor relations. Presumably he was funding this season. The idea that Letty might be quite independent of Edward never crossed Amelia's mind in her rosy picture of the indigent aunt and distant cousin fawning on her for their monthly allowance, keeping the provincials in their places.

The ideal location to get to know more about them would be at a *fête champêtre*, but the weather was so unseasonably cold, still, and any kind of outdoor entertainment would be likely to fall flat. Then Amelia clapped her hands together in delight as she had an idea. The conservatory would make an ideal indoor venue for a synthetic *fête champêtre*, and as it opened off the east gallery, that might too be festooned with plants to extend the illusion. Blue muslin draped beneath the gallery's ceiling would give an impression of blue summer skies. Amelia did not trouble herself with how this draping might be achieved; she would issue orders and it would be achieved. She lost herself in a reverie of plans, and lists of whom to invite. It would be a spectacular social success, a revolutionary idea that would be copied by all. Perhaps even when the weather was clement enough for outside entertainments, for the environment of being outside, yet inside, negated the more irritating aspects of the great out of doors, like insects, animals, breezes, and plants that bit one – Amelia had once met a thistle and had come away from the encounter much upset – and all the other evils of outside.

Letty frowned as she read the invitation.

"It's from the Hazelgrove girl," she said. "An invitation to a *fête champêtre* indoors, which is a bit of a contradiction in terms."

"Well, it's not the sort of weather to hold a *fête champêtre* out of doors," said Beth. "Anyone would think it was February, not April. I take it we refuse politely? She was not very polite at Arvendish House."

"We were not exactly friendly either," said Letty, dryly. "Perhaps it is an olive branch offered."

"Perhaps it is," said Beth. "Should we accept it?"

"I think we should. If only because she may be wanting to use us to get Edward back, so we may see what she is up to," said Letty. "I dislike her, but she has been horribly spoilt by doting parents. It might be that she was shocked that Edward has not immediately run to her side now she thinks he might be likely to be heir to the barony again, and wants to understand him better."

"Is it very uncharitable of me not to want to help her to do so?" asked Beth.

"Yes, but quite understandable and reasonable," said Letty. "Oh, I am just sorry for the girl. She has always, I suspect, had her own way, and it isn't good for anyone. It is harder to accept that the world does not always do your bidding when you are quite grown up."

"I suppose so," said Beth. "My parents were quite indulgent, but they were never foolishly fond, and I knew that there were limits."

"Exactly," said Letty. "Your parents were kindly, not foolish, and they picked you governesses who knew how to handle you, even if their learning was not extensive. Alas, it is the fashion not to teach girls very much."

"At least Edward is good at explaining things," said Beth.

Letty laughed.

"And very pompous he sometimes sounds, when doing so! But young men his age can be pompous. You should not permit him to do it too much."

"He can sound very *worthy*, Aunt Letty, but then, you see, he really is that high minded, and it just comes out that way when he speaks."

"I know, my dear. He has a good heart. But you should tease him more!"

"Well… maybe. But it seems unkind."

"Nonsense; it would do him the world of good!" said Letty, firmly.

"Is Edward invited, do you think?" asked Beth.

"Probably, but I wonder if he will decline," said Letty. "She's quite predatory, and Edward is no fool. Too much vegetation into which a young man might be lured."

"Though not quite as much as with a real *fête champêtre* at least," said Beth.

"Oh, I don't know; most young ladies like their outdoor entertainments to involve as little wildlife as possible, and choose manicured gardens or fields with grass lately shorn by sheep, and very few bushes that might turn out to have thorns," said Letty, cynically. "I wager she'll be making use of an Orangery or similar, with plenty of vegetation, and divided into areas of different kinds of plants, divided with artful bushes or climbing plants, trellises and pergolas and so on."

"I have never seen an Orangery," said Beth. "Papa was of the opinion that if a plant could not stand a good English climate, it should not be permitted to grow here. I had cucumbers for the first time ever at your table."

"Oh, conservatories and the like are something of a conceit," said Letty, "but I am glad of my own small greenhouse, which is not grand enough to warrant the title of conservatory. It is pleasant to have a wider choice of food."

"I enjoy the wider choice," said Beth. "Does Edward have a conservatory?"

"A massive one," Letty told her. "And being Edward it is devoted entirely to vegetable growing. Why, I recall once when he had not got a flower to wear in his buttonhole, he went and picked the flower of a cucumber, and all of those who were not gardeners complimented him on his exotic plants and asked what it was called."

"What did he say?" asked Beth.

"*Curcubita*," said Letty. "He could not recall off the top of his head the correct taxonomy, which is *Cucumis sativus*, but it is of the curcubitae family, and it did well enough to provide an answer that still told the curious absolutely nothing."

"He has a wicked sense of humour," ventured Beth.

"Yes, and it is why I do not fear too much for him becoming, or remaining, too pompous," said Letty. "Because he can still laugh at himself as well. Shall I write and ask him to accept this invitation?"

Beth considered.

"No; let him make his own choice," she said. "I will not make him dance attendance on me, just because he is good-natured enough to do so."

Letty nodded.

Beth was being sensible.

Chapter 14

The Hazelgroves were not a family to permit the exigencies of nature to spoil their enjoyment of its offerings in a suitably tamed and manicured state, and the conservatory felt hot and steamy in comparison to almost anywhere else.

"The consumption of coal for this conceit would heat several foundling asylums," murmured Beth.

"It's their money to spend," said Letty, warningly.

"I shouldn't be so rude as to comment to anyone but you, or to Edward," said Beth. "It would be gross ingratitude to our hostess, but it does seem a little profligate. The amaryllis are spectacular, though."

"They are," said Letty. "And some splendid camellias and azaleas. Really it is a very extensive conservatory for a town house. I wonder if they use the used hops as a mulch and how good they are for the plants?"

"I beg your pardon?" said Beth.

"Miss Hazelgrove's grandmother is a beer princess," said Letty. "Her father made his fortune brewing porter, and sold out the business when he had only a daughter to inherit, who married a gentleman who had no intention of carrying on the trade. The Hazelgroves like to forget that, though I, for one, admire a man who can make his own fortune. I was indulging in facetiae; they have nothing to do with hops nowadays."

"Yes, I, too, have every admiration for a man who can build himself up; as you told me that Edward has built up and increased his own lands."

"There is a lot of foolishness regarding the so-called 'Cits'," said Letty. "They may not always know the rules of the society we take for granted, and into which they are wishful to move, but they would learn soon enough if those of the *ton* were not so high in the instep and would teach them how to go on."

"It does seem foolish," said Beth. "But I suppose some of the *beau monde* think that they are trying to buy their way into an exclusive society, which is exclusive because some of them bought their way in two hundred years ago by purchasing titles from James the First, and most of the rest either did favours for Henry the Eighth or came over with William the Bastard to steal lands since they had none of their own."

"Exactly," said Letty. "However, let us enjoy the splendid display of flowers in the well-appointed conservatory, and appreciate how cleverly arranged is the way the greenery spills out into that gallery. And no doubt Miss Hazelgrove will wish to talk to us at some point, depending on what her motives were for inviting us."

They did not have long to wait, as Amelia drifted over, her large mouth stretched into what was probably intended as a smile of welcome.

"Ladies! How good of you to come!" she said. "We hardly had any time to chat at the ball, and Edward was decidedly out of sorts, was he not?"

"He was in good enough spirits when I danced with him," said Beth.

"Dear Edward! So kind, so indulgent to his relatives, you must be *so* grateful to him!" said Amelia.

Beth felt her eyebrows draw together in confusion.

"He has been kind enough to squire us to a number of entertainments and to drive in the park, though it was too cold to stay out long," she said.

Amelia gave her tinkling laugh.

"I meant that he was providing your Season, of course!" she said.

"No he ain't," said Letty. "I'm a lot warmer than Edward is, and I don't need to hang on the sleeve of my nevvy. Grey was in cloth, and it may not be as profitable as beer, but he did very well for himself."

The laugh was a little forced this time.

"How very fortunate for you! I am so glad you are well able to provide for your…ward. How was it that you were both related to dear Edward?"

Letty clenched her teeth at the impudence of hinting

that Beth was her natural daughter.

Beth had missed the nuance, fortunately.

"Oh, it is quite simple! Aunt Letty is the younger sister of Edward's mother, and I am a daughter of their cousin. When I was orphaned rather unexpectedly, Aunt Letty gave me a home, as she had recently been widowed, and I have been able to repay her kindness by being a companion to her. My father had too many mortgages on the estate for me to have anything to look forward to but a life as a companion or governess, so you may be assured I was delighted!"

"And yet you have waited for a season?" asked Amelia.

"Never crossed our minds before," said Letty. "Like Edward, we prefer, on the whole, a quiet life in the country, though may I say you have made a delightful indoor space here to hold a *fête champêtre*; so very clever of you!"

Amelia was diverted from the irritation of Edward's preference for the country by the praise, and she almost preened, a smile of satisfaction creeping across her face.

"It is rather splendid, is it not?" she agreed. "I think it has worked out even better than I hoped when I had the idea. Though I am disappointed that not everyone I invited has come. I suppose they might come later."

"Perhaps some people were wary of the idea of an indoor *fête champêtre*," said Beth. "Aunt Letty and I were merely excited, and eager to see your conservatory.
We have only a small greenhouse, but perhaps we might be persuaded to extend it."

"It is rather exciting," said Letty. "The fountain is very attractive too, and I must say, I would rather like to use something similar to grow watercress for the table."

"Oh, there are sections for the vegetables as well, but of course they are not on display; such things are think that was rather a high in the instep comment?" said Beth.

"Well, yes, it was, and I cannot say I am anything but a little ashamed of myself," admitted Letty. "But her continual slights, implying that you are my natural daughter, that we are poor relations, and that final blatant suggestion that she is planning on marrying Edward really made me angry. So I'm afraid I ranged the eleven generations of aristocracy behind me, that I had almost forgotten through my happiness with Grey."

"She implied all that?" said Beth. "I am very stupid."

"No, my dear, just not wise to the ways of those who know how to give their words a cutting edge," said Letty. "And I am capable of cutting back, I fear. I learned a lot by listening to what Grey's diplomatic friends said, and what they said by not saying anything. Dear me! I have not met someone I wanted to be so rude to in a long time!"

"I fail to see how she thinks she is going to marry Edward, when she turned him down, most fortuitously for him," said Beth.

"I suspect she believes she can re-captivate him, now his incipient barony looms handsomely before her," said Letty. "Dear me, I can think of a few rather well-turned phrases I might use regarding his attraction that are not at all suitable for the current age; we were less mealy-mouthed when I was young."

"As if you were old, Aunt Letty!" protested Beth.

"I am not old, but I am not a babe in arms either; and the things that were said in my young days would make your hair curl," said Letty.

Beth laughed.

"Then perhaps you should try to give me ringlets!" she said.

"Hmm, I think not; you would end up with it as frizzy as a Dutchman," said Letty. "No, I will not tell you what I thought. You are likely enough to repeat it to Edward and he is certainly too delicate for the same"

Beth giggled.

"That's a hum!" she said.

"Possibly, but I prefer not to risk it," said Letty, primly. "Shall we remain for the whole afternoon and continue to exacerbate Miss Hazelgrove's nerves by our presence, or shall we withdraw, having discovered her plans?"

"Have we discovered her plans?" asked Beth.

"I believe so," said Letty. "I think she rather hoped to be able to patronise us a little, thinking us to be poor relations, and to ingratiate herself with Edward by being kind to us. I suspect she will continue to try to look good in Edward's eyes by being nicer to us than she wants to be, and I suppose it would be uncivil not to meet her half way. It won't make the slightest difference to Edward."

"No, indeed; he seems to think me a suitable sort of wife," sighed Beth.

Letty elevated an eyebrow.

"Suitable? Oh dear," she said.

"I could hope for love," said Beth, wistfully.

"He's a man; and most men are idiots," said Letty. "Depend upon it, he will realise what is creeping up on him sooner or later."

"Do you think it is?" asked Beth.

"Oh, I think so," said Letty. "So long as he does not fall into another fit of idiocy such as he had over La Hazelgrove!"

It was, perhaps, a shame that neither Letty nor Beth realised that the heavy bush of myrtle they were standing beside concealed the entrance to a small grotto, where Amelia Hazelgrove was currently standing, listening to this conversation with growing fury. She controlled her rage with unwonted fortitude in order to listen to the close of the conversation, unaware of the old adage that says that eavesdroppers rarely hear good of themselves. So! Edward was planning to marry the dumpy nobody who liked grubbing in the dirt like a peasant! Amelia planned to put a spoke in that plan; and as soon as she might. The Renfield girl must somehow be shown to be as much of a slut as Tiffany Pelham had apparently turned out to be, for Edward would not do the chivalrous thing and marry a ruined girl if there was any chance she was with child by another. Arranging to have Beth Renfield ruined might prove harder, but Amelia was certain she would find a way. It only required that Beth be somehow induced to go somewhere with a man, or where a man might meet her, and spend the night with him. Even if somehow she retained her virtue under such circumstances, nobody would believe it, and she would be forced either to marry whoever did the deed, or retire to the country, her reputation in shreds. Amelia was wealthy; and there were plenty of gentlemen whose reputations were not of the best and who would always do anything for money. It surely would not take too much effort to find one such man, who would be happy to deflower a virgin and get paid for it; and indeed, if Letty Grey were rich, doubtless Beth was her beneficiary, and an heiress for a wife would please such a man too. Amelia smiled to herself at her own cleverness.

And during the meanwhile, Amelia vowed that she must also smile until her jaw ached at Letty and Beth, and seem to be friendly to these horrible provincials!

Chapter 15

London was swiftly flooded with soldiers returning from France, officers who swelled the ranks of the gentlemen at balls and routs, and common soldiers too, destitute in the case of many after their discharge from an army which no longer wished to pay them; and Beth noticed that there were many more beggars on the streets. Many of them were crippled by their experiences of war, missing one or both legs, or an arm, or with eye-patches over ruined sockets, and many of them suffering cruelly from the effects of frost on stumps of limbs.

Beth gave largess where she might, and spoke to Edward, when he came, he said, to take his leave for a week or two.

"I just wanted to talk to you about something if I may, before you go," said Beth.

"If it's about what you should wear for some ball, I have less idea than one of my pigs," said Edward. "I have very little idea of fashion."

"It is nothing so frivolous or foolish," said Beth indignantly. "It is that the government has served its soldiery very badly. Do you not think it would be a good idea to help these men out, before they feel tempted to become criminals?"

"By Jove, Beth, it's a capital notion," said Edward. "And I'll certainly speak to others I know. I have to go and see to the planting of the wheat and barley, but while I am in the country, I shall turn my attention to what work may be found."

"Some may have come from the land in any case, and even if not suitable for work on the land, for being too crippled, might yet be able to train young boys bound over to keep the peace that you had in mind initially," suggested Beth.

Edward nodded.

"It's a good thought," he said. "And one I shall bear in mind. I'll be back before too long, dear Beth; I shall miss you, you know!"

He sounded faintly surprised.

"I miss you when you are not here, too," said Beth.

He kissed her hand, with a flourish, and left her.

Beth knew she would miss him, but immersed herself in the social round whilst she had the opportunity, to store up and remember, for she could not imagine having another time like this. And nor, being honest with herself, would she want to! She gave herself to helping her friends with their own romantic problems, not so much of a problem in Elizabeth's case, for she was becoming very close to Mr. Grindlay! And Elizabeth could choose to wed where she wished, and her parents likely to permit any reasonable choice. Mr. Grindlay was undoubtedly a gentleman, and hence an impeccable choice for any young lady, allowing for his means being modest.

Lady Cressida was another matter. As Mr. Chetwode was part of Beth's group of intimates, the rather poker-faced lady had been drawn in, and teasing by Beth and Elisabeth revealed her to be merely shy, and hating the idea of being sold to the highest bidder.

"We are in the same situation, Cousin Cressida, except I am supposed to be the purchase price of a title," said Madelaine.

"It is a very trying thing to have determined parents," sighed Cressida. The girls were in the ladies' cloakroom in a break in the dancing, fixing each other's escaping hair. "I ... the only person I have ever met whom I can respect is Mr. Chetwode, and I fear my parents might not accept a penniless musician."

"Ascertain if he has enough for you to live on and then elope with him, Lady Cressida," said Beth.

"Oh, call me Cressida, I pray you!" said Cressida. "It is hard to know how to raise the subject without being indelicate!"

"Why, Cressida, I think that sometimes one has to be blunt; and ask him if he can support a wife, and a couple of servants," said Beth, "for you are not used to coping without servants, I think."

"I can at least cook," said Cressida, dryly. "Someone had to step into the breach when Mama offended the last cook but one, and he left in high dudgeon. I used Mrs. Rundell's excellent book of Domestic Economy."

"Now that's resource," said Elizabeth.

Cressida shrugged.

"Needs must, and after all, French aristocrats have had to learn to make shift for themselves. And I am English, and at least as capable as any Frenchwoman."

"I wish I were so resourceful," said Madelaine.

"I am sure that you would be, if you had to be," said Cressida. "Look here! You have money, and we have the title; I'll ask Lucien if he won't make sheep's eyes at you just to make your mother think you have snared the heir to the Earldom. It's what Mama thinks she wants."

"But he's just a schoolboy!" said Madelaine.

"Yes, but it won't be real," said Cressida. "He'd be as horrified as you, if anyone wished such a marriage on him, because he wants to do his own choosing, as I do! But he's a sport, and he'd play along!"

"Well, that might help," said Madelaine. "Thank you! Even if he says no, thank you for asking him. Why was he in trouble for playing?"

Cressida chortled, startling the other girls, who did not realise she knew how to laugh!

"He was playing a piece called 'the trooper watering his nag' which is full of innuendo, and he explained it to me, and I blushed merrily, I can tell you!"

"I don't want to know," said Abigail, hastily.

"And Edward would not tell me," said Beth, mournfully.

"And I think I should spare my blushes as it would probably shock Mr. Grindlay," said Elizabeth, blushing.

"I hope he will not explain it to me!" cried Madelaine.

"I pestered him," said Cressida.

They returned to dance, and Beth found herself with Philip Devereux.

"A ladies' meeting to pull apart we men, I suppose?" he asked as he led her into the country dance.

"Oh, you flatter yourselves," said Beth. "You men must ever think you are the sole topic of the conversation of women!"

"And we are not? I am devastated. Quite cast down, indeed," said Mr. Devereux.

"No, you are not," said Beth.

"Well, no, I am not, and I can hide disappointment that my hopes are unfulfilled," said he.

"Idiot," said Beth, amicably.

The notice, meanwhile, of a criminal conversation suit, brought by Baron Darsham, duly appeared in the newspapers, naming Evelyn, Marquis Finchbury as the defendant, and the trial date was set. Edward thought himself well out of it; and anyone who thought to ask Letty and Beth, as relatives of those most nearly concerned were met with fishy looks.

"I can hardly comment on people not known to me," said Beth, firmly, when Amelia asked what the news was. They always seemed to be meeting Amelia, who was determinedly friendly.

"It affects Edward so nearly, though; are you not interested to know if he is likely to become the next baron?" asked Amelia.

"Not in the least," said Beth. "If he is the heir, why

then, he has been trained to it, and will accept the duties with resignation, and will do his utmost to perform such duties as fall to him to the best of his ability. If Lord Brandon remarries again and produces a son, then he will be relieved to avoid such duties. He told me that if he became baron, he would have to sit in the House of Lords and take an interest in politics, and I know that he is not particularly interested in politics."

"Oh, pooh, most of the peers do not bother," said Amelia.

"Perhaps not; but this is Edward of whom we speak, and he is very conscientious about his duties," said Beth. "He would find it such a nuisance, having to come to town to sit in the House; it would interfere with his farming plans. He has been driving back to Suffolk regularly, you know, to oversee the spring planting."

"Oh!" said Amelia, "is *that* what he's been up to? I wondered if he had a mistress hidden somewhere."

"Not unless her name is Wheat and Barley," laughed Beth.

"Well! I would think more of him as a man if he had a mistress, rather than dabbling in the dirt," said Amelia, crossly.

"I think more of him as a man for taking care of those who are dependent on him, and caring for the land he holds, not just for the benefit of his dependents, but for those he holds it in sacred trust for, his descendants," said Beth.

"Oh, you would," said Amelia crossly, thinking that if Beth Renfield were much more bovine, she would chew the cud!

Beth hated the little seed of doubt that Amelia had sown as thoroughly as Edward was sowing his crops; what if he did have a mistress? She decided to ask Letty, once they were back in the privacy of their temporary home.

"Amelia suggested that Edward might be visiting a

mistress, not his lands," she said. "Oh good, that was a most unladylike snort."

"I thought most unladylike thoughts about that little madam," said Letty. "Edward is a babe in arms where women are concerned; I could never picture him with a mistress. Oh, I expect he learned what was what in his youth, but he's too fastidious to, as you might say, flit from flower to flower, and he's too transparent for me to fail to pick up the idea of him having a long term mistress. And if he did, he would hardly have been sitting in Miss Hazelgrove's pocket since she came out in the Little Season. And I can't see him neglecting his lands for a few hours dubious pleasure in any case. Edward is far too dutiful and worthy! Indeed without his saving grace of a sense of humour, and an eclectic taste in reading matter, he would be quite boring!"

"He is not boring!" said Beth.

"No, that's what I said," said Letty. "He has a broad knowledge of all kinds of things, which he loves to share, and which bore the likes of Miss Hazelgrove, but which fill people like you and me with delight, for he shares what he knows in a spirit of enjoying what he has discovered, not in the spirit of imparting knowledge to less well-read people. Now, that Major who is making a cake over you, he likes to tell poor ignorant females what they ought to know."

"He's a boring ass," said Beth.

"Quite. Asinine in the extreme, and has no idea of how to impart knowledge without turning it into a lecture. He was explaining to me how cucumbers need a greenhouse."

"Oh dear!" laughed Beth. "Did you point out how little you need telling?"

"No, my dear, I'm afraid I put on a look of vapid and vacuous interest, all wide eyes, and let Edward explain to him that I send cucumbers to all my neighbours."

Beth chuckled.

"I wish I had seen that," she said. "Was that why he was so huffy when he was dancing with me?"

"Probably. He deigned to sit out with me while you were giving a fine impression of taking a spider for a walk whilst dancing with Mr. Chetwode."

"Mr. Chetwode may look like a drunken spider when he dances, but he is a fine musician," said Beth.

Letty raised an eyebrow.

"You are not preferring him to Edward?" she asked.

"Oh! No!" said Beth, "but I am a conspirator of his, to enable him to get close to Cressida, as he is hoping to marry her."

"I cannot see that her parents would disapprove; they have despaired of finding a husband for her that she has not scared away, and Mr. Chetwode is very wealthy," said Letty.

"*Is* he?" asked Beth. "Why, then, there should not be a problem; Cressida is under the impression that he is as poor as a church mouse and is trying to work out how to break it to her parents that she loves him and will have him, no matter what. I told her to ascertain if he could afford to keep her, and then elope with him."

"Oh Beth! Not perhaps a good comment to make, even in jest," said Letty. "He is not as well born as perhaps they would like, but as it is money the family needs, I cannot see a real bar to the union. I am glad to see less of Mr. Devereux around, he is a pleasant rattle, but I am not sure that he is of serious enough mien for you."

"Oh I like him well enough, but too much levity may become as tedious as too much seriousness," said Beth. "I dare say he will make a good husband to someone when he finishes growing up. Edward enjoys recounting the misdeeds of his youth, Mr. Devereux regrets not reliving them, I fancy. He does not take himself seriously at all, and until he does, he will not take anyone else seriously."

"Ah!" said Letty. "You have not, then, met anyone

you prefer to Edward?"

"No, Aunt Letty; I love Edward, and I could hope that he learns to hold me at least in affection," said Beth.

"He'd be a fool not to," said Letty.

Chapter 16

Beth was assiduous in helping her friends, including newer friends like Cressida, who was so hard to get to know. Consequently, she spent much time dancing with, and chatting to, Mr. Chetwode, boosting his confidence.

"She asked me if I could support a wife, is she having a laugh at my expense?" asked Mr. Chetwode, anxiously.

"Not at all," said Beth. "A girl who has been economising in the hopes of marriage to someone who can support her in some style is going to want to know if there will be enough in the house to eat, and better yet, a servant to cook it. I'm sure Cressida is more than capable of cooking and doing housework, but I have no doubt that it might put a strain on love for her to have to do so unaided."

"I'm a nabob," said Mr. Chetwode.

"Yes, I know that, because I can see the quality of the cloth of your clothes, and that they are cut for comfort not fashion, and the violin you play is a Stradivarius, I think. But not all people are so perspicacious, and as you do not throw your blunt around, they assume you to be fairly impecunious and buying as good clothes as you can get as an economy."

"And wonderful Cressida thinks that? And would still marry me? I could scarcely dare believe it!" said Mr. Chetwode.

"She was wondering how to confess to her parents that she wanted to marry a poor man," said Beth, "Which is why I told her to elope with you. It might still serve. Her father might not listen to explanations once Society has made up its stupid mind about you."

Mr. Chetwode looked shocked, but chuckled.

"And I have to say I shouldn't be so deucedly awkward or likely to fall over myself in a quiet wedding over the anvil as I might if I had to have a big society wedding as befits an earl's daughter," he said. "And the wealthy are always forgiven for unconventional behaviour. Blessed if I won't actually consider it ... If you don't mind being my go-between to Cressida, I'll go ahead and arrange it."

"Good man," said Beth. "Let me know of the arrangements, and I'll tell her where and when to meet you, and persuade her to stick to no more than two band boxes."

"Do you think she'd be likely to bring more?" said Mr. Chetwode in lively horror.

"There's no telling what girls raised to expecting silver spoons might do, as her parents are very conscious of what's due to her consequence," said Beth, dryly. "I have no doubt her mother would be likely to pack all the family silver and a couple of footmen to polish it, but Cressida does seem to have a practical turn of mind. She says she learned to cook when they were between cooks."

If Beth suspected that Cressida had merely invaded the kitchen armed with a book of domestic economy and issued orders to lesser servants, it was at least more enterprising than leaving it all to a scullery maid.

"What a wonderful girl she is!" sighed Mr. Chetwode, looking quite, thought Beth, like a moonling in his throes of adoration.

She left him contemplating his adoration to dance with Edward.

"What revolting faces that fellow was pulling!" he said.

"He's in love," said Beth, "as well as being a musician. I suspect it takes artistic people more violently than it does ordinary beings like you and me."

"Good G-d! Are you in love then?" demanded Edward, conscious of feeling guilty that he had possibly gazed on Amelia in such a rapt fashion.

Beth blushed and lowered her eyes.

"Beth!" Edward was suddenly furious with Mr. Chetwode. "He ain't worthy of you!"

"I beg your pardon?" said Beth, looking as confused as she felt.

"That Chetwode fellow you're in love with!" said Edward forcibly.

"Whatever gave you the idea I'm in love with another woman's man?" said Beth, indignantly. "Don't you dare go spreading that around, or poor Cressida will be quite cast down and fear that I'm going to wreck her chances with the daft creature!"

Edward stared.

"You mean... you're not in love with him? But you blushed when I asked!" he accused.

"You asked if I was in love, which was a slightly indelicate question, but you never mentioned Mr. Chetwode, who is a pleasant companion, but not someone I should ever be in love with. I expect I might even have to tell him which inns to stay at on the Great North Road when he elopes with Cressida, he is singularly hopeless at detail," said Beth.

"You will not. I'll advise him," said Edward, assuming that this was mere levity, and half ready to find any way of making sure Mr. Chetwode was as far as possible from Beth. "Not that I know the road any further than York, but I'm sure he can improvise for the rest of the way."

"Oh thank you, Edward, how kind you are, and how nice of you not to make a fuss about me advising them to elope!" said Beth.

Edward came to the realisation that she might be serious, and decided that the best thing to do was to treat it lightly, as Lady Cressida was, he felt sure, unlikely to do anything so shocking.

"Oh, I daresay it's the only way to unfreeze Lady Cressida," said Edward. "And a couple of days on the road with a dreamy type like Chetwode will either show her how she has to manage him, or will send her fleeing for home to accept any choice her parents make for her."

"I doubt she's likely to flee," said Beth. "It's his brains and his music she's interested in; I daresay she can manage to procure a hack in the rain for herself if he can't, which is one of my criteria for a marriageable gentleman."

"Well, it's not hard," said Edward.

Beth laughed.

"It's not hard for the sort of gentleman who can also catch a waiter's eye to be served, and who never is at a loss how to deal with a situation where a lady is in need."

"Suppose I had not been the sort of man to manage such things?" said Edward.

"I should not have accepted your proposal," said Beth.

"But how could you know?"

"Partly from my own observation, and partly from Aunt Letty's stories of you, after allowing for some degree of partiality," said Beth.

"What a dear girl you are!" said Edward.

Edward was not the only person to assume that Mr. Chetwode was enamoured of Beth; for Amelia also noted this earnest conversation, and made plans accordingly, and smiled encouragingly at Mr. Chetwode. As the young man was trying hard not to make a spectacle of Cressida, he cheerfully asked for an introduction to this smiling young woman, so he might dance with someone else, and hope she would not mind his clumsiness.

Amelia was not looking forward to the unhandy nature of Mr. Chetwode's dancing, but it was something to have to put up with for her plan to work.

"Oh, Mr. Chetwode," she cooed, "I could not help noticing you speaking with my friend Beth Renfield!"

"Ah?" said Mr. Chetwode, hoping that his plans had not been overheard and that this female, pleasant as she seemed, did not hope to make him reconsider.

"Indeed! And seeing how much in love with her you are, I am certain that Beth is quite as much in love with you, but of course she does like a man to prove that he may be *masterful* you know. And your best way to win her is to wait outside her house for the ball on Friday, and hustle her into your carriage and drive straight to Gretna with her!"

Mr. Chetwode made a strangled noise of mixed irritation and incomprehension. Amelia misunderstood.

"Oh, you poor man, I know, you have not the funds to undertake such an operation!" she said, with her tinkling laugh, "but I will readily give... or loan if you prefer... whatever you need, for Beth will be able to pay me back when she comes into her inheritance."

Mr. Chetwode found his voice.

"I think, Miss Hazelgrove, you are labouring under several false apprehensions," he said. "Miss Renfield is a dear young lady who has been like a sister to me, helping me to gain the courage to ask the woman of my dreams to be mine. But I do not love her, and she does not love me, which is just as well, for her playing on the pianoforte is bearable but only just, and only if one does not have to listen to her doing more than accompany equally inept people."

Amelia stared.

"But... but I thought... your expression... when you were speaking to her..."

"Oh, but we were speaking of the incomparable... of the most beautiful and accomplished woman in the world," said Mr. Chetwode.

Amelia tittered.

"Do you make a habit of praising this female when in the company of other women?" she asked.

"Oh! No, but you asked," said Mr. Chetwode. "I do not need to discuss her, usually, for phrases of music in my head whisper about her, and then I do not have to listen or talk to any other female who is present."

Amelia promptly left him before they reached the top of the line to dance.

"What did I say?" said Mr. Chetwode to thin air, then shrugged and left the line. If this silly creature did not want to dance after all, he did not have to. He hesitated over whether he should go and sit the rest of it out with her, and decided it would be more convivial to go and find his hostess' music room and play the music that he was writing for Cressida.

Amelia stormed off in a rage, because he had not even pretended to be attracted to her, and because he was of no use to her after all.

Well, if there was nobody she could persuade to elope with Beth Renfield, she must see which of the idiots lost too much at cards, and offer one of them a way to earn his way out of his debts.

Edward was busy puzzling over who Beth might be in love with, and whether there was a problem, that she had not asked to be released from their secret betrothal. How dare someone make Beth look so wistful as she had when she had blushed! Some idiot had not realised that Beth loved him, and was not returning her regard! It made Edward want to grind his teeth, and long to plant a facer on someone who was upsetting his Beth!

Edward suddenly realised that he was jealous, and wondered guiltily if his own behaviour had driven away a suitor before he might properly appreciate Beth.

He must speak to Letty about it.

Amelia racked her brains for who might be rakish enough to consider abducting a girl for money whom she actually knew. Her first choice fell upon Sir Leomer Byesby, who was said to gamble very deeply and to be a dangerous man. Accordingly she used her smile, and her fan to let him know that she wanted to dance with him, and managed adroitly to meet him on the dance floor before her mother might expostulate. Amelia's mother gave her a great deal of leeway, but she would be likely to protest over so gazetted a rake as Byesby dancing with her daughter.

"What did you want of me, Miss Hazelgrove?" asked Byesby.

"La! Can it be that I wanted anything but the pleasure of a dance with you?" said Amelia, plying her fan.

"Unlikely. Why not come to the point and then we may enjoy the rest of the dance?" said Byesby.

Amelia nearly left him standing partnerless at that point, but decided to pass it off with her tinkling little laugh, that had taken her so long to achieve.

"Why, My Lord, you are blunt indeed!" she said. "Very well; you have a problem of debt, and I have a problem of a stupid girl who has somehow ensnared into betrothal the man I intend to marry. I pay you to compromise her by abducting her, and we both have no more problem. Her guardian is rich, and she is likely the sole heir."

"What a poisonous little snake you are, to be sure," said Byesby, his lips curling slightly in a sneer. "And which poor girl are you planning to so betray to a bridegroom most definitely not of her choosing?"

Amelia flushed.

"Are you saying you won't do it? I can pay you all you ask!" she said.

"Mercenary as a Cit, too," said Byesby, managing to combine boredom with scornful amusement in his voice. "I am not to be bought; no gentleman would ever accept such an infamous suggestion, even if it were his last chance to stay out of the Marshalsea. You are a thoroughly unprincipled girl to even consider such a thing. Which poor girl are you hoping to enact

133

this wickedness on?"

"I shan't tell you, so there!" said Amelia. "How dare you call me a Cit, and poisonous?"

"Because you are," said Byesby. "Though I fancy it's more a case of being too thoroughly spoilt to realise how wicked you are; you should have been well spanked as a child. It's probably too late now."

For the second time of the evening, Amelia flounced off the dance floor; and those who had been inclined to censure the behaviour of Mr. Chetwode for driving her from him changed their minds to argue that a girl who left two dance partners must surely be the one at fault, since there was nothing wrong with Byesby save a fatal attraction to gambling and a fatal attraction for women.

Byesby laughed, and took himself out of the measure to find the nearest waiter with a drink, whereupon he sat and watched Amelia Hazelgrove quite narrowly, to see if she would be likely to reveal who was so unfortunate as to be the object of her designs.

Amelia was in receipt of a scolding from her mother for behaving badly in two dances.

"To leave a known rake like Byesby is one thing – and you should never have accepted an offer to dance from him in the first place – but to do that after leaving an inoffensive creature like Mr. Chetwode, that is too bad!" said Mrs. Hazelgrove.

"He is not inoffensive, he is more interested in his stupid music than he is in me," said Amelia, who wanted to defend herself but did not dare speak of her real reasons for having felt slighted by Mr. Chetwode.

"Now that is quite childish of you, my darling," said Mrs. Hazelgrove. "For I have heard it said that he is a very fine musician, and musicians are all just a little bit mad about their music! There, I had to give my precious girl a bit of a hint, you know, before any of the old cats decide to bar you from any more balls, for being missish! I think we should go home, now, and I will drop a hint that it is *that time* for you, which is making you so badly behaved, for that will make it *quite understandable* to any hostess or would-be hostess!"

Amelia sulked. Being hustled off, and rumours of her indisposition spread widely meant that she had no time to approach any other debt-ridden rakes. She must suffer herself to be taken home early, and to stay at home for several days to lend credence to her mother's way of rescuing her from possible social ruin. Amelia did not see why it should mean social ruin to a girl, if she left a less than convivial partner looking stupid, but apparently her mother felt that it did.

Well, in the meantime she might wrack her brains and make lists of appropriate men to ruin that horrid Beth Renfield.

Chapter 17

Edward managed to get Letty alone while he escorted the ladies shopping for ribbons in Bond Street.

"Aunt Letty, I managed to upset Beth, I fear," he said.

"She said nothing of it to me," said Letty.

"Well, she might not have done so for embarrassment," said Edward. "You see, I thought for a while she was in love with that clunch Chetwode, and made a cake of myself, and I asked her if she was in love, and she blushed, and she told me it was an indelicate question."

"Edward, sometimes you are a complete fool," said Letty, crisply. "Perhaps you should ask yourself for whom might Beth have a partiality, when there is one gentleman whom she admires mightily, who is kind, and able to make sure that a lady is always comfortable, who has been assiduous in his attentions and escorting us, and who is even good-looking into the bargain."

"Why, he sounds a very paragon, but he must have been escorting you when I have been away in Suffolk, for I cannot bring to mind anyone of that nature," said Edward.

"Then you're a clunch even more so than Mr. Chetwode, and you deserve to lose Beth if you don't make a push to display your feelings for her. You do *have* feelings for her, don't you? More at least than as a convenient adjunct to your life for being restful, and kinder than the Hazelgrove female?"

"I...I believe I am in love with Beth," said Edward.

"Well, perhaps showing her that might be a good idea," said Letty, tartly. "You cannot expect a woman to make the running in a courtship; you need to court her properly so she knows she is doing the right thing in marrying you."

"But if she is in love with this other man, this paragon...." said Edward.

Letty threw up her arms in frustration.

"Edward, who escorts us shopping? Who gets waiters to serve one? Who has aspirations to aid the indigent?"

"Well, I don't know anybody else who does so," said Edward. "Kept himself secret from me, hasn't he?" he added truculently.

"On the contrary. You have been acquainted with him for twenty-seven years, four months and seventeen days," said Letty.

Edward counted on his fingers.

"That would be from my birth," he said. "Aunt Letty! Is Uncle Adam courting Beth?"

"Are you really that stupid, or did my sister merely drop you on your head when you were a baby?" demanded Letty

Edward stared.

"You.... Do you mean that the darling girl loves *me*?" he gasped.

"And I'm not sure why when you are such a nodcock," said Letty with some asperity.

"I could not dare to hope," said Edward.

"Well hope, and for goodness sake, be lover-like towards her, instead of treating her like a colleague you hope to back you in the House of Lords!"

"I don't!" he was hurt. "Do I?"

Letty sighed.

"Only a little," she said. "Here she comes, now offer her your arm do and admire her purchases."

Beth tripped over, smiling with pleasure.

"Now I may make over the gown someone spilled red wine onto, that I did not see until it had been washed," she said. "Molly was so tearful about it, and I showed her how to soak it in white wine, which brought out most of it, but there is the faintest of pinkness still near the hem. I thought to trim it with

137

flounces of the same muslin, as they still have some in the haberdashery here, Vandyked and caught at the top of the points with ribbon knots. And I know that is of no interest to you, Edward, but I was so pleased that they had not sold out. The only other thing we might have tried was to soak the whole in red wine and hope to achieve an all over pinkish tinge that at least could be worn over pink. White is sometimes a difficult colour to match, like black!"

"That sounds illogical," said Edward.

"Oh, it may sound illogical, but if you consider, the fibres may be from different places, as are the fibres from different sheep, and though they bleach it in the sun I believe, it does not always achieve quite the same shade, sometimes being creamier in colour than others," said Beth. "As for black, the dye may take differently, and some manufacturers achieve a good black by different means than others."

"By Jove, you are right!" said Edward. "One of my school coats washed corbeau-coloured the first time it was laundered, and rifle green the second, and I had to have the laundress swear it had gone to her black to avoid a whipping for gaudiness. Mama was most put out at such shoddy fabric."

"Yes, I should think so!" said Beth. "Is that why you eschew green coats?"

"By Jove, I should think it probably is, though I had not thought of it for many years!" said Edward. "How the other fellows teased me!"

"The dark blue superfine you generally wear brings out the blue of your eyes, in any case," said Beth.

"And your eyes are like the sea, ever changing, and always beautiful," said Edward.

"Oh Edward! Did you just pay me a compliment?" said Beth, looking pleased.

"Only said it because it's true," said Edward, looking flustered. "You're a very fine-looking woman, Beth, and stap me, if I don't prefer golden brown hair by a long chalk to theatrical brunette. It ain't so actressy."

Beth smiled up at him, and Edward almost kissed her. However it was not appropriate behaviour to kiss a girl in the middle of Bond Street! At least, not unless one was deucedly loose in the haft!

Beth was happy. Why Edward had looked at her so kindly, and for a moment she had wondered whether he was going to kiss her! It would be wildly improper to do so here, but Beth knew that however improper it was, she would permit Edward to kiss her anywhere!

Edward schooled himself, and was all that was proper, seeing the ladies home, and Beth hoped that he was not regretting such a display of emotion.

"Dear Aunt, Edward was not *drunk* was he, that he gave me compliments?" she asked Letty, once Edward had taken his leave of them.

"Drunk, fiddlesticks, come to his senses to recognise what a pretty girl you are," said Letty. "You ain't a beauty, but then handsome is as handsome does, and you look very pleasant indeed. He's just turned embarrassed because he said what he was thinking. It always takes him that way."

"Oh Aunt Letty! Do you think that he is beginning to feel some affection for me that is more romantic than familial?" asked Beth.

"I think he's realising how loveable you are, and how he might have nearly lost you to some other cub on the town," said Letty. "After all, hasn't he growled at all your suitors?"

Beth giggled.

"You make him sound like a dancing bear, tormented by horrid little boys," she said.

"Well, my dear, I'm sure he would enter into the feelings of such a bear, feeling tormented by thoughts that those little boys might carry off what he wants most, which in the case of a bear might be his food, but in Edward's case is his bride, you."

"Ooooh…" said Beth.

"About time he started treating you more like a woman and less like someone to harangue with his political beliefs," said Letty, "though it's a compliment that he expects you to understand them and argue if you disagree."

"I like to listen and to make suggestions," said Beth. "He is hoping to set up some kind of manufactory for wounded soldiers, where they may make things for sale, to give them dignity, with a place to stay as well and regular meals. He wrote to me from his farm that perhaps some of the woodland that needs thinning might be given over to timber for the manufacture of simple furniture that they might make, or decorative boxes for keeping gloves, or jewellery, or paperwork in."

"Edward may not be the sharpest stick in the bundle, but he is very good at seeing what needs to be done and doing it," agreed Letty. "Of course it never occurred to him that it was improper to write to you, a young unattached woman, without sending such a missive via your guardian."

"Well, we are betrothed," said Beth. "And what do you mean about him not being the sharpest stick in the bundle? Edward is very knowledgeable!"

"Yes, that is true," said Letty. "And I grant you he has taken the effort to be well-informed, but sometimes he fails to see the simplest of things… well, well, my dear, do not let it trouble you. Edward may not be as clever as some, but he has a wisdom that is more endearing."

"You *do* speak in riddles sometimes, Aunt!" laughed Beth.

Amelia's cogitations had meanwhile brought her to the decision that she knew the perfect person to abduct and ruin Beth. And she got her ideas from the newspapers.

The ongoing Crim.Con. case in the paper, regarding the foisting of a discarded and pregnant mistress onto Adam, Baron Darsham, was unfolding in some detail, since Tiffany's maid had decided to sell her story to the highest bidding newspaper, having very little understanding of such things as the concept of contempt of court, let alone the decency to preserve any of her mistress' reputation. Indeed, had she known, she might even have been pleased to take away Tiffany's name, since the erstwhile Baroness, divorced already according to the Church, had dismissed her maid in a fit of pique that the girl had backed the story after being told that she might do so. Tiffany was finding that it was not so simple as divorcing Adam and going back to being a free woman, since she was barred from most of society for her deception and prenuptial adultery. It was unfair that society did not equally bar the man who had seduced and left her, and Evelyn, Marquis Finchbury, was still received, if not permitted near to many unwed ladies.

Amelia considered that Finchbury would be the ideal candidate to abduct Beth. He was unscrupulous, and his pockets were always to let. That this was an attack on Edward's whole family never occurred to her. Contacting him was, of course, the most difficult matter. Amelia thought long and hard, and decided that the only thing to be done was to send him a letter and arrange to meet somewhere like Vauxhall Gardens, now that they were open for the Spring and Summer. A vastly improper thing to do, however, and would give the Marquis a possible hold over her. Amelia was practical enough about her own safety. However, she had a sudden idea; the illuminations in honour of the defeat of Napoleon would afford the opportunity of dark corners where the lights left pools of shadow, and yet in a more public space than, say, the dark walks at Vauxhall, one might feel safer.

Amelia began a campaign of nagging of her parents

to be permitted to view the illuminations, fairly certain that neither of them wished to go, and so would be likely to permit her to go under the care of a footman and her maid. She would be able to do that, even if supposedly under the curse of a female indisposition, as she would not be likely to be seen by many, if she was careful. Amelia gave her parents to understand that she would remain in the carriage.

Accordingly, once given permission, Amelia wrote a note to the Marquis of Finchbury, directing him to meet her that evening to learn something to his advantage, at the illuminations in South Audley Street, where the display by the Duke of Cambridge, the Portuguese Ambassador and Monsieur might be seen. Amelia planned to drive through the streets to see the other displays, at Horse Guards, the Mansion House, Manchester Square and elsewhere, but picked this venue almost at random, but she knew that she might step into Grosvenor Chapel, and even someone who was as hardened a rake as Finchbury would never abduct a lady from a church. That her own business was most unholy did not occur to her. She added the porch of the chapel as a venue to meet, and sent her favourite footman off with the message. He would doubtless be accompanying her in the evening and would do anything for her, especially with a good vail.

As it happened, Edward was also taking Letty and Beth to see the illuminations; he chose to take them to Somerset House, where the decorations were quite sumptuous, and some took the part of lit inscriptions, with the Latin tag along the front,

Europa Instaurata, Auspice Britanniae; Tyrannide subversa, Vindice Liberatis. "I may have little Latin, but even I can puzzle that out," said Beth. "Europe restored, under the protection of Britain, tyranny overthrown, the vindication of liberty."

"Near enough," said Edward. "Europe set up under the protection of Britain, Tyranny overthrown, the champion freed, as I make it."

"I like the pictures better," said Beth, pointing to another building that displayed an illuminated painted transparency caricature of Bonaparte, tumbling from the mount of Republicanism into the arms of a demon. "Why does it say 'To Hell-bay'?"

"No idea," said Edward, "unless it's a forced pun on the name of the island he is to be exiled to, Elba."

"It's not a good pun if so," said Beth, disapprovingly. "But an amusing idea to have him tumble from hubris."

They wandered the streets, exclaiming at the ingenuity of some of the illuminations, expressions of loyalty to the King and Regent, as well as praising Wellington, expressions of support to the House of Bourbon, and a myriad of coloured lamps as well as transparencies.

Edward was insistent that the ladies should repair with him to Fleet Street.

"The Knight's Gas Company have a most ingenious display," he told them.

Beth gasped as she saw what the gas company had managed, a tree made of laurel leaves and festooned with blossoms made with gas lights, and throwing all other illuminations into the shade with the unparalleled brightness of the burning gas.

"Magnificent!" breathed Beth.

"Thought you'd like that," said Edward. "One day, all London's streets will be illumined with gas lighting, and it will be a much safer place to be."

"Indeed, yes!" said Beth. "Why, I am sometimes afraid at night of turning my foot betwixt door and carriage, without having to stop to consider the possibility of footpads taking advantage of the confusion as people seek their carriages outside a house where a ball has been held, for once outside the pool of the lights at the entrance, the darkness appears the more Stygian by contrast. I cannot help wondering whether one of the reasons to continue a ball until dawn is to permit safer passage home for the guests, once the crepuscular gloom as the sun rises has given way to morning."

"I wouldn't say you were wrong at that," said Edward. "Worth braving the cold of the evening?"

"Eminently so," said Beth, determining to wrap up warmly as she saw Cressida on her way to her elopement after the ball they were both to attend. Who knew how long they might have to wait for Mr. Chetwode! She would strongly urge Cressida to dress warmly too, and tell her maid to do so; and Beth determined that she would loan Molly, who was to wait with her, her second best cloak, so that she might not get chilled.

However, this excitement was several days away, and the weather might even improve.

Not that Beth was very sanguine on this point, as the chill seemed to be set in for the foreseeable future, and the barometer held no promise of change.

She was glad to return to the fireside in Red Lion Square, where Edward was regaled with tea, and London crumpets, which were made with yeast, and had holes in for the butter to melt into. Beth thought them much preferable to the normal, flat crumpets, which were probably the same griddle cakes that King Alfred had burned, and happily consumed three, licking her fingers.

"Oh Beth, you are so sweet," said Edward. "I do love to see you enjoying yourself, whether with the illuminations or just enjoying something so simple as tea and cakes or crumpets."

"I'll be fat by the time I'm forty, you know," said Beth, seriously. "I love my food too much not to be."

"Oh, I have no doubt I shall be a trifle corpulent by then as well," said Edward, "and I love the way you accept that one ages and changes. Though I fancy you may carry it off better than I; you have the type of figure that is unchanged, no matter what you eat."

"More to the point, I go for brisk walks in the mornings," said Beth. "Because I do have my vanity."

Edward laughed.

"We shall walk together when we are married," he said, stretching out a hand to her.

"I should like that very much," said Beth, taking his hand, shyly. It was a rather buttery encounter but neither minded.

Letty heaved a sigh of relief. They would manage to declare their love before long.

Chapter 18

Amelia had meanwhile had a curt note back with five words on it: *"this had better be good"* which she had shivered over when reading. She stuffed her reticule with paper money, and hoped that she had enough to pay off the Marquis to do the job. It seemed likely that Beth was also Letty's heir, reasoned Amelia, who was still not entirely convinced that Beth was not Letty's natural daughter.

It was with some trepidation that Amelia approached the chapel. A dark figure lurked by the door.

"Well?" he snapped.

"I have a business proposition for you," said Amelia. "Shall we step into the chapel out of the wind?"

He gave a bark of sardonic laughter.

"Well, you ain't weighed down with devotion," he sneered.

"What do you mean? I am a regular church-goer!" said Amelia.

"But ready to transact trade in the temple ... I presume it is not yourself that you are selling?"

She flushed.

"Certainly not! But I offer both funds to cover any immediate embarrassments you might have, and a bride who will have a good fortune when her aunt, if the woman is not her mother, dies, should you care to marry the wretched woman, not just ravish her."

"Very well. You interest me; keep talking," said the Marquis, ushering Amelia into the church. He shut the door in the face of her maid.

"I am unchaperoned!" cried Amelia, with sudden panic, looking up into the dark, sardonic face, half afraid he might ravish any female, and half wondering what it might be like to be possessed by someone wild and untameable, not safe and conventional like Edward.

"So you are," said the Marquis. "I ain't got any desire to kiss you though; I prefer blondes with lips that ain't big enough to be likely to slobber. I don't want any witnesses."

"Very well," said Amelia, torn between eagerness to get it over with, relief that he did not demand kisses as additional payment, and outrage over his evident lack of interest in her, though he had swept her trim figure with an insolent look that almost seemed to undress her! "There's a girl called Beth Renfield, who is the ward of a Letty Grey. I want Beth abducted and ruined. You can marry her then if you will; Mr. Grey left his wife very wealthy as I understand. AWP!"

Finchbury seized Amelia by the throat, and regarded her thoughtfully.

"And would this be any kind of trap, set up by Edward Brandon, by any chance?" he asked.

"He knows nothing of it! I want to marry him, but that stupid little dab of a woman has her hooks into him somehow! And I want her out of the way!" said Amelia.

He let go of her throat as suddenly as he had seized it.

"You ain't clever enough to dissemble," he said. "Well, well! I might have suspected Edward Brandon of setting a trap for me, as he's very hot as regards family. And it pleases me well enough to do the whole family a bad turn, and sweet indeed if a bride from the same stable pays any damages Adam, Lord Darsham demands from me. Especially as I never told that little widgeon, Tiffany Pelham, to wed someone who would be likely to cut up rough because she was stupid enough to break an ankle from our fun together. Hmm, yes, and Tiff shall see that she cannot come running to me."

"I didn't know she had broken her ankle," said

Amelia. "It must be hard, missing out on dancing."

He laughed again, mockingly.

"The euphemism is for getting with child, little fool," he said. "She was so eager and not careful. Hardly my fault, but I am the one accused of criminal conversation. She was not even betrothed to Adam Brandon at the time. Yes, decidedly I will do the family an ill turn, but if you let Edward Brandon know before it's a *fait accompli* so help me, I'll wring your pretty neck if I survive that intemperate young man. He has already threatened my person over his ridiculous aunt by marriage. You will have to let me know her itinerary, and when it is best to snatch her – as well as giving me enough ready to make it worth my while, and to hire a coach, and horses on the way North."

"I have a roll of soft, almost three thousand pounds. Will that do?" asked Amelia. "It was all I could secrete from my parents."

He laughed again, and shivers ran up Amelia's spine.

"Brought it with you, did you, little fool? And only my upbringing as a gentleman preventing me from taking it from you by force! Yes, that will do. It will see to all the arrangements and keep my more pressing creditors out of the way. I need a ball she will attend to try to abduct her in the dark."

Amelia pulled the banknotes out of her reticule as he held out his hand for them, and watched in horrified fascination at the expert way he fanned and counted them.

"We all attend a big ball at Arvendish House on Friday next, the twenty-second," she told him. "Beth is bound to be there. So too is Edward, so you must be careful."

Finchbury nodded.

"My thanks for the warning," he said. "I shall endeavour to avoid him. And I wish you joy of the unpleasant fellow. He is like a march of ants, one attack negligible, but able to make a real nuisance of himself by his persistence, and he cannot be diverted once started on a march. You had better get away before anyone notices you are without a chaperone. The rest is up to me – apart from you marrying that brainless oaf. I really do not see what you see in him; they say that he is exerting his philanthropy to help those soldiers who have been invalided out, now."

"He will not waste his time or fortune on such things when we are married, I assure you," said Amelia. "I shall leave the church first; give me time to get out quickly and make myself into just one more person seeing the sights."

He nodded, and Amelia slipped out.

She scarcely took in the expressions of fervid support for the Bourbon restoration that were the major part of the display of Cambridge House, nor such patriotism equally in evidence on the houses of the Portuguese ambassador, and Monsieur, the brother of the supposed Louis XVIII. With her maid and her footman in attendance, now she had left the church, she just wanted to get as far away from Finchbury as possible, and obtain safety. She could almost swear she heard a mocking laugh pursue her as she walked as fast as she might, without running. What a loathsome man! And yet Beth Renfield deserved someone like that, for attempting to steal Edward!

It seemed an age before Amelia gained the safety of the coach, and bid the coachman to drive by other illuminations. She must study some of them, for her mother would want to know about them, even if she had not wanted to go. Amelia swallowed hard. She felt sick with all she had been through, and the cries of street vendors selling food made her heave, as they took advantage of this nocturnal excursion of so many people. But it was over now! And she should have Edward, and commiserate with him that his wanton cousin had married a ne'er do well.

Evelyn, Marquis Finchbury was thinking furiously, and was well pleased with the bargain he had been offered. This scheming little minx was probably dangerous, as much because her malice was quite ingenuous and naïve. She was likely to gloat, as soon as the deed was done, and bring Edward Brandon down on him. One did not have to be a coward to wish to avoid being beaten by the ham-like hands of a glorified farmer, who just happened to have taken lessons from Gentleman Jackson. Not because he wished to cut a dash as a Corinthian, or for any normal such reason, but just so he could keep fit, and so he could go into the roughest Rookeries to help his lame ducks! It was said he was quite a shot too, and probably had learned that for the same reason, beyond the normal urges to hunt, and it was also said that Brandon carried a sword-stick. Heaven preserve any honest rogue from a philanthropist who knew how to take care of himself!

Finchbury decided that heading out on the Great North Road was probably the last thing any sensible seducer should attempt, and decided instead to make for Wales, where a licence sufficed, as it did in England, being under the same laws, and where nobody was likely to look for him. The bride should be resigned by then to marriage, as it was still a long journey, and he should have impressed upon her by then his skill as a lover. Finchbury had every faith in his own skill to make any woman adore him, and scorned rape as the resort of weaklings. He had every expectation of making this Renfield girl a willing adjunct to her own ruin. And if she was an heiress, he might even remain moderately faithful to the girl, if she was amusing enough. Whether a girl who suited Edward Brandon was likely to be amusing was another matter; she was probably a little puritan. Well, that should be a most amusing and challenging seduction, to find out whether there was any fire behind what was doubtless a rather priggish exterior.

And as for this other girl, the one who was paying him, if she caused any trouble he would make her fall in love with him, and then laugh at her.

Amelia managed to describe the illuminations to her parents with reasonable enthusiasm. They had been spectacular enough for her to bring them to mind when she concentrated, though she was pale enough for her mother to ask sharply what was wrong.

"Oh, it is just the contrast of the illuminations and the darkness of the night," said Amelia. "Some of the wicks of the oil lanterns lighting up the display were poorly trimmed, and I have a touch of the megrim."

It was a believable lie, and Amelia might escape to her bed, with a hot brick for her feet, with a dose of the Family Pills of Grulingius, despite her protests regarding the latter.

"Now then, my darling," said her mother, "It is good for you. Why, we know 'it has been found of excellent use in Lethargies, Caras, Vertigoes, old Head Aches, Megrims, Epilepsies, Apoplexies, and other cold and moist diseases of the Brain', for it says so here on the packet. And in this cold and moist weather, it must be most efficacious."

Amelia's contemplations on her preferred fate for Dr Grulingius would not have been considered ladylike. However, it was nice to snuggle down into a warm bed, for she had become chilled by her outing, and she drifted off to sleep to dream roseate dreams of being a baroness, and only awoke sweating from a nightmare to recall that Beth Renfield would be a Marchioness if Finchbury did marry her, and would outrank her! How could she have made such a miscalculation!

But Beth Renfield would have to put up with being ruined first, and would be too much of a prude to show herself in Town, whereas she, Amelia, would make sure that Edward spent as much time in Town as possible. Finchbury would be happy to leave Beth in his country seat, wherever that was, and come to town for his *amours* since one could hardly expect him to wish to spend time with anyone as boring as Beth. Amelia had set her heart on Edward, so long as he had a title ahead of him, and she had no desire to have anything more to do with Finchbury!

It did, however, take Amelia quite a long time to get back to sleep again, though it was not her conscience that kept her awake, but the disturbing image of a dark, sardonic face.

Beth also had a slight headache from the effects of the illuminations, or, as she confessed cheerfully, too much butter on her crumpets, but unlike Mrs. Hazelgrove, Letty preferred country herbs over patent medicines, and dosed her with a tea of dried willow bark and lemon balm, sweetened with honey and flavoured with cinnamon to mask the bitterness of the dose.

"I cannot say that the honey takes much of the bitterness," said Beth, with a grimace, as she swallowed the dose down.

"No, my dear, but it is worse without it," said Letty.

"As I prefer not to imagine," said Beth. "Oh, but how pretty the lights were, and it was definitely worth a slight indisposition!"

"I agree," said Letty. "Edward showed us the best spectacles, I do believe. And what a pretty way to celebrate the end of hostilities! I do declare, I cannot readily recall when we have not been at war with France, save that brief Peace of Amiens. Why, we must have been at war more than a quarter of a century! For I was just a young girl in the schoolroom, you know!"

"It will seem strange, that one might just visit France now, if one pleases," said Beth.

"Would you like to do so?" asked Letty.

"It might be nice," said Beth. "Only think, to be able to say to my grandchildren, 'I was in France soon after the Monster was defeated', assuming I have any grandchildren of course."

"Oh, I'm sure you will," said Letty. "Now go to sleep!"

Beth drifted off happily, and dreamed of Edward holding her hand while gas lights danced just for them.

Chapter 19

Edward sent a letter round the next day to Beth, a dreadful scrawl that she puzzled over with Letty.

"He appears to have lost sleep and needs to help with deformed lavender," said Beth. "Oh! Can it be that he has lost some sheep and needs to help with the orphaned lambs? Really his steward ought to be able to manage that, though I know Edward does like to be involved," she said. "Oh, I see, something about lambs having a disease called bent-leg, deformed lambs, I see, and of course he wants to be there to make sure that he may do all he can, poor things. He writes that he will certainly be back in time for the ball at Arvendish House. Well, if he is not, he is not; he must attend to his livestock."

"And that, my dear, is why you are the perfect wife for him," said Letty, "because you enter into his concerns about his livestock, and are not jealous of the time he spends with them."

"Well, I would prefer that his livestock did not need him to post up to Suffolk, obviously," said Beth, "but when we are married, I shall not need to be apart from him, since I will be, I hope, helping him." She sighed. "I wish he might have couched the letter in more loverlike terms, though; perhaps you are wrong that he feels a partiality to me."

"He only writes such terse notes to those people he values most," said Letty. "I know Edward; he puts notes to people who are not his nearest and dearest into flowery periods, and makes sure his handwriting is legible."

Beth brightened.

"Well, in that case, we have almost a week without him which must be filled, and I confess something I should like to do is to see the sights of London. We must visit the menagerie, and see the Tower, and St

Paul's, and the British Museum. I am keen to see the black stone on which nature has inscribed the likeness of Chaucer, you know, ever since I read about it. Papa was going to take me to London to see it, before he died. Isaac D'Israeli wrote about it in an essay which was printed in a newspaper, wherein I read about it."

"Well we must certainly see that!" said Letty, "Though if I were you, I would be prepared for some disappointment, for what some people see easily with their imaginations, may not be as clear to others."

"Well, there must be some resemblance, or the curators would have sent away the finder of it with a flea in his ear," said Beth, "but I shall allow for some exaggeration."

"We shall not, however, go tomorrow," said Letty, "for I recall reading a rumour that the Grand Duchess of Oldenburg is to visit the British Museum, and we do not wish to be caught up in the crowds looking at her as much as at the exhibits, nor do we want to be trammelled by her people, who will naturally wish to keep her at a distance from ordinary folk."

"I should hate to be a Grand Duchess, even if we had such things in England," said Beth. "But I pray you, let us go and see her; for I should like of all things to have seen Grand Duchess Catherine, for she is said to be as beautiful as any princess in a fairy tale!"

Letty laughed.

"Oh, very well," she said, "and then we might see St Paul's today, and the museum on Monday."

Beth was suitably impressed by the grandeur of St Paul's Cathedral, and she and Letty amused themselves by testing the tales of the whispering gallery. However she was looking forward to seeing the controversial Grand Duchess, whom, rumour whispered, disliked the Regent almost as much as he disliked her. Russia, however, was an ally in the defeat of the monster Bonaparte, so rumour must not be spoken too loudly. Some said that the Grand Duchess was in England, on behalf of her brother the Tsar, to break the betrothal of Princess Charlotte to the Prince of Orange, the alliance not being to the liking of Russia. Beth just wanted to see the spectacle!

The crowds waiting to see the Grand Duchess were considerable, and as the carriage was held up by them in any case, Beth suggested to Letty that they climb up beside John Coachman, the better to see. It lifted them too above the noise and bustle of the crowd, and the smell of bodies packed closely together.

Letty smiled, and agreed, though it might not be entirely ladylike, there was nobody of consequence to see, and it was no more than if they were driving a high perch phaeton for themselves. Beth would need a chaperone in so exposed a position, but Letty had not the heart to spoil the younger woman's fun, and readily climbed up with her. John Coachman grimly flourished his whip to make sure that any lewd fellows who might think to make game with two ladies would be thinking again; and any ribald comments died unspoken at the determination on his face.

The ripple of excitement running through the crowd at the far end of the street told those waiting of the impending arrival of the Grand Duchess, and the ringing of the hooves of horses was heard above the ragged cheers that thronged the way.

The sound of so many hooves was explained quickly since Grand Duchess was accompanied by outriders of cuirassiers in splendid uniforms, and aggressively Russian military moustaches. The plumes on their golden helmets bobbed as they trotted in step, a prodigiously difficult thing to do, as many of the crowd were knowledgeable enough to realise, applauding spontaneously. The Grand Duchess herself was in an open carriage, despite the chill weather, clearly adoring the adulation of the crowd, and waving occasionally a languid hand. Her dark curls and smouldering eyes attracted attention of all, as did the many and massive pearls that adorned her person!

"Why, how jealous Amelia Hazelgrove would be," said Beth, "for I know that the Grand Duchess is in her thirties, yet she outshines Amelia, for having the look that Amelia would like to have, seductive and smouldering."

"She's also reputed to be quite as unpleasant as Amelia can be," said Letty. "However, at least we do not move in the sort of circles where we have to avoid the spite of someone as influential as a Grand Duchess; for though Amelia Hazelgrove is giving the appearance of all that is amiable, I cannot help thinking that she is still pursuing poor Edward, and likely to do you an ill turn if she knew that he was betrothed to you. But she at least has little enough influence! Well, that was a pleasant spectacle, to be sure; and we shall enjoy the museum the better when illustrious persons are not there. Come, Beth, let us resume the carriage!"

Beth climbed down.

"I should like to purchase a book that I saw advertised in the papers, it is by Mr. Ackermann, and is the first volume of something called *The Microcosm of London*," she said, "for I believe it features the British Museum in its pages."

"We must see if it is available," said Letty. "It will be an instructive volume, I am sure! And I very much admire Mr. Ackermann's prints, so I hope it will be illustrated, as is the *Repository of Arts*. There is so much to be seen in the museum of course, one might take all day and not see it all! There are many Egyptian artefacts of course, for some were seized from French ships conveying them to France, and other antiquities too, from Greece and Rome and other ancient places; and there are the natural exhibits, stones and minerals, animals and birds stuffed in a most lifelike way, and so on."

It may be said that Beth found that the visit to the British Museum felt somewhat flat without Edward present to discuss the exhibits, though there was much to marvel at with the Egyptian artefacts, some donated by British antiquarians, as well as those captured from the French. There too was the celebrated sarcophagus of Alexander as well as all the Etruscan, Greek and Roman antiquities, which could only be enhanced, as Beth said, by the addition of the Townley collection, whose purchase for the museum was to be debated in the House of Commons.

As both the second and the fifth rooms contained portraits of Oliver Cromwell, Beth went back and forth from one to the other, and studied them closely.

"Now I shall definitely recognise him, if he should indeed haunt us," she laughed.

"Oh Beth, you are funning! But I think so austere a fellow would scorn to do anything as frivolous as haunting, as we were agreed when first told the story!" said Letty. "Did you not see the exhibition of native boats, clothes and weaponry from Australia and the like? It is most quaint!"

"It did not interest me so much as the antiquities of our own ancient Britons, nor the classical or Egyptian displays," said Beth. "I cannot think, however, that Cromwell would be found to be very happy, if his portrait might only speak of it, to be found in company with heathen idols from all over the world in the one room, and with a royal companion like Tsar Peter the Great in the other room."

"Oh, I beg to differ, my love," said Letty. "For Peter the Great came incognito to Britain to work in a shipyard, to take back techniques to his own country. He was as practical as Edward!"

Beth gazed anew on the portrait.

"Somehow I could not imagine the current Tsar being able to turn an honest day's work, and still less can I imagine it of the Grand Duchess," she said.

Letty chuckled.

"I agree!" she said.

Beth thought that her favourite exhibit was in the banqueting hall, where a portrait of George II stared down on an amazing table all inlaid with different samples of lava.

"Oh dear, it is a shame, perhaps that we have done the whole in order," she sighed, "For I have wanted very much to see the lavas, spars and minerals, and too the shells and petrifications, but I fear I shall be too tired to enjoy it as much as I hoped, and I cannot, just cannot go on to view the natural history of animals and serpents."

"Why, my dear, we have plenty of time, and might view them another day, and the minerals and petrifications too, if you wish," said Letty.

"No, I am determined to see the stone that looks like Chaucer," said Beth.

Alas for Beth's determination, the stone resembling Chaucer appeared to no longer be on display! It made a disappointing end to a day not entirely as well enjoyed as might have been expected, but Letty smiled.

"Cheer up, Beth! Perhaps Edward will be back before too long, and will be able to escort us another time."

Beth brightened.

"That would be splendid," she said. "It is not that I do not enjoy your company, dearest Aunt Letty, but…"

"But it would be wonderful indeed if a young woman did not prefer the company of her young man," said Letty.

Beth sighed.

"I would rather be feeding orphaned sheep through a fine glove finger or whatever is needful than dressed in finery in the Capital of the world, as some call London."

"Of course you would," said Letty. "But most ineligible until you are wed!"

159

Edward was missing Beth's company as well, for he would have welcomed her thoughts on the disease of bent-leg, which he had read about, as most common in young tups between six and twelve months. Edward suspected that it was a form of rickets, and was sorry that the grass was poor with so little warmth from the sun. His shepherds had not thought to supplement the feed of the sheep, and Edward was certain that being hungry had contributed towards the lambs having succumbed so readily to the disease as they weaned, which was not a condition he had come across before.

"I seen it afore, master," volunteered one of the shepherds. "When we hed wet, winter and spring, ar, must be ninety-seven. It's when there be-ant much sun jew see? Thass a bad thing. Moi ol' granpa, he say 'dew yew feed un on milk and butter, thass gwine ter help, John moi lad, and get 'em in th' sun', and thass what I done, and thass helped some back then. An' when the weather got better, so did they, them as wasn't deformed permanentually."

"Milk and butter, eh?" said Edward. "Have you been trying that?"

John Shepherd shook his head, and spat.

"Them ow' steward o' yourn say 'do-ant yew be so daft-loik, John-bor' oony he say it his jaw-crack voice wass come outa thinkin' as how he moight be a gen'lman which he aint, nowise."

"I'll speak to him," said Edward. If he put it diplomatically enough, he might even have Michael Fowler volunteering John's suggestion scornfully, and then be able to suggest that it was worth trying anything. "I know it's cold, John, but shear them along their backs too, leave the belly wool for warmth, because if it is a lack of sunshine, odd as that may seem, letting what little sun there is reach to warm them when it is out might help. If you build shelters out of hurdles for the night they should take no harm. I recall seeing something similar in city children, who were also pale, and saw little of the sun; and though it seems unlikely that sun alone can cure it, we have no harm in trying."

"Ar," said John. "Reckon thass as good a thing to try as any, master."

Michael Fowler was willing to animadvert about the old wives' tales of John as Edward believed; and Edward listened.

"Let John do as he will," he said, "and provide him with as much milk and butter as possible, which is precious little at this time of year in so cold a spring, I fear. But it cannot harm, save to our meagre dairy profits, and if it works, then the old wives' tales are vindicated. We have little to lose because this year's hoggets will all have to be killed if we cannot cure it in a hurry."

"Well, Mr. Brandon, if you say so," said Mr. Fowler. Edward hid a smile at the accuracy of John's description of his jaw-crack voice. Mr. Fowler's father was a bailiff who had managed to send his son to a grammar school, even if he had not managed to penetrate the haunts of gentlemen so far as to go to university. Edward decided he might leave matters in the hands of an obedient and well-educated, if not especially innovative or brilliant steward, so he might return to Beth.

Chapter 20

Edward arrived at his London house too late to escort Letty and Beth to the rout party he knew they were attending, at Elizabeth's house, and he debated putting his feet up for the evening, and going to call on the morrow, because he was tired; but then, the thought of Beth gave him the impetus he needed to put on evening clothes and go to the rout to meet them there.

As it happened, there were other people arriving as late as Edward, but they were arriving fashionably late, and treated the Medlicotts as though they were doing them a favour in turning up at all. Edward apologised punctiliously, explaining that he had just driven into town from Suffolk.

"Oh, I .d..do hope your sheep are d...doing better, Mr. B...Brandon," said Elizabeth. "Beth t...told me you write a t...terrible hand, but that she thinks they have b...bandy legs."

"Essentially, yes," said Edward. "It's a form of rickets, I think; and I have hopes of relieving the condition, but nobody really knows how to cure rickets, so I'm going with the old wives' tales of my shepherds in the hopes something works."

"Well, I h...hope they know what they are t...talking about," said Elizabeth. "Beth is p...playing for some dancing, perhaps you will like to r...relieve Mrs. Grey of t...turning her pages?"

"I'd be delighted," said Edward.

He was doomed to be delayed.

"EDWARD!" cried Amelia. "*Where* have you been? Beth tried to tell me some hum about sheep with bent legs!"

"No hum at all," said Edward. "It's a serious condition and could make a huge deficit in the farm profits, even if there is a profit this year, which could be doubtful, if they have to be slaughtered early."

"Oh pooh, I have enough money for both of us, when we are married you won't need the farm," said Amelia.

"My good Miss Hazelgrove, even if I intended to marry you, which I do not, I should not permit you to pursue such a *laissez faire* attitude to money," said Edward. "Why, your grandfather must be turning in his grave! He amassed your fortune, and it is not there to be squandered. Money is like a farm, if you do not nurture it and care for it, it withers and dies. I take my farm very seriously, as a result of which I am quite well off."

Amelia flounced, and tittered.

"Why, you cannot expect ladies to understand money!" she said.

"Actually, I do," said Edward. "I might not expect a lady to have been taught how to understand consols, shares and compound interest, but I consider that the blanket assumption that women cannot understand money at all is insulting on the part of a man who says so, and wilfully foolish on the part of a woman. A woman has to understand, if nothing else, how to hold a household, and oversee its accounts."

"That's for the housekeeper," said Amelia, sulkily.

"And how do you check whether the housekeeper is cheating you?" asked Edward, gently. "I think you might be pleased to have avoided marriage with me; because discovering such an appalling ignorance in any lady I took as my wife would mean that I felt it behoved me to hire a tutor for her."

"I suppose Beth Renfield is a paragon who understands how to play the stock market," said Amelia, sulkily.

"No, but she knows how many beans make five, and is amenable to being given instruction," said Edward. "But that is neither here nor there; and speaking of Beth, I am supposed to turn pages for her, your servant, Miss Hazelgrove!" he bowed punctiliously and moved off. Amelia stamped her foot. Edward had no right to want to insist on her changing; he was the one who would have to change. With that wretched Renfield woman out of the way, he would stop being so tiresome.

The smile Beth gave him made Edward feel that it was well worth having scrambled into his evening clothes. He did not know that his answering smile made Beth's heart sing.

Letty readily ceded her place to Edward, and Beth played another measure and declared it was time someone else took a turn.

"How are your sheep or lambs or sleep or lavender?" she asked.

"Was my writing that bad?" he looked contrite.

"Worse, I assure you," laughed Beth. "I believe you were talking about deformed lambs with bent legs."

"I was," said Edward, soberly, and explained all about it.

"In which case, if it works for sheep, as it might, then perhaps you should be looking to give country holidays to foundlings with the same problem" said Beth.

Edward brightened.

"Indeed, or even perhaps set up a foundling asylum in the country specifically for children with rickets, and then I may employ old soldiers to teach them skills, and women who wish to turn aside from crime too, and kill two birds with one stone!"

"I think that is an excellent idea, Edward!" said Beth. "And now the war is over, perhaps we might experiment with taking a few children to warmer climes to see whether or not it might work!"

"And even if it don't, it ought to make them feel better for not being hurting in this dreadful cold," said Edward. "I took two wounded soldiers I had encountered with me to Suffolk, and they told me the frost makes wounds hurt cruelly. One was a farm hand before he was wounded, and knows how to build hazelwood hurdles, so I have set him doing that, and the other can cook, which will help in the kitchen, which is stretched when feeding all the hands. Naturally his cooking is a bit basic, but the shepherds and swineherds and other hands won't mind that he can't manage any fancy sauces or *haute cuisine*."

"No, indeed, and they would probably rather that he did not," said Beth.

"You are probably correct," said Edward. "As someone else is about to play, will you dance a measure with me?"

"I should like it of all things, dear Edward," said Beth.

"Dear Edward? I like that," said Edward. "Oh Beth, I have missed you! And I only hope that you can feel some regard for me after I made such a cake of myself over that little fool Amelia!"

"Hush, someone will hear you being censorious of the poor thing," said Beth. "She is most terribly spoilt, poor girl, and cannot help not having had the advantages of being made to learn how to do anything much."

"I was saved from making a terrible mistake," said Edward. "How could I think I was in love? I was a cawker!"

"I believe a lot of young men make cawkers of themselves over beauties," said Beth.

"You are not jealous?"

"How could I be jealous? I am the gainer from her making you lose your temper."

Edward blushed.

"I did not behave well," he admitted. "But oh Beth! I am come to love you!"

"Oh Edward, I have loved you since I first met you," said Beth.

165

"And you watched me make an idiot of myself without trying to stop me, and attract me to you instead?" said Edward.

"Edward, it never occurred to me that you would ever look at me as an eligible female – especially when you were heir to a barony too – when I was a poor relation, with nondescript hair and a poor figure," said Beth.

"What's wrong with your figure? It looks quite perfect to me," said Edward.

Beth laughed.

"Now I know you love me truly, my dear; because I am short-waisted and rather overly well-endowed above, with nothing much to speak of below, rather like a man o' war in full sail."

"Well, I rather like watching ships sailing too," said Edward. "Oh, I know that a large fundament is fashionable… I can't say that, can I? You are giggling at me."

"There are worse words to call it," said Beth, "and at least you are not being a total farmer to refer to it as a *rump*, but actually it is not a part of the anatomy generally mentioned at all."

"The clothes are designed to show it off though, especially in a stiff breeze," said Edward.

"There is a difference between what is displayed and what is mentioned," said Beth, "not that it troubles me. I have no doubt we shall have earthier conversations over the breeding of animals."

"True," said Edward, brightening. "And our own children."

"Sir! You cannot want me merely as a brood mare!" said Beth with mock severity.

"I don't. I want children, but if it don't happen, I have a heap of aunts with brats for the wretched title to pass to, and we shall have our foundlings to keep us occupied," said Edward.

"I admire your compassion, Edward," said Beth,

softly.

Amelia was not pleased to see that Beth had abandoned the piano to dance the impromptu measures for which Elizabeth was now playing the accompaniment. At least Beth would be out of the way soon, even if she might end up being a marchioness. That would be hard to swallow. But then, a poor little dab of a thing like Beth would never be able to stand up to a terrible man like Finchbury, as she, Amelia, had stood up to him. Amelia's recollection of the encounter, which had left her feeling bruised, was becoming rapidly tinged with the roseate hue of time, which permitted her to see her actions as brave and uncompromising, ordering the wicked rake to do her bidding. People always did what she wanted, after all. And Edward would be no exception when he realised that it was inevitable.

Only another couple of days. Amelia managed to smile at Beth and Edward as they finished the measure, and politeness dictated that Edward should ask her to dance.

"I am sure that dear Beth is such a comfort to you about your sheep," said Amelia.

"Beth enters into my interests regarding my stock," said Edward, stiffly.

"Yes, one would not think her to be so clever, from looking at her," said Amelia, with a tinkling laugh.

"Why not? Beth has intelligent eyes, you can see that she thinks deeply," said Edward.

Amelia fought not to grind her pearly teeth. He had totally missed the innuendo!

"Why, yes, indeed, and as one discovers, quite clever enough to entrap a man in the throes of disappointment into promising, marriage; she must have guessed that Tiffany Pelham would play your uncle false. And you put such a good face on it, dear Edward!" said Amelia. "But I wager if a higher title came along, Beth would soon be after it, for all that she looks like a sheep chewing on the cud."

"Sheep don't chew on the cud, and how you can think pretty Beth looks like a sheep, I do not know," said Edward. "It is cows who chew on the cud, since they are ruminants, and have several stomachs. The digestion is incomplete without the regurgitation of the partially digested cud to be re-chewed and…."

"Edward! That is not a fit subject for the ears of a lady!" said Amelia, almost gagging.

"Oh, sorry, of course, you are less capable of dealing with country matters than Beth," said Edward, hiding a chuckle that Beth would chide him for using a misquote from Shakespeare with rather improper overtones. "You seemed interested enough to have brought up the subject of cud-chewing. For your information, I am not trapped into anything. I wish you will realise that I have no intention of marrying you, and I am not about to change my mind."

"Well, I shall be here when you have been let down by her," said Amelia.

"I shan't be," said Edward.

Amelia permitted herself a small, knowing smile. It had worked out all for the best that Finchbury was a marquis, because it would look as though Beth had abandoned a putative heir to a barony for a certain marquis, because Adam Brandon might yet remarry.

When she was married to Edward, Amelia decided that she would just have to make sure Adam Brandon never remarried. One might easily find ways to scotch a budding romance. And as he had fallen in love so hard, it was said, with Tiffany, after having mourned his wife for many years, he was unlikely to be so trusting again. It would all work out very nicely.

Evelyn, Lord Finchbury, was making his own plans. The mail might manage London to Bristol in nineteen hours, but that was with a huge infrastructure of changes of horses and such. With the roll of soft the Hazelgrove girl had given him, it made sense to hire six good horses and a postillion as well as his own coachman to drive, but travel more than eight hours in one stretch, Finchbury refused to do. With six horses they might make it to Marlborough overnight, and there they might rest, and then drive on, avoiding Bath like the plague, and heading north of Bath and Bristol for Gloucester, and thence into Wales. Having once got out of London, the pace might be taken more slowly, as the likelihood was that Brandon would go haring off up the Great North Road. Finchbury intended sending his man ahead to arrange another team of horses at Marlborough, which would mean a quick change would be possible if necessary. He hoped, however, that the girl would be ready for a bit of a tumble by then, once fortified by coffee and breakfast. He could work on her in the coach, inuring her to the inevitable and wooing her. And it was another reason not to take too hurried a pace, because it would merely give any woman the megrims. Maybe heading for Marlborough was too ambitious. It was not as though he seriously feared pursuit. Newbury was some six hours away, perhaps less with a good team of six horses pushed to their limit, and a safer distance than Reading, more comfortably situated at perhaps four hours distant. Well, at that, if his man had a change of horses ready at Reading, he and the wench might afford to rest for a couple of hours and then press on, past Marlborough, and then take a more leisurely trip to Wales. If he could bed her, she'd be willing to put up with the discomfort, and if she was missish, well, a turn of high speed would dampen her spirits and make her more grateful for proffered kindnesses in return for a kiss or two. And Finchbury was confident enough of his skills in kissing that once a girl was kissed she was ready to do anything for him. He chuckled nastily. He could have easily had the Hazelgrove girl; he had repelled her and attracted her in equal measure. Once kissed and pleasured she would have been his to command. But then, he did not like brunettes, and he did not like scheming hussies. He had his standards. The Renfield girl was not precisely blonde, but she was more akin to the type of girl he preferred, and being quite plain she should be pleased to attract a man of the world like himself. And if he did decide to marry her, he would treat her kindly. Finchbury was very well pleased with himself.

Chapter 21

The day of the ball at Arvendish House arrived, and Beth dressed with care, just for Edward. She also laid out a heavy cashmere shawl, woollen spencer, and heavy cloak, both for travelling to the ball, and waiting to see Cressida off, helping her with her bandboxes. Molly was sworn to secrecy and would help Cressida's own maid bring Cressida's band boxes where they were to be secreted under the seat of the Stonhouse family carriage. This had necessitated some negotiations with the Stonhouse coachman too, but so long as he had not got to do anything to actively help, the man was willing to give tacit support. Cressida was cold and unbending with others of her own kind, but was a much loved mistress, who saw the needs of her servants and addressed them to the best of her ability. Molly would be wearing Beth's second best cloak, which as Beth also said would mean that she was less likely to be questioned if moving around someone else's coach.

"I hope Lady Cressida will be very happy!" said Molly, "Ooh it is romantic!"

"It is," agreed Beth, reflecting that at least Cressida had a practical head on her shoulders as well as a sense of romance, and had been quite ready to live on a small income for her beloved Mr. Chetwode. That Mr. Chetwode was also very wealthy was to Cressida merely a bonus, not one of the reasons to wed him.

Beth greeted Cressida warmly when she saw her at the ball.

"How are you feeling?" Beth asked.

"A bit numb," said Cressida. "Scared. Excited. Happy. Worried. Mostly excited, I think. Lucien has been a Trojan; he caught me smuggling bandboxes down, and helped. He likes Brook; and Brook has promised to pay for him to do university, which Lucien wants of all things. Even if it is more to get away from home than for the study, I fear!"

"Oh, I expect young men need to find themselves one way or another," said Beth. "Lucien will doubtless settle down to work if he respects Mr. Chetwode's kindness."

Cressida brightened.

"Yes, he will. He's not a bad boy, just a bit wild, but then what do you expect at sixteen? He feels it very deeply that our parents expect him to marry an heiress as his duty to the family, and he doesn't like it above half. So he kicks over the traces a bit."

"University will give him the chance to cut larks without being under your parents' eyes," said Beth, "and get it all out of his system, or at least, so Aunt Letty has said. I'm glad you had a chance to talk to him, I had a feeling something was worrying you about this elopement, and it was your brother, wasn't it?"

Cressida nodded.

"Indeed," she said. "I did worry how he would take it, but he has given me his blessing and promised to break it to our parents, not only that I have gone, but that Brook is a very Croesus. I can't help wanting to giggle at the thought that I'm running away with a man my parents would almost force me upon if only they knew of the extent of his wealth, especially as he has no hint of shop about him. But at least this way he won't have to put up with a big wedding, and being afraid of falling over his own feet in front of too many people. His family are as clever with speculation as with music! He says the Stock Exchange is as nice and regular as a Bach Cantata, which I cannot see myself but I am glad that he can."

"The Stock Exchange makes my head ache," confessed Beth, "Though I do try to follow and understand it."

"I suppose I shall have to make an effort to do so," said Cressida. "How nice it is to know people like you and Elizabeth who are willing to admit to learning things for sheer interest! I am no bluestocking like Elizabeth, but at least I am no prattling ninny. Why are you laughing, Beth?"

"The haughty Lady Cressida is the last person anyone in the world could accuse of being 'prattling', ninny or otherwise," said Beth.

"It's a way of keeping people at arm's length," said Cressida. "I don't stammer like Elizabeth, but I do find people intimidating. The idea of a quiet wedding by special licence away from my family pleases me as much as it pleases Brook. I think that being drawn into the coterie of you girls by Brook is the best thing that ever happened to me, and when we are wed, I will do what I can for poor cousin Madelaine, to rescue her from her horrid mama. And have Abigail's next brother to stay, along with Lucien, and hope they will be friends but not drag each other into too much mischief."

"You are kind, Cressida," said Beth.

"I have much kindness to pay back," said Cressida, simply. "You accepted me, without shying away and whispering behind your hands about me being stuck up."

Beth linked arms with her and gave her arm a friendly squeeze. Mr. Chetwode was engaged to Cressida for the supper dance, and was to slip away two dances earlier, to ready his carriage, and Beth and Molly, Cressida and her maid, would transfer Cressida's bandboxes from her coach to his, and bid her farewell in time to go back in for the supper dance with Edward. And since Cressida and Brook Chetwode were supposed to be dancing and dining together, there would be no outraged partners looking for them; Cressida had been careful to leave her dance card vacant after supper, pencilling in some spurious names in scrawling handwriting.

Aspirants to her hand for a dance would, perhaps, have

been outraged had they been able to read that she planned to dance with J.S. Bach, Henry Purcell, George
F. Handel and John Gay.

So far as Cressida was concerned it was barely a lie, since she anticipated living with these composers and more for the rest of her life.

Amelia was quite as wildly excited as Cressida, in arranging her own future marriage. That satisfying her own desires meant degradation and misery for another girl did not really enter her head, or only in a superficial way with the thought that it was only what such an encroaching creature as Beth Renfield deserved. Somehow she had to persuade Beth to go outside before the end of the ball, but if necessary she could ask Beth to come out with her as she felt faint, and view the illuminations left up for the ball. Amelia was sure she could get gullible Beth outside for Finchbury. She had to separate her somehow from that icicle of a woman, Lady Cressida first, a female who looked at Amelia as if she knew about the family fortune coming from beer. If Amelia had but known it, this was Cressida's normal expression to people outside of her new group of friends, with which she guarded herself, but Amelia did harbour enough insecurities about the origins of her fortune to take it personally. Elizabeth, more nearly connected to trade than she, never saw that expression directed at her, for Cressida appreciated Elizabeth's frank friendliness and indifference to the difference between them in social rank. Had Elizabeth attempted to toad-eat at all, Cressida would have frozen her out, but such never occurred to Elizabeth. Amelia, on the other hand, had been sufficiently impressed by an earl's daughter that her manner to Cressida had put Cressida's back up from the first time they had met.

Amelia was meanwhile giving quite abstracted answers to her many admirers, for trying to keep an eye on Beth, and wondering how to prize her away from Cressida that she quite opened the eyes of one love-struck swain, by saying "oh yes, quite so, I agree," when the unfortunate Honourable Mr. Thomas Hawkesbury had stammered that he had a poem for her, even though it was not very good at all. The youthful poet was cut to the quick by such a slight, and stalked off, to brood in what he hoped was a Byronesque manner. Mr. Hawkesbury would have given his eye teeth to resemble in any particular the hero of *The Corsair*, who was as much a household name as Byron himself since it had been published in February. However, nature had cursed Mr. Hawkesbury with a slight frame and pale, wispy hair, and eyebrows so blonde as to appear non-existent. However, he did have aspirations of poetry, when perhaps his own epic heroes might be spoken of in the same breath as Byron's Conrad, and perhaps add their lustre to his rather overlooked frame. Mr. Hawkesbury was under no illusions about his own physical charms for the ladies, but he did fancy, self-deprecation aside, that his poetry was both good, and witty, and to have his self-deprecation agreed with by a beautiful, but undeniably hen-witted girl was a blow to his ego, and his infatuation, that may have left him a wiser man, if no better as a poet.

Amelia was not to discover the defection of this swain until later, when she was to wonder who had dared steal one of her court, being entirely unaware of her own foolishness. However in the meantime, the 'fair cruel one' showed her court that she had weightier things on her mind than their adulation, until such time as the dance before the supper dance.

Suddenly Amelia was aware that both Cressida and Beth had left their accustomed place, near to Elizabeth, Abigail and Madelaine, and appeared to be moving towards the vestibule.

Amelia lost another swain, whose shy devotion was

too devastated to ever consider approaching her again, when his Goddess of Beauty got up and almost ran out of the ballroom as he approached her to collect her for the dance. It would not have improved his blighted ego to have been told that Amelia had not even noticed him. Amelia almost screamed with frustration when her hostess stopped her and asked if she felt quite well, as she seemed flustered, and Amelia had to invent a sudden spurious faintness and a need to visit the ladies' dressing room. Which she did, in case the other girls were there, but to no avail.

The operation to go outside had been accomplished with speed. The maids were already dressed for outside, and had their mistresses' spencers, cloaks and other accoutrements ready for them. They had left the dressing room, and indeed the house, before Amelia caught up with them. Wrapped up warmly the two young women and their maids slipped outside to cool their faces, as Beth said gaily to the footman. He goggled slightly, but shrugged; they really did want to cool their faces, not use it as an euphemism for seeking out the closet.

"The lights are so pretty," added Beth. "I did not have a chance to look at them properly on the way in. You will let us back in again presently?" she slipped the young man a vail.

The footman's face cleared and he nodded comprehension. Some of these poor young ladies were positively chivvied by their mamas, almost as much as if they were prime dells with Haymarket ware, he thought in his own idiom. Ay, and bargains struck with no more sentiment than such common streetwalkers sold by their bawds. Let the poor things have a few minutes freedom!

The one that followed them had a sly look to her face, and Tom the footman had no intention of telling *her* where those nice-looking ladies had gone, when she asked. He pocketed the shilling vail though.

"Why miss!" he said. "The Jericho is out through there, for them as wish to cool their faces."

It was not a lie. There was a convenient office where he indicated, as well as the Jordans provided for the ladies in their dressing room. The look of blank confusion on this other lady's face was right funny. Thought she'd caught them out at something no doubt, and planned on tattling to whichever harridans had the keeping of them. Tom watched her go out of the back door, hoping, no doubt, he thought, to catch them at some illicit dalliance. Well, if they were meeting anyone on the sly, good luck to them! he thought.

Amelia's search outside showed her where the earth closet was; and she ran back indoors again as she discovered that this was where the men cooled their faces, and any female approaching those waiting to use it might be subject to a few ribald remarks. She could not see either naïve Beth nor frosty Cressida coming this way! When she returned, Tom had prudently made himself least in sight, and another footman was on duty. Well, they must have gone out the front, thought Amelia, and hoped that Finchbury was sufficiently up to snuff to keep his side of the bargain.

Outside, the four young women rapidly removed the band boxes from Cressida's carriage, ably assisted by Mr. Chetwode, who had fettled his team with promptitude. Cressida kissed Beth on the cheek.

"Thank you," she said.

"Godspeed, and good luck," said Beth, kissing her back. "Invite me to the christening."

"I shall," said Cressida, blushing.

Beth and Molly watched the carriage as it went down the road.

"Oh Miss Beth, I do hopes they don't go off the road in the dark!" said Molly.

"Mr. Chetwode is very capable," said Beth. "The illuminations are pretty, are they not? I like the transparency of the Prince of Wales' feathers, it is delicately painted.

"It is pretty," said Molly, critically, "but if you ask me, men didn't ought to wear feathers; they should leave it to the ladies."

Beth laughed.

"Oh, it is but a heraldic device, such as knights of old had painted on shields, so people would know who they were inside their armour," she said. "Our Princes of Wales have used it since the time of the famous Black Prince, who took it from the King of Bohemia."

"Fancy!" said Molly, who had no idea who the Black Prince was, and less of the King of Bohemia.

They were standing in shadow, the better to see the lights, the contrast marked, when a carriage came clopping up beside them. It was unusual, having six horses and a postillion riding one of the leaders, so both Beth and Molly turned to stare. The door opened and a male voice asked,

"Miss Beth Renfield?"

"Who wants to know?" asked Molly, before Beth could say a thing.

"I do, Miss Renfield," said Finchbury, for it was he! He was certain that this must be Miss Renfield, brought out by Amelia Hazelgrove. They were a little early, but then perhaps the Hazelgrove girl had bethought her of getting the girl well on the way before she would be missed at supper. And probably she had to take what chances she might, in any case. No matter! He lifted Molly bodily by the arms to pitch her into the carriage, and jumped in after her, slamming the door.

Chapter 22

For a moment Beth was stunned; then she realised that her poor maid had been taken in mistake for her! Why anyone would wish to abduct her, Beth had no idea, but plainly someone did, and there was no time to lose. She scrambled up behind the coach, using the steps for the convenience of those stowing baggage, and found a platform where a tiger might be expected to cling. She hung on grimly, glad that she was wearing heavy woollen gloves over her soft kid gloves, and that she had stopped to pull on her overshoes to go out.

The door opened and she saw the friendly footman.

"Oh footman! My maid has been abducted! Pray tell Edward Brandon!" she called.

Tom goggled; and almost fell back inside. A swell mort caring enough for her maid to hang onto the back of a coach was something to see! She'd fall off and be killed of course, but that was pluck to the backbone! Tom wondered if he dared tell Mr. Brandon about it at all, but if the lady wasn't killed, then at least Mr. Brandon would want to know to go looking for her mangled body.

Edward Brandon, meanwhile, was looking for his partner for the supper dance. Elizabeth, Abigail and Madelaine were in something of a huddle, looking concerned, and Edward decided to confront them.

"Where's Beth?" he asked, without preamble.

"Oh M...Mr. Brandon!" said Elizabeth, "She w...went to see C...Cressida off, and she has not returned, and m...my maid c...cannot find hers either!"

"See Cressida off? Off where?" demanded Edward.

Guilty glances were exchanged.

"Eloping," said Madelaine, "With Mr. Chetwode."

179

"And her family will come round, but with a *fait accompli* it makes it easier for the happy couple to explain that," said Abigail.

"Well a right bunch of fait accomplices you are," said Edward, who was less pleased with the pun than if Beth had been there to share it. "They actually meant it? Good Lord!" as he assimilated that Lady Cressida really had eloped. Well, the chit was none of his business.

"Amelia followed them out," said Abigail, "and Oh! I know it is uncharitable of me, but I cannot like that girl!"

"She did, did she?" said Edward, thoughtfully. "I wonder if the wretched female thought it a laugh to push Beth into a cupboard or something and lock her in?"

"Oh, Mr. Brandon, I am glad you do not consider my feelings about her entirely unfounded," said Abigail. "You know her quite well?"

"Know her? I had a lucky escape from being leg-shackled to her," said Edward, with feeling. "Thank you, ladies, she is looking very pleased with herself, I shall go and find out what she knows."

Amelia was feeling very pleased with herself. Neither Cressida nor Beth had returned, so one might assume that Finchbury had seen her outside, and taken his chance to seize her. Or both of them until he could ascertain which was which, which would be inconvenient with regards to providing her with a chaperone, but he could always abandon Lady Cressida in some inn somewhere.

Amelia blenched suddenly as she saw the look on Edward's face and turned quickly to her partner.

Edward strode across the room, and said 'excuse me' to Amelia's partner and seized her arm.

"I say, sir, you can't come and barge in and take my supper partner!" bleated the youth, a young man in immaculate regimentals who appeared to have faced no worse danger in the Battle for Paris than assault by the ladies of the city.

"I can when I think she's done something to my partner," said Edward, grimly. "You can have her back when I've finished questioning her, and the less fuss either of you make, the less of a scandal it will cause."

Amelia tittered. She was too angry to consider the consequences of telling Edward what had happened, secure in the belief that he would readily assume Beth to be another such as Tiffany Pelham.

"Oh, I'll tell you, because it's too late now for you to do anything about it," she said. "That precious trollop of yours wants something better than a barony that is still uncertain, and has run off with a marquis – Lord Finchbury."

She gave a little cry as Edward gave her a shake.

"What have you done?" he demanded.

"Why, what should I have done? Let go, Edward, you are hurting me!" said Amelia.

"I'll do a lot more than hurt you if you've arranged to have my Beth hurt," said Edward, "because I'll have you whipped at the cart's tail as a common bawd and exposed in the stocks."

Amelia went white and swayed.

"Here, I say!" protested the subaltern.

"I wouldn't, if I were you," said Edward, through gritted teeth. "If you say too much I might just call you out as an accomplice of this little madam. Now take her away before I forget what is due to my hostess and give her the hiding she richly deserves."

"But Edward! I did it for you! Because she had her hooks into you and meant to marry you!" wailed Amelia.

"Madam, that's an admission before witnesses," said Edward, with awful coldness. "And whatever may happen to my Beth, I will still marry her, and no other. And God help you if she is hurt."

He turned and strode away.

Amelia had hysterics.

"We shan't be inviting her again, my dear," said the Duke of Arven.

"Certainly not," said the Duchess. "Putting Mr. Brandon out of countenance too; the girl is a skirter."

As Edward strode for the door Tom the footman reached him.

"Mr. Brandon sir!" he cried.

"Not now," snarled Edward.

"But it's about the lady who shouted to me to tell you!" said Tom.

Edward stopped in his tracks.

"I'm sorry m'lad, what is it?" he said.

"She said to tell you her maid had been abducted, oh and SIR! She was hanging on to the back of the coach like a tiger, pluck to the backbone!" said Tom.

"Her MAID?" Edward was nonplussed.

"Yessir! Her maid were wearing a fine cloak, see," said Tom. "Reckon the swell cove made a mistake."

"Only one of many that he has made," said Edward. "Here, my lad…" and he gave Tom a sovereign.

Tom reckoned that Mr. Brandon probably did rate a swell mort like Miss Whoever.

Edward was in love, hot-headed and impulsive, but he was also no fool, and rapidly made his apologies to his host that he was called away, and extracted Letty from the gaggle of dowagers into which she had been drawn.

"Aunt Letty, Amelia arranged to have Beth abducted, but it seems the abductor made a mistake," he said, tersely. "He has Molly, and Beth is clinging to the back of the coach. Will you drive at high speed to rescue her?"

"Of course," said Letty, paling and swaying. "Yes. And we must take a flask of brandy and blankets, and some clothes; ten minutes delay at Red Lion Square will make little difference, my dear, and you should change also."

Edward nodded.

"I'll drop you there and pick you up when I have changed," he said. "Half an hour will be closer than ten minutes, but Molly is resourceful. And for all his faults, Finchbury is a seducer, not a ravisher."

"*Finchbury?*" demanded Letty. "Of all people!"

"Yes, and I will see Miss Hazelgrove in court for this if either Beth or her little maid take any harm," said Edward.

"She has done this deliberately?" cried Letty.

"Yes, and she should be whipped," said Edward.

Molly was terrified.

Having been abducted once for immoral purpose, she had a better idea, perhaps, than Beth would have done, of the ordeals in store, even without having been ravished. She shrank back in the corner and regarded the man with big, terrified eyes. If he knew she was only a maid would he let her go? Or would he take her anyway, as revenge for having been fooled? Molly fancied that he would probably take her anyway.

Finchbury regarded the terrified young girl. She looked younger than he had anticipated; scarcely old enough to be a debutant, though it was hard to see, huddled deep in her cloak as she was.

"Do not fear me, Miss Renfield," he said, in a gentle tone. "I will not hurt you, at least, not by design. We are going to be married, and if you please me, you will find me an indulgent enough husband."

Molly decided that the best course for her to take was to pretend to be Beth for as long as possible, and hope to have an opportunity to escape. And if she spoke, that would give her away. She shrank further into the corner, and permitted herself a whimper which was not entirely acting. Whimpers of sheer terror were quite egalitarian sounds. She buried her face in her hands and made a show of sobbing.

"Egad!" said Finchbury, taken aback. "I thought from what that Hazelgrove female said that you were a woman of some spirit. I should have thought the wretched woman would have managed to find some way of overcoming a watering pot like you, without involving me. Not that I object to having an heiress as a bride, especially a tolerably pretty one. If I engage not to lay a finger on you until we stop, will you come out and talk to me?"

Molly was hard pressed not to disclaim being as hen-hearted as he apparently thought her, but lowered her hands sufficiently to glare, balefully at him.

"Come, that's better," said Finchbury. "A fine pair of eyes to be sure, that should not be drowned in tears. Let me loan you my handkerchief."

Molly cautiously accepted the fine linen handkerchief and blew her nose with unladylike vigour. She balled up the handkerchief and kept it to dab at her face from time to time. Her brain was working rapidly. He would have to stop at some point to rest the nags, and there doubtless alight for bodily comforts. She might have a chance of slipping away then, hiding the fine cloak, and blending in with other maids in the inn he chose, working hard enough that nobody would question that she was anything but a maid, and the fine gentleman would doubtless be likely to go haring off to see where his quarry had run off to. He wouldn't look for her hidden under his very nose. Molly felt comforted by this. And maybe she could sell the cloak to take the Mail back to London, and hope that Miss Beth would forgive her for doing so.

Finchley spoke again.

"My name is Evelyn, Marquis Finchbury. I don't mean to hurt you. I hope you will find me agreeable, for I don't want to scare you. I'm not given to bad moods or temper, and I don't usually drink to excess, which you will of course wish to know. We can while away the journey chatting, and you choose the subject, or we could play cards. It's a deucedly abrupt way of making your acquaintance, but it's no worse than any other arranged marriage, and at least I'm sober and not about to force you to do anything you don't want, except accept my name. And in doing so, Beth, gain yourself a title, and a better title at that than as a baroness, one day, and only when the current Baron Darsham has turned up his toes. He's a vigorous man, is Adam Brandon, and not likely to make Edward become baron any too soon. You will be a marchioness, and if your fortune is sufficient, I shan't object if you want to spend part of each season in Town. I beg your pardon?"

Molly had sniffed, eloquently. It was an unladylike sound, but then, Mrs. Grey at least was known to express herself thus. And Mrs. Grey was undoubtedly a lady.

Finchbury laughed.

"That sounds remarkably like Letty Edgeby, or Letty Grey as she now is; easy to see she had the training of you. The Hazelgrove girl thinks you are her natural daughter; as she's the right side of forty by some years, I'd say she'd have to have been a bit of a prodigy to manage to breed and then come out as the innocent she undoubtedly was then. I'm somewhere between you in age; a little older than Edward, but not by much."

Rattling on inconsequentially would hopefully put the chit at her ease. Finchbury was most uneasy with a frightened girl; scared but eager he was used to, but not girls who just shrank in on themselves. Four hours to get to know her, he promised himself.

Molly had made an involuntary noise of indignation at the idea of Miss Beth being a bastard child of Mrs. Grey; the idea was very silly! Mrs. Grey had been respectably married, and Miss Beth was some kind of cousin of hers, and had talked from time to time about her childhood and her parents, encouraging Molly to speak of her own much loved family.

Finchbury smiled at her. He had a winning smile.

"Yes, I did rather discount that spiteful little piece's guesses as far off the mark," he said. "And no, I didn't like her one little bit, but you see, my pockets are entirely to let, and likely to be more so in the future."

Molly managed an interrogative sort of noise, whilst dabbing at her face with the handkerchief.

"Why, did you say?" said Finchbury. "Well, it's those dratted Brandons. Adam Brandon is doubtless going to hold out for his pound of flesh in damages, and the joke of the matter is that I never did actually cuckold him. I laid that flighty piece, Tiffany Pelham, but it took two of us to make her brat, and she was more than willing, you know! She knew my reputation, unlike you she did not have to make sure she was alone with me. And I succumbed before temptation. I had no thoughts of marriage of course, her portion was insufficient to tempt me. I have no idea what your expectations are, but as you are supposed to be Letty Grey's heir, it will be a considerable amount. And with luck the Brandons will avoid scandal by letting me off whatever damages are set. You know," he added conversationally, "I am in favour of making women responsible in law for their actions. If Tiffany had not decided to give Adam Brandon every expectation that she was having his child, I should not be in this pickle. She should have done what other women do, and go away quietly to a country house run by such doctors as are discreet about such things, and then the baby might have been farmed out in the usual fashion. One might see advertisements for such things in the papers, very discreet and no mention of bastardy of course."

Molly made a noise that could have meant anything.

"Cat got your tongue?" said Finchbury.

Molly had a sudden idea, and made noises as though she was about to be sick. Finchbury reached under the seat and produced a useful utensil.

Molly took it, and heaved a few times, then shook her head, and passed it back.

Finchbury regarded her thoughtfully.

"Now, I do wonder if you were genuinely overcome by nausea, but had an empty stomach, on account of not having yet dined on supper, or whether you were hoping I might stop before we left London," he said. "If Miss Hazelgrove thinks you a nuisance, I wager you were hoping I would call for the coach to be stopped in the hopes of escape. I'm sorry, my fine lady. I cut my eye teeth before yesterday, you know! And if you need to use the Jordan for other reasons, I'll turn my back but only with the doors secured. Ah, that does make your eyes flash. I'm glad, my dear. A sobbing bride would be rather dreary. But I'll be wary."

Molly cursed herself for giving away her intent to escape; she would have to be very careful from now on. She hunched a shoulder in an imitation of the petulant way some ladies had, and settled down in the corner as if to sleep. And if he did not intend touching her, sleep would not be unwelcome.

Finchbury mentally shrugged.

It was a long way to Wales, and at least she was not attacking him with fingernails.

chap. If Miss Medlicott hadn't taken a liking to that Grindlay fellow, I'd have introduced her to Gil."

"Well, I'm sure he can manage to find his own young lady," said Letty.

"Doubt it. Poor fellow stutters at the best of times, and turns beetroot when in the presence of a female," said Edward. "You mean, it's none of my business, well, you're right, it ain't, but then it wasn't Beth's business to be helping Lady Cressida Stonhouse to elope, either, but if she hadn't been doing so, she wouldn't be in this pickle," said Edward. "And someone had to shove Chetwode in the right direction."

"Oh dear, I should have guessed," said Letty. "How fast are we going?"

"These bays can do sixteen miles an hour in ideal conditions," said Edward, "which it ain't, nowise, but I don't believe we're going a thread below ten miles an hour."

It did not take long to be out on the open road, Letty throwing the coins to the toll keeper after Edward alerted each with a horn. Edward was grinning maniacally, as they accelerated out past Hampstead.

"I dare say they think you and I are eloping," said Letty, "for it is too dark to see that I am too old."

"Let them!" said Edward. "This is a good road, it's a shame the moon is new, and long since set, but I know the road as far as Baldock, in any case. And my lantern is good and the wick newly trimmed."

"How comforting," said Letty, with an edge to her voice. "We surely cannot continue at this pace, can we? Even the Mail only travels at an average of eight miles an hour."

"Well, the mail travels by night as well to avoid traffic, where it may," said Edward, "and that's one thing that cuts our speed, having to keep an eye on the road where the lantern shines. And of course the lantern on a Mail doesn't extend so readily in front of four horses, where we only have to have it light the road beyond two, and more closely fettled at that. So I can afford to go a bit faster."

"I see," said Letty. "I'd feel safer with a full moon."

Edward laughed.

"With a good moon you hardly have to slow at all, once your eyes have adapted to the low light. In a couple of hours it's like daylight."

"Indeed," said Letty, a little faintly, wondering whether to be glad or sorry that the moon's sickle had struggled to its bed before they had left for the ball.

Edward smiled at her.

"I've driven at night before, you know," he said. "And I'm not reckless, even though I am fairly desperate to catch up with poor Beth before she falls off with exhaustion."

"I hadn't thought of that," said Letty, worried. "I do hope she will be safe!"

"I suppose it all depends on whether she thought to put on heavier gloves," said Edward. "Light kid gloves would help somewhat, but the cold will soon strike through, numbing her hands and making her let go. But Beth is a resourceful girl, I imagine if she feels her hands growing numb she will kick on the back of the coach to alert Finchbury, and hope that she and Molly between them can overcome him."

Letty nodded. Beth would risk ruin rather than permit herself to die needlessly; because Edward would always love her, no matter what. And she and Molly between them were quite likely to be a match for any man.

"I do believe there's a coach ahead!" said Edward, excited. "I see a glimmer swaying like the lantern on its side. I can't overtake here, there are some deucedly tight bends, but watch us catch up to it because we can corner better!"

Letty tried to take pleasure in Edward's skill, and in his obvious pleasure in his skill, rather than worrying about being overturned in that frightening-sounding manoeuvre called 'cornering'; however, she need not have feared, though she felt tremendously bruised by being thrown first left, then right, and back again several times. By the time this uncomfortable sensation had subsided, Edward was giving a shout of triumph, for they were now right behind what was quite plainly a coach or carriage, its flickering and bobbing light clearly revealing the shadow of it on the ground, and even some of the colours on its dark bulk. Edward frowned in concentration, and then he was drawing the curricle out to the right, taking it past the coach, and shouting to the coachman to pull over, using the curricle to push the leaders towards the edge of the road.

It took a while for the other vehicle to rumble to a halt, for it was heavier by far than the curricle. Stop, however, it did, and Edward was frowning, for there were but four horses and no postillion.

The door opened and a man jumped down, the white face of a lady visible, staring out of the door.

"What is it?" said the man.

"Chetwode?" said Edward. "Is that you?"

"It is I," said Mr. Chetwode. "What's to do, Brandon? If Miss Renfield thinks that Cressida left her toothbrush behind, I am sure I might purchase her a new one."

"Nothing like that," said Edward. "You left her at Arvendish House?"

"She waved goodbye to me," said Cressida, from inside the coach. "What is wrong?"

"She's only hopped up behind a coach and six to prevent an abduction," said Edward.

Cressida gasped.

"Oh, how very brave and foolhardy!" she cried. "How kind Beth is, but that was not a good thing to do! I trust you may find her, but oh! Mr. Brandon! No other vehicle has passed us."

"Are you sure?" asked Edward, wondering if they had been too busy billing and cooing.

"Positive," said Brook Chetwode. "And take those dirty thoughts out of your noddle, Brandon, we have not been misbehaving ourselves at all."

"My apologies, Chetwode, Lady Cressida," said Edward. "Well, if they haven't overtaken you, why haven't we overtaken them?"

"Isle of Man?" suggested Mr. Chetwode. "Used to be as popular as Gretna. Can't recall why it isn't still."

"The marriage law there changed before our grandsires were old enough to elope, you nodcock," said Edward, cheerfully.

Mr. Chetwode, much flattered to be called a nodcock in so affectionate a tone by a man he quite admired, chuckled amiably.

"Well, maybe the villain don't know that either," he said.

Edward frowned.

"Dammit, I have no other lead," he said. "Back to London, Aunt Letty, and onto the Bristol road for Cheltenham, Gloucester and Liverpool."

"You won't make it if you tire the prads," opined Mr. Chetwode.

"No, I know," growled Edward. "Sorry to hold you up. Good luck!"

"Oh, Mr. Brandon, I do hope you find Beth safe and sound," said Cressida.

"She'll be fine," said Mr. Chetwode. "Never knew a girl with so many plans; I wish you joy of her, Brandon, exhausting sort of girl to live with if you ask me."

"I find her quite restful," said Edward, a little stiffly.

"Yes, Edward, dear, but if we were all alike it would be a boring world," said Letty, hastily. "Let us not waste time quarrelling over matters that are too personal to ever agree on."

"You are correct, as always, Aunt Letty," said Edward. "I will drive on ahead and find a place to turn."

"If it is an inn, it might not be a bad idea to rest the horses," said Letty. "I fear that now we shall not catch up with them until the morning at the least."

Edward frowned, but nodded.

"I don't want to overtire them," he said, "for then we shall be sunk. We shall see if a dish of tea is to be procured anywhere, and then drive back to London, and I shall see to hiring post horses, that we may then exchange for fresh ones as we take to the road again. I am certain that if we take some rest, I can go twice as fast in daylight as any coach may manage at night, and though Beth will be compromised, even if she has not been in the carriage with him, we are already betrothed."

"Indeed," said Letty. "Edward, if she has to reveal that she is there, he might…." She left the sentence hanging.

"I know," he said tightly. "If he has, I will kill him. And I will have to show her that it need not be like that. I will not repudiate the betrothal if he has… violated her."

"And I will work on her to persuade her that she has no reason to release you from it," said Letty. "And now that we have discussed the worst that can have happened, let us put it out of our minds until we find out what has happened."

"Easier said than done, but I'll try," said Edward. "There's a coaching inn, and an ostler ready to take the horses. I will just ask to make sure that there has been no coach and six pass by."

The ostler was looking frankly interested at a lady and a gentleman approaching so precipitously, but his face cleared when asked if a coach and six had passed, or even stopped. Must be some eloping couple's relatives.

He pulled his forelock as he accepted a vail from Edward.

"No coach and six, mister," he said. "The Mail for York, and a coach and four, going with all the enthusiasm of a hodemedod with gout."

The image of a gouty snail was too much for Edward's equanimity and he laughed.

"Well, thanks for that, m'lad. We must have taken the wrong road," he said.

"Well, it be the best road for Gretna," said the ostler. "But I wouldn't say as how it might be a clever man who took off for Scotland up the west country."

"I was coming to that conclusion," said Edward. "Take care of my bays, lad, while my aunt and I have whatever refreshments are on offer."

"There's allus ale or beer, coffee, and bread and cheese and ham," volunteered the ostler, and pocketed another vail with pleasure.

Edward and Letty moved into the comforting warmth of the inn for a rest.

"How lowering to be fooled by Finchbury," said Letty.

"Yes; but we'll overtake him yet," said Edward.

Chapter 24

Beth was most uncomfortable. Her legs did not belong to her, her head pounded and her hands hurt. She might try to attract attention by banging on the coach, which would at least end this physical ordeal; or maybe that would be out of the frying pan and into the fire. If there was only a way she might simulate a problem with the carriage or the horses! If she had a parasol, to thrust between the spokes of the wheels… but that would break the parasol, and possibly her arm sooner than it would break a wheel. If she had something to hurl over the top of the carriage to strike one of the horses, it might shy. But then, she had to have something heavy enough to hurl, and be certain of hitting a horse in a place that would discommode it without hurting it. She had several sovereigns in her reticule, where she had thrust it into her pocket, but wasting money that might be needed to get back to London would not do. There was baggage tied onto the roof; would the abductor notice if she cut through the straps with her penknife so it fell off? Probably not. Besides, some of it might be female apparel for the girl he had abducted. Which meant it might be dreadful clothes such as poor Molly had been wearing when first they met, or it might be quite ordinary day garb. Probably that would be in the band box; the trunk would be the gentleman's own clothing. And whilst it might be both safer, and more fun to masquerade as gentlemen to get home, though Molly might pass as a youth, Beth knew that her own shape was against her, and that a gentleman with bosoms would be too remarkable. She laughed wryly to herself for even briefly considering the idea.

Beth was seriously considering making a noise and courting discovery when nature took a hand. There was a sudden lurch, and a creaking splintering noise, and the coach slowed as the coachman called to the postillion to hold his horses, and used the reins to indicate the need for a stop.

The sound of the window between coach and driver's seat opening was a sharp clatter, and the muffled voice from within asked sharply,

"What is it?"

"That's this blurry weather, milord," said the coachman. "I thought we was on the flat, but reckon we went through ice on a puddle what's a deep enough rut to cause some damage. I'll just take th' lantern and have a look-see."

"Be quick about it," said the voice on the inside.

Beth cowered back as the coachman lifted the lantern from the side of the coach and came back towards her; but he was looking under the coach, not at its back. The side window opened.

"Can you see what the trouble is?"

"Yes, milord, it's the back axle; it ain't broke but it's not in good fettle. It's have fractured-like. Reckon I could put a cord round it to hold until we come to an inn. What sailors call woolding."

The man in the coach sighed.

"Do it," he said. "Have you cord?"

"Ar, I don't never stir without a bit o' cord, sir, you never know when you might need it," said the coachman.

It took him half an hour to effect the temporary repair, and Beth thankfully rested, seated on the back step. She tied herself hastily back on as the coachman returned to his seat on the front. It would be easier to help Molly to escape at an inn, where she would doubtless be permitted out of the coach, if nothing else to use the Jericho. The coach proceeded at a sedate pace, for the coachman had no intention of losing the axle if he could avoid it, short of somewhere to lay up and make proper repairs. There would be bound to be someone who could make a new axle.

In the coach, Finchbury gave Molly a wry smile.

"The best laid plans fall apart as a result of nature's interference, my dear," he said. "And we shall doubtless have to rouse an irritable innkeeper in an establishment not anticipating coaches at every hour of the day or night. I am going to tell him that you are my wife, and I strongly suggest that you do not contradict me. If you do, your reputation is gone in any case, and I might feel strongly enough not to want to actually marry you. I am sorry to use threats, but I'm sure you understand my position?"

Molly gave a snort of derision.

"Will you play along, Miss Renfield?" asked Finchbury, dangerously quietly.

Molly nodded assent.

She had her fingers crossed inside her cloak.

The inn was indeed dark; it was impossible to even work out what its name was. The coachman went to knock thunderously on the door, while the postilion unhitched the horses and led them round to the stables.

A tousled head appeared at a window.

"Who's making that devilish row?" it demanded.

"My master's coach is damaged! He and his...wife need to come in immediately, come down and let us in!"

"Be damned if I shall; that's the innkeeper's job."

There was a pregnant silence.

"Well who do you be, then ef you bain't the innkeeper?" demanded the coachman.

"I'm a clerk and I'm just staying here," said the head.

Another window opened.

"Now then, now then, what's all this?" the new head demanded.

"Are you the innkeeper?" asked the coachman.

"Naow, I'm the queen of the fairies," said the new head. "Of course I'm the ruddy innkeeper!"

"My master and his wife find themselves distressed upon the highway," said the coachman. "Lord Finchbury and his lady need lodgings."

"Do they, now," said the innkeeper. "Well I'll come down, but I'll see the colour of his money afore I let his supposed Lordship in. Honest folk don't travel by night unless they go by mail."

"My master travels at night for the same reason the mail does, to avoid traffic," said the coachman.

The head withdrew abruptly, and the window slammed shut. The coachman knocked on the door of the coach.

"Did you hear all that, milord?" he said.

"Of course I did! Contumelious yokel, but doubtless once paid he'll be an oleaginous yokel," said Finchbury.

There were sounds of bolts being drawn back, and Finchbury strode forward, holding Molly's arm through the folds of the cloak, as though solicitously. Finchbury waved a handful of sovereigns under mine host's nose, which quivered happily in his red face set above its woollen wrap, which could not deserve the name of banyan, and voluminous night rail.

"Come in, my lord, you and your good lady, I shall have the best chamber prepared for you right away! Come into the parlour and I will make you coffee while your bed is warmed! If your man brings in your baggage, I can show him where to take it!"

Beth slipped first to the coach, where she made search in the pockets of the doors; then over to the inn, keeping to shadows, and waited for the coachman to start undoing the luggage to slide in the door, listening for the sound of the now quite loquacious and, as Finchbury had suggested, oleaginous innkeeper. There were other rooms to hide in while the innkeeper made and brought coffee, and then he would retire above to sort out a chamber for Quality.

Molly went into the coffee room with fear in her heart. Mine host fussed around lighting candles, and kicking the embers of the fire into enough life to throw a log on. The room was warm, at least compared to the cold coach.

"Come, my dear, you can take your cloak off now," said Finchbury. Molly undid it with trembling fingers, and threw it off.

"There, milord, you can see what I am now," she said. "You grabbed the wrong one, and I loves my mistress enough to let you think I'm her so you don't go back for her."

Finchbury stared.

"By Jove, girl, you have courage and loyalty! Nay, don't look so afeared, I'll not touch you. If I'd known who you were earlier, I'd have put you down at the first inn we came to, with enough to get home. I'm no coward to only ruin maidservants and tavern wenches! Not that I'd turn down a tumble with a good wench like you if gold should tempt you... no? well, my loss," he added as Molly drew back.

"I didn't know you was a real gent, as well as an abductor," said Molly. "Why did you want to steal away my mistress?"

"Because I was paid to do so by a lady named Amelia Hazelgrove," said Finchbury. "Who held out the added bribe that Miss Renfield was possessed of an elegant inheritance."

"She told you a hum, then," said Beth, coming in the door. "I do not own a thing, milord whoever you are. Amelia makes up what she does not know, though to do her justice, I believe she believes her own tarradiddles. I have heard what you said to my maid, which is why I have not shot you."

Finchbury regarded the carriage pistols which Beth carried.

"Do you know how to use those?" he asked.

"Oh, yes," said Beth, mendaciously. She knew

enough to make sure the safety catches were off.

"Well, then, I believe I shall be very careful," said Finchbury. "My name is Finchbury."

"Finchbury? That should be familiar," said Beth, moving round towards the corner, where she could also see the door. Finchbury looked on her with wry approval.

"Ah, not the usual mistake of Gothic novels, wherein you might be overpowered from behind by my man," he said.

"I cut my eye teeth long since," said Beth. "Why do I know your name?"

"Because I seduced that little idiot Tiffany Pelham who tried to foist her bastard onto a blonde man," said Finchbury.

"Singularly idiotic," said Beth. "Now, Molly and I wish to escape from here, and I fear you are an impediment, and though I mislike the idea of either shooting you or hitting you over the head, I shall have no qualms about doing so if I have to."

"Funnily enough, I believe you," said Finchbury. "And demme, if you wanted to marry someone, even without a fortune I shouldn't mind. You have ten times the spirit of any of the usual girls in town; aye, and so does your maid, whose loyalty I admire."

"That's all very well, milord, but I ain't a-trusting of you for all the Spanish coin you can muster," said Molly.

"You are a good girl," said Finchbury. "Are you sure you wouldn't like to be my mistress?"

"No, thank you, milord," said Molly. "Miss Beth, shall I hit him with the poker?"

"I don't think you need to do so, Molly," said Beth, "but if you keep a good hold of the poker it might not be a bad idea. I thought perhaps milord might like to stay to drink brandy while his wife and her maid are shown to the bedchamber, and he will stay perforce since I was planning on tying his legs to the chair, and his right arm too, so he has one arm free to drink with, and to work the knots loose eventually after we have escaped."

"What about bodily comforts?" asked Finchbury.

"I'll get the Jordan out of the cupboard and you will have to fumble about and hope to aim in the right direction," said Beth.

"It was worth a try," said Finchbury.

"Oh, in your shoes I'd have tried it myself," said Beth.

"Do you really prefer a slow-top like Edward Brandon?"

"Yes, Lord Finchbury. He is a practical man and a compassionate one, and I like him very well, as well as loving him," said Beth.

"Dear me! There must be more to him than I realised," said Finchbury. "I wish you will tell him though, and ask him to tell his uncle, that I had no idea that the Pelham girl was stupid enough to foist her brat onto someone as unlike me to look at as possible, rather than quietly have her child and have it farmed out, as most girls who misbehave tend to do."

"It takes two to misbehave, and you're old enough to know better," said Beth. "Molly, pray use your netting skills to fasten Lord Finchbury to his chair, while I keep a pistol trained on him."

Molly hastened to do Beth's bidding, sacrificing the wool from the stocking she was knitting, and had carried in her pocket. Unfortunately, she moved between Finchbury and Beth; and the Marquis seized his chance.

He grabbed Molly by the arms, and held her in front of him.

"I really do not want to be tied up," he said. "I don't intend to hurt you, girl," he added as Molly squirmed and kicked him in the shin. Beth said loudly,

"DUCK, Molly!" and as Molly obediently bobbed down as low as she might, Beth fired!

The crash of the gun startled Beth as much as it did Molly, who screamed. Finchbury cried out, and clutched his shoulder.

"Demme. girl, I didn't know you were that good!" he exclaimed.

"Nor did I," said Beth. "I even hit where I aimed!"

"I should be thankful you didn't aim for my head," said Finchbury.

The landlord came crashing into the parlour.

"What's all this, what's all this?" he cried.

"My Lord Finchbury is a trifle bosky, and wanted to shoot the flames off the candles," said Beth, smoothly, "And I tried to take the gun from him. Unfortunately it went off."

"Shoot the flames off candles? With a coach pistol?" said mine host, disbelievingly.

"Exactly; madness," said Beth. "I wish you will send for a doctor and let my maid and me put him to bed, and I pray you find another chamber for me. I have no desire to sleep with a drunken wounded idiot."

"Yes, my lady, of course, my lady," said the innkeeper, bowing and scraping. He had not seen a maid at first and had wondered if this was something haveycavey, but the lady had the manner of a marchioness. Shooting flames off candles indeed! The aristocracy were more trouble than they were worth, almost made one wish to be a Frenchman, but for the obvious disadvantage one would then have of not being English.

Chapter 25

Beth and Molly between them cleaned the wound and dressed it with mine host's own bandages – and Finchbury's own cravat which had the advantage, as Beth said, of at least being approximately clean – and put him to bed. They retired to the adjoining room with the bandbox of clothes.

Beth rummaged.

"His taste is good at least," she said, "and he had brought round gowns that may be adjusted with pins to almost any size. We shall bolt our doors, and sleep here for what little remains of the night, and then we shall consider how to get back to London."

"Oh Miss Beth, you take it so calm!" said Molly.

"There is no point falling into hysterics," said Beth, "Though I confess I have felt like it a few times! How clever and brave you were!"

"Oh and Miss, how brave you were! Was you riding like a tiger all the way?"

"I tied myself on," said Beth. "Really, I fancy it is just as well that we are both resourceful."

"I am mortally sorry I got in the way," said Molly.

"Never mind, Molly," said Beth. "No harm done – except to Lord Finchbury. And if he had only submitted to being tied up, he would not have ended up with a hole in his shoulder. A doctor will have to dig the ball out. And by the way, I have the other pistol just in case, for I do not know how to reload the first."

"Good job there was two, then," said Molly, taking off her dress, and looking with distaste at the floor.

"We'll share the bed," said Beth. "It's just about wide enough unless you kick."

Molly giggled.

"I don't think so," she said.

"Well, well, my shift is a little fine to sleep in

without getting cold, so I will see…. On second thoughts, my shift is a lot thicker and more decent than these confections purporting to be night rails in here," said Beth. "Ah well, there is a hot brick in the bed, and plenty of good woollen blankets."

Without further ado the two young women got into bed, and if Beth took longer to go to sleep than Molly, who just curled up and slept, it was not by much. Beth was exhausted after an evening dancing and then her ordeal on the back of the coach!

Edward had bespoken rooms and asked to be awoken at first light, and ordered breakfast in bed to be prepared for his aunt half an hour after that. He did not sleep well, for he was worried about Beth. However, he knew that he would do her no good by driving haphazardly about the countryside in the dark. And after snatching a couple of hours sleep, he knew he had been right to do so. The horses would be fresh to take him back to London, and he might then hire horses to head west. He had no other clue as to what way to go.

"Edward," said Letty, as she tripped into the parlour, where Edward was discussing an excellent breakfast, after seeing to his team, "Correct me if I am wrong, but isn't Finchbury's mother Welsh?"

"You're right," said Edward. "I recall once he was boasting that he knew the border country like the back of his hand. Well, the route will be the same as far as Gloucester, so we have nothing to lose by following the same plan as if he were going to Scotland up the western side of the country. We must just hope to catch up before we have to make a decision to turn towards Wales, or head further north."

"When you have finished eating, I will be ready to set off," said Letty.

"Bless you, best of aunts!" said Edward.

Letty laughed.

"That is less complimentary than it sounds, as I

know Cassandra, Daphne *and* Eglantine, dear boy," she said.

"Well, there is that," said Edward. "I have finished; let me just settle up, and then we can be on the road."

Beth woke crying out in pain as she stretched.

"Oh Miss Beth!" Molly sat up, rubbing at her eyes. "What is it?"

"I'm stiff, Molly, from hanging on to the back of the carriage," said Beth. "I'm sorry to wake you."

"Well, I can hear a hum and bustle of people, so it's past time to rise," said Molly. "I find when I'm stiff, if I rub my legs and arms it helps."

"Thank you; I shall try it," said Beth. "We should get breakfast and then attempt to get away. I have no idea where we are, and if we can find that out, we can find out where we need to go."

"I'll go down to the kitchens and arrange you a tray, Miss Beth," said Molly. "And ask nosy questions that a maid can ask where a lady cannot. You stay here, and don't let anyone see you; no sense in letting anyone make scandal."

"A good point," said Beth. "And make sure you bring enough for yourself too; we shall eat together."

"That ain't right, miss," said Molly, disapprovingly.

"We've been through a lot together; we can worry about what's right or not when we get out of it safely," said Beth. "I'm tempted to choose the plainest of these gowns for me, and the next plainest for you, and then we try to travel as sisters, country girls but of good enough estate not to be molested by anyone."

Molly looked doubtful.

"I'll get some breakfast, and then we can discuss it, Miss Beth," she said.

Over buttered eggs, plenty of toast, tea and apricot preserves, Molly said shyly,

"I think it's a good idea pretending to be sisters, if

you would so condescend, Miss Beth, because we shall be less remarkable. A lady with her maid would raise eyebrows if she had no gentleman escort, and the gowns he has packed seem to be mostly quite plain, and a heap of ribbons and silk flowers and braid in the bottom of the band box."

"I have to say that as abductors go, he has been moderately considerate," said Beth. "I suppose that as he was intending marriage, he wished to begin in a conciliatory fashion, and no wise man tries to second guess the sartorial tastes, that is tastes regarding clothes," she added, as Molly puzzled over an unknown word, "of his wife. What he does regarding his mistress may be very different, but a wife should be given respect. I think we should see to his shoulder before we leave, and thank him for the consideration he intended towards me."

"Just take the other pistol, Miss Beth," said Molly.

After breakfast, the girls arrayed themselves in some plain muslins, putting on two gowns for warmth, and Beth put her spencer back on. There was a plain navy blue spencer which would do for Molly, and they had their cloaks. After checking that the coast was clear, Beth led the way to the Marquis' room, only to pause on the threshold to see his coachman tending him.

"You may go, Spalding," said Finchbury. "You look quite charming in the clothing I chose for you, Miss Renfield, and so does, er, Molly."

"I ain't having that virago shoot you again, milord," said Spalding.

"If she wanted to finish me off she could have done so last night," said Finchbury.

"Have you removed the ball, Spalding?" asked Beth.

"No, miss; doctor is coming to do that," said Spalding. "It ain't one of your skills I suppose, like flourishing barking-irons like a bridle-cull?"

"It isn't, and I have no idea of half of what you said," said Beth. Spalding grinned like a gutter-snipe, nodded to his master, and left her without explanation.

"Barking-irons, guns; a bridle-cull, a highwayman," translated Finchbury. "He has packed the wound with basilicum powder, Miss Renfield, and renewed your competent bandage with linen he boiled overnight, having discovered me indisposed after seeking fruitlessly for someone to mend my axle. You have missed anything vital."

"Oh good," said Beth. "I am glad, because I have to say that from all that Molly has told me, and from the way you left trims separate, you have been prepared to be a most considerate and even conciliatory husband. And I am sorry to have caused you pain, and indeed in some respects to deprive you of the fortune I don't have. If only your reputation were not against you, you would have made some girl a very kindly husband."

"Thank you, Miss Renfield," said Finchbury. "My problem is that I dislike the... well, shall we say, ladies for hire. And yet I have my needs, and there are plenty of girls willing to satisfy them. And I have never been ungenerous to a mistress who has not been ungenerous first."

"Tiffany Pelham?" asked Beth.

"Oh, I won't talk out of turn, but she was ... difficult," said Finchbury, "And not so much fun as I thought she was at first. I expect Darsham found that too."

"I wouldn't know: I don't know Lord Darsham," said Beth. "Edward said she was a superficial mercenary little ninnyhammer."

"Brandon *is* wiser than I am," said Finchbury. "I was a fool to amuse myself with her, but there you are. What's done is done."

"I don't think that for all you are supposed to be a ladies' man that you are at all clever about women," said Beth, "for you fell in easily enough with Amelia's plans."

"Yes, I did," said Finchbury. "And to be honest, now I know you better, I'd have loved a chance to bed both you and the redoubtable Molly, but I don't take any woman against her will. That can never be a charge levelled at me. I was hoping to bring you willingly to my bed, Miss Renfield, whether quickly by the sheer force of my ineffably marvellous personality, or in resignation when, reputation in tatters, you had no choice but to wed me. Whereupon I would have hoped that you would have learned to enjoy the experience."

"You really do not know Edward very well," said Beth, "for I know that whatever my reputation might be, he would wed me, even if I had been ... if you had been less scrupulous."

"He's a remarkable man then, and probably actually deserves you," said Finchbury. "May I kiss your hand and we part friends? I promise I mean no harm."

"You are a gentleman, so I will trust your word," said Beth, extending her hand.

He gave her a crooked smile.

"Had I intended trickery, by saying that you would have defeated it in shaming me into recalling that I am a gentleman," he said. "Enjoy the clothes."

"I should like to pay for them but I do not have enough on me," said Beth.

"Oh, do not worry," said Finchbury. "Amelia Hazelgrove paid for them. And I have not accomplished her purpose, but I do not intend to pay her back. Let her sue me for breach of promise, I say."

Beth laughed.

"Indeed and it would be an interesting case if it came to court!" she said. "I bid you fare well, and I mean it. And I hope you meet an heiress who will love you for yourself."

He gave a sardonic laugh.

"So do I," he said.

As it would look strange to travel without any clothing, Beth and Molly elected to take the band-box, in which was laid also Beth's ballgown and Molly's maid's clothes, which it would be profligate to leave. Molly was to wear the one straw bonnet within, a few of the silk flowers pinned onto it securely, and Beth fashioned a toque from her cashmere shawl, earning much admiration from Molly at her cleverness.

"What are we going to do, Miss Beth, to return to London?" asked Molly, who had ascertained that they were at a village rejoicing in the name of Burnham, or rather outside its normal boundaries, the inn being on the main road in the hopes of gaining more trade. Being between Maidenhead and the coaching town of Slough, it might be a forlorn hope, save for those looking for a quieter hostelry.

"And it was bad luck for Finchbury that his axle broke on the wrong side of Slough, where he might have had it repaired in a matter of a couple of hours, I wager," said Beth.

"Instead of which he has ended in quite a Slough of Despond," Molly giggled.

"Oh, you are familiar with the '*Pilgrim's Progress*', are you?" said Beth.

"Yes, the vicar read parts of it instead of a sermon some Sundays," said Molly.

"Well, then, as Slough must be some three miles or less, I suggest that we trudge along the road, in our own pilgrimage and there await either the Mail, or take a yellow bounder," said Beth. "The Mail goes faster, but I wager the postchaise is more comfortable."

Molly nodded.

The next adventure was to leave the inn unobserved; and to achieve this end, they decided to wait until the doctor arrived, since he might be expected to command the attention of the innkeeper at the very least, and possibly some of the other servants.

As the doctor sent for boiling water, and brandy, he

set the whole inn in an uproar! Beth and Molly were able to walk boldly out of the back door, as if going to the Jericho, and walk round to the road without challenge. Indeed they were looked upon with some admiration by the Marquis' hired postillion, who did not for one moment suppose that either of these obvious country ladies was the fine lady he had seen coerced into the carriage the night before. Of her fate, he was not paid to ask, and what he did not know he could not be tried for in court!

Beth and Molly walked on to the road, arm in arm, without a backwards glance, and set off towards the east quite merrily.

Chapter 26

The day was chill, and frost crackled underfoot in the early morning; but Molly had stout shoes, and Beth had warm overshoes, and as both were country girls, they were used to walking briskly, and did not notice the cold too badly. A thin, unwilling sun was burning through the early morning mist and haze, and if the frost on the skeletons of the previous year's Queen Anne's Lace did not exactly sparkle, it had a filigree delicacy that no silversmith might improve upon. The beauty brought a smile to Beth's lips. The new fronds of this year's Queen Anne's Lace were sulkily unfurling in the frosted grassy verges of the road, and soon would reach tall, and fill the sides of the ditches with their ferny leaves.

"I wonder what the time is," said Beth.

"Does it matter?" asked Molly.

"It might. It depends when the coaches run. I'd hate to miss one because we slept on a bit."

"Oh, it was only an hour or so after dawn that we rose," said Molly. "And an hour perhaps after that when we left. It won't take as much as an hour to walk into Slough I shouldn't think, and that will make it about nine of the clock."

"I hope you are right," said Beth, dubiously, thinking that by the time they had breakfasted and seen Lord Finchbury it was somewhat more than an hour. They had been overtaken by several vehicles, and one had been yellow, and carried a guard behind with a yard of tin. The Mail had gone through from Bath long since, but that could not be helped. Beth had no idea whether it stopped at Slough or whether the guard merely threw down an appropriate sack of mail and caught the sack of mails incoming. The question was academic since it had flashed past before they were even on the road!

The walk took perhaps three quarters of an hour, delays mostly involving getting off the road as traffic came along. Pedestrians customarily walked on the right, towards oncoming traffic, to be able to see it coming and move off the road.

"Did you know that the French drive on the right hand side of the road?" Beth asked Molly.

"No! Go on, it's a hum, how do they use the whip freely to crack, without it tangling in trees and bushes?" asked Molly.

Beth shrugged, and winced as it jarred her arms.

"I don't know, Molly, perhaps they cut back the trees or something. But it was the idea of Robespierre, who was a lawyer and a politician but had obviously never driven, or even, like you, observed people driving. Because pedestrians walk on the right, and peasants never had carriages, the right had to be egalitarian, and the left elitist."

Molly snorted.

"And what about the farmer and his carts, and the carters, and all the honest folk with ox-carts or dickey-carts or cart-horses what go to market?" she said. "They ain't aristos, nowise."

"Oh, I don't pretend to understand the French mentality," laughed Beth, "but I thought you might find it amusing, that they drive on the wrong side of the road all on the political whim of a barrister."

Molly gave an eloquent sniff.

Slough was an unremarkable small town save for being perhaps busier than some, for its coaching in at the Crown. It smelled strongly of horse, and horses being cooled were being led about near the inn.

"We must ask about what coaches pass through," said Beth. Molly nodded.

"There'll be a board up at the inn which gives times," she said. "See, I've travelled on the stage coaches when I came up to London, so I know more'n you do, Miss Beth. And look, it says 'second stage' on that, which is good, because that means it's a place where the horses are changed, so most of them will stop, and there's that blessed yellow bounder that passed us on the road on its way out!"

"Oh, how irritating!" cried Beth. "They won't stop if we wave, I suppose?"

Molly shook her head, and had to retrieve one of her fabric roses that fell off at this uncalled for vigour.

"No, Miss, they don't stop for no-one. If you take too long in the Jericho, even if you're booked to ride and have paid, they've gone."

"Oh, dear, I wish now we might have hurried a bit more," said Beth, "and you must remember to call me Beth as we are sisters."

"If we'd hurried that much, likelihood is we'd of turned an ankle in a rut, or slipped over in those puddles that were still frozen," said Molly. "There'll be others. If it's second stage out of London, it'll be last stage into London. And look at the board, that must have been the Reading coach, and they come from Bath, Bristol, Oxford and all over. Oh, I know! It's one of the places the Young Gentlemen get off for Eton, I think. I seen that somewhere."

"Well, we must peruse the board and not be disappointed that we have missed three coaches that an earlier breakfast might have seen us catching," said Beth. "The York House coach leaves Bath at six in the morning, dear me, Slough must be about two hours out of London, so that should arrive at about eight of the clock this evening, for it is sixteen hours to Bath, I believe; and then there is a Sunday coach from Reading which leaves Reading at nine in the morning, so I suppose it will stop here some time between ten and eleven."

"You are clever to work that out so quick!" said Molly.

"I'm having to do a lot of guessing, though," said Beth. "Slough is about two hours from London, fifteen or sixteen miles, so I have to take a couple of hours off the time of travel from Bath. Which I may have misremembered, you know."

"I am sure you have not, Mi….Beth," said Molly. "Look, there is a daily coach from Oxford, leaving at half-past six in the morning; how far away is Oxford?"

"It must be at least thirty miles," said Beth. "For Oxford is a good fifty miles from London, and the road by this route will be longer. So the coach will not arrive here until at least half-past ten. This might well be the best coach for us."

"So we have time for a dish of tea and some toast?" suggested Molly, hopefully. Beth laughed.

"We do indeed," she said.

Fortified by tea and toast, most of which Molly ate, and warm within the parlour of the inn, Beth and Molly awaited the arrival of the coach from Oxford. The tavern wench who had served them said that the coach was due in at eleven, so Molly had asked for hard boiled eggs, bread-and-butter and some ham to be put up in a parcel for them to take as a nuncheon to eat on the way into the city. The girl came out with the parcel which she tendered with a cheerful smile.

"Best be waiting outside, misses, to make sure you get a place," she said. "If there's room, that is! There's time to use the Jericho too."

Beth slipped her a vail with thanks, and she and Molly took turns to make themselves comfortable before waiting outside in the yard.

The coach rumbled in, and ostlers leaped to the heads of the horses, and began to unharness them, the new team being led out to replace them. Two or three of the passengers leaped out to hurry to make use of the facilities of the inn, or to take a hurried cup of coffee and buy hot pies for early nuncheon. Two of them who came off the roof were young men who ogled the girls and nudged each other.

"Please may I have two tickets to ride?" asked Beth, timidly, of the guard.

He looked at her and Molly, and smiled kindly, but sympathetically

"I'm sorry, Miss, but unless any of those as have gone into the inn are too late back, we be full," he said. "Not that you'd much enjoy it, there being two young gentlemen sent down from University, and kicking up every lark they can think of. I reckon one of them thinks he might persuade the driver to let him take the ribbons."

"Dear me!" said Beth. "I have read in the newspaper of accidents engendered by the over-estimation of skill on the part of gentlemen so engaged. If anyone is late, I may hope it is those young gentlemen!"

The guard laughed a rather bitter laugh.

"Alas, miss, no such luck," he said. "I'd throw them off if I dared, but they've paid to travel, and causing such nuisance as using a fishing rod to fish through the carriage window for anything to cause annoyance ain't mentioned in the book of rules, and no more it isn't for them to make indelicate noises every time I sound the yard of tin."

"What ill-bred little brats," said Beth.

"Yes miss, you might say so, but I couldn't possibly comment," said the guard lugubriously.

Nobody was late back to the coach; and Beth sighed as the young men made it at a sprint, scrambling up as the coach started to move; for having ridden on the back of Finchbury's carriage just a few hours before, Beth did not feel able to brave the roof, even if they were late.

"Perhaps it is as well," said Molly, timidly. "Those young gentlemen must be making the ordeal of travelling even worse for the other travellers."

"Indeed so," said Beth. "It makes me angry, because although I have no desire for a university education for myself, Elizabeth would have relished it, and would have done the work assiduously, and yet young men who are permitted to go so often seem to waste the privilege."

"It don't seem fair," agreed Molly. "And poor men who are clever enough to better themselves if only they could go don't get the chance neither."

"You are quite right," said Beth. "When Edward and I are taking care of foundlings we must send the cleverest ones to such schools as will enable them best to learn, and to send those that deserve it to university."

"They will be bullied for being poor and low born," said Molly.

"Not if they have learned the speech to support the position into which they wish to elevate themselves, and go as our wards," said Beth. "They need never mention their birth. It would be a fine thing to give doctors and scientists to the world, who would otherwise have no education. "

"Oh yes!" said Molly, nodding agreement.

They retired back within to await the next coach to London, a tedious wait, but at least better accomplished in the warm.

Coaches out of London also stopped off, and the inn was full of bustle, frenetic moments of passengers desperate for coffee, hot pies, the Jericho or just to rest a moment from the discomfort of the seats in a coach. Some stopped here, or were changing coaches. An endless stream of disparate people flooded into and out of the door, some settling down to wait as Beth and Molly were, others in too much of a hurry to even notice who else might be there. Beth quite enjoyed it.

"Oh Molly, how tempting it is to make up stories about people!" she said. "That little man, positively bouncing with irritation at the delay, like a cockerel who has had his crow subdued somehow, I can imagine him being a lawyer on his way to make a deathbed change to a will, and worrying that he will not be on time and will lose his fee!"

Molly giggled.

"Or maybe he is just desperate for the Jericho and it is full of the rather vulgar ladies who were travelling with him, who will not hurry!" she said.

"Well, that would account for some choler, but he seems to have something more on his mind than that," said Beth. "Maybe his daughter has run off with someone unsuitable and he is trying to get there in time to stop the wedding."

"Or he has chilblains, and can't get anyone to heat him a brick to warm his feet or find him some Whitehead's essence of mustard to ease the itching," said Molly.

"And the vulgar ladies must be a mother and daughter, off to confront a young man in Oxford about the ruin of the daughter, for weren't they trying to be *grandes dames*!" chuckled Beth.

"Oh, I hadn't thought of that, I thought they had been up on the town hoping to catch a husband for the younger, but couldn't get anywhere and were going home in high dudgeon and pretending to despise everything including London to cover disappointment," said Molly.

"Your guess is probably closer," said Beth. "Indeed, all your guesses are probably closer; I must read too many novels."

Molly giggled again.

"Most people get more exercised in the mind over bodily discomforts or embarrassment than about anything else," she said. "That's why that lady, Miss Hazelgrove, wanted to do you a bad turn, because she felt an idiot that she had not managed to hang on to Mr. Brandon."

"I should think you probably have the right of it, Molly, my dear," said Beth. "Dear me, I wish you were my sister, I never had anyone to giggle with, and speculate over people with. But if you are my personal maid, I am sure Edward will be quite tolerant of us sharing a friendship as well."

"He's a lovely man," said Molly. "And he's going to have a lovely wife too!"

"Bless you, Molly!" said Beth, quite overcome. The pair passed the time quite happily in their innocent enjoyment of making guesses about those who came and went, being careful to speak in low voices, and not to stare, so as not to embarrass anyone. Molly had learned not to stare, and really, thought Beth, was doing a very good job of passing for a young gentlewoman of rustic background. Perhaps as Molly was so young, she might be able to learn to be a companion more than a maid. It was something to consider!

Chapter 27

Edward was tired, but the thoughts of Beth spurred him on. He insisted that Letty should stay at home and go to bed, for there was far less impropriety in driving with a girl and her maid in daylight than overnight. Edward breakfasted again in London where he hired fresh horses, on the principle that food could take the place of sleep, according to the tales of some of the soldiers he had been helping. And that was a good point, thought Edward. He never bothered with a coachman in London as he drove himself, but one of the soldiers he had not yet transported to Suffolk had experience with driving; and driving a curricle on good roads probably needed no more skill than getting a baggage train over the Pyrenees.

He went to seek out Sergeant Ned Hoskins.

"Someone's abducted my bride," he said. "He didn't take her on the great north road. I need someone to drive while I snatch some sleep, who can return by Stage if need be. Can you handle a curricle?"

"Reckon I can handle anyfink," said Hoskins. "Strewth, Mr. Brandon, ain't I used a ruddy high perch phaeton to transport me Colonel's fancy woman and her baggage, though if you arsts me she was the biggest baggage of all, to safety?"

"You did? Well if you can handle one of those, and with a Female of that calibre aboard, I'd say you probably can manage anything," said Edward, relieved. "Obviously I'll pay you for your time."

Hoskins spat.

"I'd rescue a lidy from that sort o' Captain Hackum gratis," he said.

The drive out on the Bristol road was quite busy, but after Edward had watched Hoskins covertly for a few miles, and noted that he overtook with ease and skill, if not style, he decided to leave it to the sergeant, and permitted his weary head to droop. Hoskins smiled affectionately. Mr. Brandon was a good sort of cove to place that much trust in him!

Edward slept for over an hour, and awoke as they passed through Cranford.

"Where are we?" asked Edward.

"Cranford, sir, but I'm not sure where we're heading."

"Nor am I," said Edward. "I'm looking for a coach with a crest showing two small birds and a crown, which I should have told you before."

"We ain't passed one, and that's a fac'," said Hoskins.

"How can you be certain?" worried Edward.

Hoskins spat over the dash.

"Because we ain't passed any coaches wiv any crest, coming nor goin' acoss I was looking out particular in case you got arahnd to tellin' me if we wus lookin' fer one," he said.

"Hoskins, you are an excellent man," approved Edward.

"Thank you, sir," said Hoskins. He hesitated briefly and then added, "I was hoping you might have a position for me as a driver. I know I wheeze from that bullet in the chest, but it don't stop me driving."

"It doesn't," said Edward. "I'll certainly think about it. I was considering asking you to train children to drive, when Beth and I start taking on foundlings, but in the meantime…"

"Well, sir, if I was to be useful as a driver, you might want me just fer that, I ain't never had anyfink to do wiv nippers," said Hoskins.

Edward laughed.

"Well, nor have I, bar my extremely pampered and singularly unprepossessing younger cousins," he said.

"Got many?" asked Hoskins.

"I couldn't tell you the numbers," said Edward,

honestly. "I don't get on with my father's sisters and each one of them appears to be a horde. Each one of my paternal aunts is so forceful as to seem like a horde," he added. "Not to mention my female cousins and their offspring."

Hoskins nodded.

"Difficult to assess the enemy when they're milling about," he said.

"Well, for all I know some of them may turn out well enough, but not my cousin Jane, who's as Friday-faced as a parson in a Methodee Chapel," said Edward. He lapsed back into silence, contemplating how many cutting things his aunts and cousins would manage to say about Beth, and wondering if he could just manage to forget to invite them to the wedding.

It was during his musing that Edward suddenly sat up straight.

"Hoskins!" he said.

"Got a crest on it, I'll pull in," said Hoskins, doing so. "Heh, two liddle birds an' a dirty great crown, 'swotyousaid."

Edward nodded, grimly, and leaped down, heading purposefully for the inn.

"Where is Lord Finchbury?" he demanded of the landlord.

"In his bedchamber, sir, but...."

"The VILLAIN!" roared Edward. "Take me there at once!"

"But...." Mine host was not happy.

"But me no buts, you old goat, just take me to Finchbury now, and pray I don't call you as an accessory!" growled Edward, having visions of Beth raped solidly all night and half the morning.

Mine host grumbled to himself, but the word 'accessory' was a powerful cantrip upon his compliance. He had no idea what he might be an accessory to, but as this was a young gentleman who was plainly very well blunted indeed, and as there had been something deucedly havy-cavy about Milord Finchbury, he suspected fraud or theft. At least Milord did indeed seem entitled to that form of address.

He showed Edward up the stairs to the door and scurried away, as Edward booted the door in.

He fetched up short at seeing Finchbury in bed with his arm in a sling.

Alone.

"Where's Beth?" demanded Edward.

"In London by now, I shouldn't be surprised," said Finchbury. "*What* a virago; I declare you're welcome to her."

"*What did you do to her?*" demanded Edward.

"Not a thing, old boy," said Finchbury. "I never bed unwilling females; didn't you know? And besides, she never gave me a chance to work my charm. She shot me."

"Beth?" said Edward. "I didn't know she knew how to handle a gun."

"She's either very good, or very lucky," said Finchbury. "Do be a good fellow and help me with the Jordan. I'm as weak as a cat."

Edward found himself helping the man he had planned to kill.

"And what about little Molly?" he asked.

"That's a brave, loyal little girl," said Finchbury. "Turned down an offer from me though. Pity. I might even have ignored the due to my family and married her.
But she and your Miss Renfield set off as soon as they might this morning."

Edward groaned.

"She was with you all night?" he cried.

"No, she was with Molly all night," said Finchbury. "They called in to say goodbye and change my dressings. We parted amicably enough."

"Amicably?" Edward ground his teeth, hardly able to believe it.

223

"Why not?" Finchbury looked down his hawk-like nose. "I like her more than I like the little hussy who hired me. And once she had it plain that I despise ravishers, then we were able to have a plain conversation. Lud, she's boring about you, Brandon!"

"I was planning on beating you into a paste," said Edward.

Finchbury shuddered.

"Then I must say, I am for the first time quite delighted that Miss Renfield put a ball in me. You're far too much of a gentleman to do so when I am *hors de combat*."

"I am," said Edward. "But I might come and seek you out when you heal; I've another family matter to blame you for."

"Oh, acquit me of anything to do with Tiffy's idiocy in trying to fix the brat onto a man who looks nothing like me, or indeed any man at all," said Finchbury. "Really, the girl turned out to be quite addled, I can't see what I saw in her, and before you go saying anything ugly, it was touch and go whether the brat would be mine, or that of the pugilist I caught her with. Or the groom I suspected her of having her pleasure with too. Couldn't get enough of it from me once I'd showed her the way. Is the brat mine?"

"Yes; she has sallow skin and your ears," said Edward.

"Lud! Well, she might have had black ringlets and a long nose, the pugilist was a protégé of Mendoza's," said Finchbury.

"Well, I have to take your word on it," said Edward, "But I never knew she was so lost to shame!"

"My dear fellow! It's only what plenty of married ladies do, you know," said Finchbury, in an amused drawl. "Just like the matrons of Rome and the gladiators, you know."

"Good G-d!" said Edward, shocked.

Finchbury decided that perhaps he had better not

mention some of the dubious transactions he had overseen, which gave him the entrée into so many places and made sure his pockets were not entirely to let. Besides, it would be indiscreet.

"I wish you might tell Lord Darsham that I did not intentionally cuckold him," said Finchbury. "This Crim. Con. is most inconvenient."

"If you've even frightened my Beth, inconvenient is going to be the least of your worries," said Edward.

"I don't think she knows the meaning of the word, 'frightened'," said Finchbury. "I hope you will take good care of her without trying to mollycoddle her; she's as spirited a piece as any I've ever seen, and clever, and I'd hate to think of her being trammelled by someone who doesn't appreciate her worth."

"Well of all the cheek!" said Edward. "I know her worth all right, and I have no intention of trammelling her!"

"Good," said Finchbury. "Give her my regards when you catch up with her, but for pity's sake go away. You're very tiring."

"I'll go away when you tell me where she was planning to go," said Edward.

"London, she said," said Finchbury. "She and young Molly were planning on walking to the nearest coaching inn; which to my reckoning must be Slough. There's enough coaches through there that I'd imagine she might well be half way to London by now. Resourceful pair, those girls. They were both wearing the plain gowns I bought, without adding any of the trim, and hoping to be taken as sisters. Looked enough like a pair of parson's daughters for anyone to leave 'em alone, if you ask me," he added.

"Well! Thank you for that," said Edward. "By the way, were you headed for your mother's country in Wales, or using the Western route North?"

"You know about my mother? I'm impressed," said Finchbury. "I was heading for Wales, to delay pursuit."

"It did," said Edward. He strode back out to the curricle.

"Is he dead?" asked Hoskins.

"No. He has a pistol ball in him, though," said Edward.

"You shot him?" asked Hoskins.

Edward shook his head.

"My betrothed did that last night," he said.

Hoskins whistled.

"She's quite some lady!" he said, remembering not to use cant.

"She is," said Edward. "We're heading back the way we just came, and checking at the 'Crown' in Slough whether she's been there, or indeed is still there. And we'll be looking on the way for two girls in cloaks, looking like a parson's daughters."

"Two?" inquired Hoskins.

"My betrothed and her maid, being remarkably clever, because a lady and her maid travelling without male escort might be remarked upon, whereas two sisters in genteel poverty would not," said Edward. "Most people like as not would either take them as visitors to London for the time of their lives, or travelling to take up positions as governesses or some such." Edward reflected that but for Aunt Letty, being a governess might yet have been Beth's lot in life; and shuddered. He knew well enough what sort of a dance his cousins led their various governesses.

"Well, if they've gone on, will anyone remember them, sir?" asked Hoskins. "If they're being unremarkable, with coaches coming and going all day and night, will two ordinary looking young ladies be noticed?"

"Damn," said Edward. "I think Beth is beautiful, but she ain't a classic beauty by any means. And Molly is just a child ... well, we can ask, and maybe someone will have seen them."

"Have they got money enough to take a stage?"

asked Hoskins.

Edward looked horrified for a moment, and then relaxed.

"Beth won't have let go of her reticule," he said. "And she will have had money in that for vails at the ball. It ain't going to be more than ten shillings from Slough to London, so a quid will cover the pair of them. And I know she takes a couple of guineas against need, she threw one to the footman to bring me message.... It won't have been more than a shilling or two for a room for the night and a meal," he added. "And if I was her, I'd leave Finchbury to pay the shot anyway, except I ain't her, and Beth ain't one to leave debts behind her. They'd have enough to go on the roof at least," he added, "Which ain't ideal, but Beth's determined enough, getting home would be the main thing. And she might very well have more with her," he added.

"No accounting for what women have in their ridicules," said Hoskins, with a spit.

"No indeed," said Edward.

The frost had largely thawed by the time Edward and Hoskins travelled the road that had been so sharp with frost some hours earlier; and the Queen Anne's lace did not draw Edward's attention as it had done Beth's, being now nothing but sad and damp vegetation. Its foetid smell as it dried in the watery sun made Edward's nose wrinkle; he would have found it hard to believe that Beth had found it a thing of beauty!

It took much less time for the curricle to reach Slough than it had for the girls on foot. Hopkins tooled the team into the inn yard, and Edward leaped down to leave him to sort out the cooling of the team and hiring fresh horses for the homeward journey, as he strode towards the inn.

There appeared to be some kind of altercation going on inside, including raised female voices which were not shrieking and sounded well bred.

Edward groaned.
One of the voices was, he was certain, Beth's.

Chapter 28

"This is boring, Miss Beth," said Molly. "And I longs to get out cleaning things and clean up in here a bit; look at all that mud on the floor, and smears on the furniture!"

"Well, the servants can hardly hope to keep it pristine when there are people in and out all the time, tracking in mud," said Beth. "I know it's a bit quieter now, but I don't blame them for taking a brief rest. And to be honest, I'd rather be bored than have the excitement of fighting off the attention of any young gentlemen or other would-be gallants."

"You have a point, Miss Beth," said Molly. "About being bored, I mean. But it's not showing proper pride in the place to leave mud on the floor when there's a couple of hours between coaches."

"We don't know what else might be needed elsewhere," said Beth. "They may be cleaning the chambers in anticipation of people staying overnight, and you don't know what state they were left in. I doubt there was anyone bleeding over it, as poor Lord Finchbury did, but mayhap there was vomit and overflowing Jordans, as I recall having to clean up once for a gentleman who was staying overnight with poor Papa, and one could not ask the servants to deal with so much mess. He was very drunk when he arrived and carried on drinking. Papa never invited him again, you may be sure!"

"What had he come for?"

"To buy horses; Papa was retrenching, even then. But he would not sell a horse to a man like that. He was horrible," she shuddered. "I was about your age, Molly; and Papa sent me to bed early and I was glad to go. He made me feel dirty and I did not understand one half of the comments he made."

"Prob'ly just as well," said Molly. "Well, I should

think they might have such problems in an inn, but it's the downstairs that people see first."

And from this position she would not be moved, and Beth had to agree that she had a point.

They sat huddled over the tiny fire, for it was still bitterly cold, and Beth leaped up and jumped back as there was a fall of soot.

"Oh that is too much!" said Molly. "This inn is not well kept-up!"

"An insalubrious inn," murmured Beth, enjoying the play on words.

There was a sudden influx of people from, presumably, a coach that either went no further, or from which it was possible to catch another coach heading elsewhere. A stout woman with an umbrella eased herself down at the table, while a prosperous-looking but bucolic fellow with gaiters took up a place before the fire, and stood with his feet apart, blocking its heat from everyone else. The other two men gave him a flat, unfriendly stare. They looked like clerks to Beth, neatly and conservatively clad, with shiny cuffs to their right hand sleeves.

A few other people started drifting in, and Beth was beginning to wonder if she should cede the fireside seat to one of them, for what good it would do, with the yeoman farmer of bailiff or whatever he might be, in the way.

Molly gave a sudden cry as a further fall of soot cascaded down the chimney, billowing up in a plume of dust as it choked the fire.

"The devil!" cried the yeoman, leaping away.

"Merely soot, and pray do not use such language in front of ladies," said Beth.

He gave her a look that he plainly thought was sneering contempt, and made him look constipated.

However, he did at least move away to the window, muttering to himself, and banging at the behind of his breeches to remove the soot.

"Looks like he's farting soot," giggled Molly.

"Hush!" said Beth. "Dear me, I think we may wish to move, too."

As she spoke, there was another roil of dusty soot from the fireplace, a muffled scream, and a chimney brick, sending up more clouds of the soot in which it landed. It was swiftly followed by a very dirty child, who was yelling in pain and terror.

Beth, her handkerchief pressed to her mouth to try to stop herself coughing, sprang forward, and plucked the child quickly away from the fire, such as was still visible.

"Are you burned?" she asked the choking child.

"Only me feet," said the child, coughing again and rubbing a dirty hand over its running nose. "Old Jonesey, he lit a fire under me to make me climb, dirty owd mundungus!"

"Oh you poor child!" said Beth, lifting the child onto her lap, regardless of Molly's exclamation of horror. "Molly, be silent; muslin launders well enough. He needs a cuddle more than I need my gown to stay clean."

"He needs a bath," said Molly. "I suppose we're keeping him?"

"I'm a her," said the child. As she was wearing nothing but a ragged breech clout it was hard to tell.

"Surely that must be illegal!" gasped Beth. "Are you hungry?"

"Oh yes! I'm right gutfoundered!" said the child.

"Molly, see about some food for her," said Beth. "What's your name?" she asked.

The child, who must have been no more than six years old, considered.

"It ain't '*you darty kinchin*'," she said. "I... I fink it wus Kate."

"You poor little girl," said Beth, holding Kate closer. The child burst into tears and clung to her.

Beth tried not to shudder as the snotty, sooty nose

was wiped on her bosom. Molly returned with bread and cheese, and Kate stared in delight.

"All for me?" she whispered. "All for you," said Molly. "And mind you try to eat slow, or it'll come up again if you are empty." Kate looked at her; and nodded. She tore into the bread with eager teeth.

"Chew it well and slowly, as Molly said," said Beth. Kate tried, but was plainly ravenous.

The landlord was busy hustling over.

"Oh Miss, I am sorry this dirty little brat has troubled you, I will remove it immediately," he said, reaching out for Kate, who cowered, hiding her food behind her back.

"You will *not*," said Beth, "This child is hurt, hungry and distressed, and the sweep who has put a little girl into the chimney with a fire below her is an evil fellow."

Those waiting in the parlour ranged themselves on two sides at this juncture. There were several compassionate murmurs of 'that's quite correct' and 'aye, as miss says' on the one hand, and the spit into the now soot-smothered fire from the individual of the sooty behind, who said,

"'Tain't a her, it's an it, these animals of whore's brats need to work to work off the shame of their condition."

Beth fixed him with a steely gaze.

"And even if there was a mite of Christian charity in those cruel words, what makes you think she's a whore's child?" she demanded.

The stout yeoman farmer shrugged.

"Must be. Them sweeps get the brats from foundling asylums. And why would they be in foundling asylums if there mothers' weren't whores?" he rocked back and forth from heels to toes, thumbs hooked in his waistcoat, and a smile on his face that plainly said this was a clinching argument.

"Nonsense, my good man," said Beth. "What an ignorant attitude! Some may well be the children of fallen women, but others might well be orphans who have no family to care for them; the children perhaps of heroes, of sailors or soldiers, who have been away at the wars and the unfortunate mother of the family dead from disease, or the baby born while her man was away. Or the children of good girls ravished foully by those of a social position that makes it hard for them to find recourse in law, as happens too often!"

Those who had wavered from Beth's side came back to it.

"Ar, my neighbour's girl went into service, with a Judge an' all, and was done over by one o' his sons, and her turned out on her ear!" said the stout woman. "'Anged 'erself she did, pore thing!"

"At least she had the proper feeling to hide her shame in killing herself and her bastard brat," said the Yeoman farmer.

The stout lady lost her temper at this point and hit him over the head with her umbrella.

"Bravo, madam!" said Beth.

Before an affray could develop, the sweep himself marched into the room and strode up to Beth.

"Gimme. the brat," he said.

Beth drew back, and half turned, shielding Kate from him. He stank of stale tobacco of a most unpleasant kind as well as of soot and sweat, and his own appearance was almost as begrimed as that of Kate.

"No," Beth said. "You have hurt this little girl, and it is not right. As well as keeping her half-starved. Why don't you use Mr. Glass's patent sweeping machine? It is morally indefensible to put children up chimneys, even if you have not burned her feet by lighting a fire under her."

"Well, 'ow else am I s'posed ter git the brat t'go

233

up?" said the sweep, one assumed a Mr. Jones if Kate called him 'Jonesey'. "It ain't no good stickin' pins in their feet, the little bastards get sick an' die on yer. Likes yer has ter feed 'em just enough to keep goin' but not enough to get fat."

"So you admit to causing the deaths of other children? And pray let me not have any more of the immodest words you and certain others think suitable to use before ladies," said Beth.

"I di'n't cause no deaths," said the sweep. "It were their own fault for not shiftin' quick enough. If you doesn't 'and the brat back, I'll 'ave the law on you for stealing; I paid good money t' git the indenture of a good skinny one."

"Then I will buy her," said Beth. "I will give you a note of hand, and will redeem it when I am back in London, where I might reach my funds."

Jonesey laughed. It was a wheezing, grating laugh.

"Oh hoity-toity!" he said. "Do you really think I'd be taken in by that, my fine dimber brimstone!"

"I haven't the least idea what you called me, but since you did not care to couch it in the King's English I can only assume that it is something that you should be ashamed of saying in the presence of any female, let alone a lady or a child," said Beth. "You scoundrel! How dare you imply that I should abscond without paying you off? A lady's word is her bond!"

"Hah! If you think I believe a doxy like you is a lady..." began the sweep.

"Don't you mind him, dearie," said the stout woman. "You bennish clunch! Can't you tell from the way she do speak as how she's a lady? And you didn't ought to talk like that afore honest women like me, neither."

"I say we call for the magistrate," growled the yeoman farmer. "These yere viragos oughta be whipped at the cart's arse, I say."

"I do pray you, to moderate the coarseness of your

tone," said Beth. "As for whipping behind a cart, my good fellow, it is not generally employed for women of good character such as the goodwife here and myself. You are sadly out of line, I fear."

"I got the watch in," said the landlord, triumphantly, reappearing in the doorway. "I don't want no trouble, miss, and you're causing it by trying to keep the brat. Ain't a peck o' use bein' compassionate about brats like this, they'll only turn round and steal from you. Now be a good lady, and give her back to her master; you done your Christian duty by feeding the wretch."

"Ar, and thanks for that, she won't need no more until termorrer," said Jonesey.

Beth stood, and drew herself up as well as she was able with Kate in her arms, clinging like a limpet.

"I would never forgive myself if I gave up this poor little girl to that monster!" she declared. "He has starved her, and admits it; lights fires under her; and probably beats her. He has admitted that other children indentured to him have died because of sticking needles in their feet, the wounds becoming infected, as well might any wound with soot in it! He is not a fit person to have control of another human being."

"But she ain't a huming bein' she's just a foundling brat!" whined Jonesey.

The constable of the watch cleared his throat.

"I'm sorry, miss, but the law's the law, and he's paid fair and square to have the child indentured to him," he said. "And he's his apprentice and that's that."

"She's a girl, not a boy," said Beth, firmly and loudly. "And have you seen his papers of indenture?"

The constable wriggled his shoulders uncomfortably.

"Well, no, but why should he lie?" he said, miserably.

"Why should he lie? Well if he picked her up off

235

the street, he might lie to avoid a charge of kidnapping," said Beth. "And he accused me of lying about giving him the price of her, once I was back in London, and in my experience, people who accuse others of lying are generally liars themselves. I've seen it in several maidservants," she added.

The constable looked even more uncomfortable; the lady might be better connected than he had thought.

"Well, I'm sure you don't want to take it before a magistrate...." He tried.

"I will happily take it before a magistrate," said Beth, "and doubtless when he questions Kate he will discover all manner of abuses that are forbidden in indentured service."

"You hatchet-faced dell! I don't have to take this from Mistress Princum-Prancium here!" yelled Jonesey, and fell into a fit of coughing, as he disturbed the soot again with his shout.

"Constable, if that is cant, don't you think he knows too much for an honest man?" said Molly.

"Well he do know plenty," agreed the constable, "but he still do have the right."

"If he can produce the paper of indenture I will take it to the magistrate, otherwise I will not pay him a penny, for he is a lewd fellow and I am most displeased," said Beth.

"You'll be hied off to gaol!" howled Jonesey. "You hear her, constable, plain as a pikestaff, declaring she plans to withhold my property!"

"And I understood that we had had a law of abolition, so that you cannot own a slave," said Beth, angrily.

"Sorry, miss," said one of the clerks, "But it only means you cannot trade in slaves; those slaves already enslaved or those born to it are still slaves out in the West Indies, and indentured servitude for a foundling is the same as an apprentice, and legally binding."

"But can be bought out," said Beth.

"But can be bought out," said the clerk.

"I ain't going to sell the brat, she's mine, and if you knew what's good for you, you xanthippy you, you'd step right away. Or you don't know who might come down your chimbley, do you?" he leered.

"I believe that's threatening behaviour," said Beth.

"Mr. Jones, that is," said the constable.

"Here, whose side are you on?" demanded Jonesesy.

"The law," said the constable.

"I will not let this horrible man hurt this little girl," said Beth. "Surely morality sits above the law?"

"Not in front of the bench, it don't," said the constable with feeling. "Miss, I ain't got no choice but to put you under arrest, until I can get this heard by the Magistrate, and he ain't here today."

"Oh how ridiculous!" cried Molly. "How can you take that awful stinky man's side when he is plainly mistreating the child?"

"Now, Miss, you and your... sister is it? ... didn't ought to take that attitude," said the constable. "It's the law it is, and that's how it has to be."

"The law, sir, is in that case quite unfair," said Beth. "Did not our Good Lord say 'suffer the little children to come unto me'? And isn't His law superior to any laws of mankind? How would He feel about this child's sufferings? Can you kneel in church tomorrow or on any other Sunday and pray with a clear conscience if you permit her to be delivered up to pain and probable early death from blood poisoning or suffocating?"

The constable shifted uneasily.

"Don't listen to the jade!" howled Jonesey.

At that moment, the inn door crashed open, and Edward stalked in.

"Oh *EDWARD*!" cried Beth, running to him, casting herself and Kate into his arms.

Chapter 29

Edward found himself with a rather unexpected armful of lovely Beth and most unlovely dirty and smelly child. Still, if Beth could hold the child so tenderly, he could hold both of them equally tenderly, and he paused to absently ruffle the wary child's filthy locks before enfolding both in his arms. Kate relaxed somewhat.

"Very well, perhaps someone can manage to explain what all this is about?" said Edward, looking down his nose at the assembled company.

Quality was plainly Quality, and if Edward did not ape the top sawyers in his garb, his heavy coat was of excellent cut and quality, and sported a sufficiency of capes to impress most people who had never met a Corinthian. As the rest of his figure also spoke of a man used to the best, and wearing it comfortably, and unconcerned about the possibility of having to replace any clothes soiled by a climbing girl, there was a subtle shift in the atmosphere to grant deference to the newcomer.

"Mr. Brandon, my *sister* Beth wished to purchase the indenture of little Kate because of the way Jones has ill-treated her," said Molly.

Edward nodded to her.

"I knew I could rely on a straight story from you, my dear," he said. "It's good to know my sister-to-be can keep her head. And my bride, of course," he said, kissing Beth on the forehead.

"Oh Edward, I am sorry to throw myself into your arms like some missish female," said Beth, drawing away.

"I ain't. I was quite enjoying it," said Edward. He winked at Kate. "We had a chaperone," he added.

Kate managed a watery smile.

"Oh Edward, what a most excellent father you are

going to be!" approved Beth.

"And what a fine mother you will make!" said Edward.

"You'll excuse me, sir, and all the billing and cooing is all very well, but can we get this business sorted out, please?" said the constable.

"Certainly," said Edward. "I am Edward Brandon, nephew to the Baron of Darsham, and in my own neighbourhood I'm a Justice of the Peace, so I believe I am qualified to take charge of the proceedings here."

"Take charge o' protectin' your doxy you mean," said Jones.

Edward stepped forward and punched him, hard, in the sternum. Jones doubled up.

"I won't lay you out as I need your testimony, but you cannot call a gentleman's betrothed wife a doxy and expect to get away with it," said Edward, calmly. "I might instead have had you imprisoned for slander, but I really can't be bothered. Miss Renfield is my cousin, several times removed each way, and whilst I might wish you removed a lot further in any direction, I fear I will have to put up with your presence a bit longer, you disgusting article."

"I paid four guineas for the brat," said Jones, when he had finished wheezing and coughing.

"Oh? And she's a parish pauper?" said Edward.

"Yes," said Jones, looking shifty.

"Jones, indentures for parish paupers cost nothing to their master save the cost of caring for the said child, if I recall the wording correctly, which I do for having signed enough of them, requires that you, er, *'shall and will during all the Term aforesaid, find, provide, and allow, unto the said Apprentice, meet, competent, and sufficient Meat, Drink, and Apparel, Lodging, Washing, and all other Things, necessary and fit for an Apprentice.'*. Now, as this apprentice is half starved, has no apparel to speak of, is certainly unwashed and looks more like a feral dog in Fleet Street than a child,

I rather fancy that you have fallen down in your duties. It's a ten pound fine, I believe."

"You can't make me pay!" blustered Jones. "I did pay for her, I did, it weren't the parish, it were, er, a private foundling asylum!"

"You would still be required to sign similar indenture papers," said Edward, "Which are countersigned by the local Justice. Where is this private asylum then?"

Jones' eyes looked this way and that, and he wheezed harder.

"I di'n't ask when she were offered to me," he said, sullenly.

"Ah, now we are getting somewhere," said Edward, pleasantly. "Kate, if you please, would you tell me whence you came? Where you were before Mundungus Jones took you?" he clarified.

"At 'ome," said Kate.

"I see," said Edward. "Home being with your parents?"

"Yerse," said Kate.

"And who took you to Jones?"

"Me da," said Kate.

"Your father sold you to this creature?" Edward tried to keep the incredulity from his voice.

"Yerse," said Kate.

"Have you any idea why your father would sell you?" asked Edward.

"To buy booze," said Kate. "Girls don't count."

"You poor child," said Edward. Beth was holding Kate tighter.

"Me ma useder give cuddles like that," said Kate, snuggling.

"Poor woman, she must be so worried," said Beth.

"I'll have someone find her, and reassure her," said Edward.

"Oh Edward, you are so wise and clever and able," said Beth.

"Lawks, they'll be off again if someone don't stop 'em," said the stout lady, beaming upon the couple beneficently.

The constable cleared his throat.

"Are you saying, sir, that any transaction entered into with regards to this child was illegal?" he demanded.

"Highly," said Edward. "And even if it had been legal, he has failed to comply with the terms of normal indenture. He probably ought to be thrown in gaol and made to suffer the full rigours of the law."

Jones howled in real anguish and sought to sidestep Edward to escape the inn. Edward neatly tripped him up.

"I di'n't know it was illegal!" howled Jones.

"For which reason, I am inclined to not prosecute you, and even to let you go on your smelly way," said Edward. "I am even inclined to reimburse you the money, on one condition."

"Wassat?" asked Jones, picking himself up, his eyes sparkling with venality.

"That you purchase one of the chimney cleaning machines and do not make any further use of children or even of geese with their legs tied," said Edward. "And I will be checking up on you, Jones; your ill-spelled advertisement is in the paper and it gives your direction."

"GAWD!" cried Jones, "The queer-cuffin's bleedin' omniscient!"

Edward permitted himself a small smile. It had been a fortuitous guess.

"Edward," said Beth, "I do pray that you might enlighten me on some of the cant; for both you and Kate have used the same word to refer to Jones, and I would like to know what the horrid little man just called you, if it may be translated with sufficient roundaboutation for a lady's ears."

"Oh that one ain't a problem," said Edward. "A

queer-cuffin is a magistrate. And mundungus is someone who stinks of rank tobacco. And I prefer not to translate what he called you, or it would make me want to hit him again."

"He called me other things as well that I didn't understand," said Beth.

Edward turned grimly towards Jones, who yelled in real terror.

"I di'n't know she was Quality, I apologises!"

"Good," said Edward. "Now there was the matter of the monies I promised you to go and get a sweeping machine...." money changed hands, and the sweep rapidly started to sidle towards the door.

"No you don't," said the innkeeper. "Them chimbleys ain't swep' yet, Jonesey, you'll just have to finish them by rod, and I ain't paying you more'n half what I normally do, account o' the trouble."

Jones gave him a poisonous look.

"Sweep yer own bleedin' chimbleys then," he said, with a spit, and was gone.

"What a singularly unsatisfactory character," said Beth.

"I believe that may be the understatement of the year," said Edward. "Here, Ale-draper, mulled ale all round on me, and then you can direct me to where I can hire a carriage. Might squeeze two slender ladies into a curricle, but not a kid, who'd freeze to death anywise. Madam, is your coach due?" he asked the stout lady.

"Not for an hour, sir," said she.

"Well perhaps you'll go find some apparel or at least a shawl or two to wrap the mite in, and any change, please keep with my thanks," Edward passed over more
money. The stout lady gasped, and left with alacrity.

"She ought to have a bath," said Beth.

"No she oughtn't," said Edward. "Travelling with wet hair? Not the thing at all. Might kill her. Hot bath back in Red Lion Square at Aunt Letty's place. Hot meal too and a warmed bed."

"How wise you are, Edward!" said Beth. Poor Kate was virtually asleep in her arms, warmer and more comfortable than she had been for a long time.

Mulled ale was served all round, and Edward spoke to the landlord about what was available for hire, and presently Beth, Molly and Kate were installed in a coach, Kate wrapped in a voluminous shawl.

"Which ain't nowise proper clothing, sir, but clothing for a child at short notice isn't easy," the stout woman had apologised.

"So long as she gets home without freezing, it's just the thing," said Edward, who knew she could have spent less and kept more. He instructed Hoskins to drive the curricle back to its rightful owner, return the horses to a staging post, and meet him at his own house, where his footmen were used to entertaining sundry soldiers and would let Hoskins in and provide him with a heavy wet and something to eat.

Letty came running out of the house in Red Lion Square and hugged Beth, before holding her away and exclaiming at her grime. She hugged Molly too, and looked in some horror on Kate, thankfully sleeping.

"I'll tell you all about it when I have had a bath, Aunt Letty," said Beth, "for oh! I do ache, and I feel as if I'd been up and down a chimney myself like little Kate here."

Letty nodded.

"I'll make up a truckle bed in your room with old sheets and the child can sleep in her grime and bathe when she's rested," she said. "Dear me, what do you plan for the poor child? She's been wrenched from her position in life to have the caresses of people much above her, like those poor little black page boys who were pampered until they grew up, and then often went from pampered pets to unwanted and homeless. Not that you would discard her so cruelly, my dear, but you have to consider her future and how you plan to deal with her upbringing."

"She's our first foundling," said Beth, "Though she has parents, but her father sold her, can you believe it? She's very young, I thought I might rear her as our ward, without any real expectations but with enough education to be a governess, perhaps in our own school when we have one."

Letty nodded.

"That would be quite suitable," she said. "I will hear it all presently!"

Bathed and attired in her own clothes, Beth felt able to explain all her adventures, nodding to Molly to tell her part. Letty exclaimed in horror at the idea of Beth riding on the back of the coach, and praised Molly for her pretence.

"And so it turned out that Lord Finchbury is not such an ogre as we feared," finished Beth, "and he was quite civil to us. I hope he will recover well enough, for I cannot bear him any malice."

"I'm not so sure I can feel so charitable," said Letty. "However, you are safe, and you and Molly were together at all times, and Molly a clever, resourceful girl. You are not, I think, compromised."

"I'm going to marry her anywise," said Edward, "if you'll only permit me to propose properly."

"You already did propose," said Beth.

"Only in anger, and not because I loved you then," said Edward.

Letty shooed Molly out of the room, and Edward sank to one knee.

"Beth, I adore you. Will you marry me?" he said.

"With all my heart, but only if you get up right now," said Beth.

Edward rose and swept her into his arms.

"No Kate in the way this time," he said, and kissed

her firmly. Beth clung to him, and knew that he really did love her, and that she loved him, and that the getting of children would prove to be a joyful matter, with the feelings he aroused in her.

"Oh Edward! I do love you!" said Beth. "Let us get married as soon as we decently might, and move to Suffolk, and begin babies!"

"What a nice idea!" said Edward, and kissed her again.

finis

Historical notes

This novel is set in a very specific time period, being at the end of March through beginning of April in 1814. This period saw the defeat of Bonaparte at the Battle for Paris, and his surrender, to be confined on the Island of Elba. There was much rejoicing since the country had been at war with France for more than two decades. It was a calm before the final storm, of course, but nobody knew that. It led to much celebration, and too to a huge number of unwanted soldiery, some horribly injured, and many of them begging. That many of the able-bodied subsequently went off to fight in South America, leaving Wellington with his 'scum of the earth enlisted for drink', should have been a lesson to the British government to treat its soldiery better, but it's a lesson I've yet to see to be learned.

Criminal Conversation

Heyer mentions people gossiping about the latest 'Crim. Cons'; so what actually *is* a Crim. Con?

It is short for 'criminal conversation' which was a euphemism for adultery.

A brief foray into the rights of divorce is needed here; Men had it all their way, and women had very few rights at all. A marriage could be annulled not, as is generally believed, for non-consummation, but only for an inability to perform at all; for insanity; for adultery [if it was the woman being adulterous] or for inappropriate relationships, ie incest. A woman had to show not only adultery on the part of her husband, but also extraordinary cruelty or some inappropriate behaviour. The former was unlikely as a man was permitted to beat his wife, children and servants and considered a good man to chastise as required. The only successful divorces brought by women involved incest – ie, that the adultery occurred with the wife's sister.

Right, now the convolutions of divorce.

A couple could separate moderately amicably, and a divorce in the eyes of the church applied for. This was a divorce, but had a slight problem. Neither could marry again. For a full divorce, an Act of Parliament had to be passed on each case. And this could not occur until just cause had been proven; which meant a civil case of Criminal Conversation where the woman was caught *in flagrante delicto* or there were enough witnesses to show criminal conversation. As a married woman was not a person in law, the person prosecuted was her lover. Damages could be set as seemed appropriate, and the cases avidly reported in the press. Not all of them were high society, but the majority were of the gentry, since few other people could afford to tangle with the law.

Once the Crim. Con. case was proven, then it went to parliament, where the old coals might be raked over yet again. And it was expensive; as much as £5,000, which was a lot of money, bearing in mind that a clerk earned £80 a year, and the extremely wealthy Mr Darcy had £10,000 a year, and at the other end of the gentry, a few hundred a year might be as much as could be hoped for. Even for Mr Darcy, half a year's income was significant. It is hard to precisely equate money of the time to money of today, but sticking a couple of noughts on is a quick and dirty approximation, so we are talking about something in the region of half a million quid in today's terms. The excessive cost was doubtless mostly the cost of greasing palms to make sure it went through quickly and quietly, but it would not cost less than £1,000.

It was a horrible scandal to have associated with the family, which made it highly entertaining for the gossipmongers and bored society ladies to discuss. This is a society in which some people would go to any lengths to cover up any adultery, as the Duke of Devonshire did, when Georgiana, Duchess of Devonshire, found herself pregnant by her lover. She had to go abroad for a year to have the baby [which was adopted by her lover's family] and give up all contact with the little girl on pain of having contact with her other children removed.

Which was another thing a husband could quite legally do.

Women did not get a fair deal!

Illuminations in Celebration

I have seen several bloggers and writers who have made the assumption that 'illuminations' referred to fireworks, but this is not actually the case. The earliest reference to illuminations and fireworks that I could find was in 1717, in a letter from Fox, reported in the newspaper, viz:

Yesterday being the Prince's Birth-Day, the Arch-Bishop of Canterbury, the Lord Chancellor, the Nobility and Gentry, with the Foreign Ambassadors in town, went to St James's, to congratulate his Royal Highness; and in the Cities of Westminster and London, there was Bon-fires, Fireworks and Illuminations in an extraordinary manner in the Evening.

So what were Illuminations? As far as I can ascertain, it became custom some time probably in the late seventeenth century to celebrate nationally important events – and presumably local ones, in each town – by displaying a candle or lantern in as many windows of a house as might be afforded by the householder, showing it all lit up as a sign of approval. As time went on, and probably in the same spirit in which one today might trace the competition in a suburban street by the increase in the level of decoration of lace curtains as one walks down the street, illuminations became in many cases more than just candles or lanterns in windows. Houses 'festooned' must have had whole rows of lamps strung up outside, coloured glass doing its bit to add to the display, and by 1814 'transparencies' are described, which appear to have been painted glass with wording or pictures thus painted, and lit from behind. The Gas Company surpassed all other illuminations with their display, though it is worth noting that even gas lighting left pools of darkness, and the uncertain lighting in the shadows left by the illuminations give a sinister setting to any story… and it was not uncommon for riots to break out if anyone was felt not to have sufficiently illuminated their houses! Or, for that matter, if a mob disapproved of the reasons for an illumination…

Chimney Cleaning

Although a patent chimney cleaning machine was invented by Joseph Glass, most sweeps preferred to use geese thrown down the chimney with their legs tied, or climbing boys sent up. These boys were indentured servants, essentially slaves, as were some of the factory workers, bound to apprenticeship by parish foundling authorities. They were at risk of sticking in small flues and dying of thirst and hunger, dying of soot inhalation, being suffocated more suddenly by soot falls, and as it was not uncommon for sweeps to drive pins into their bare feet or light fires under them, the chance of sepsis from wounds must have figured in some deaths. Add to this Chimney-sweep's Canker, or cancer of the testicles, and this was one of the more miserable lives to be led. Campaigns to prevent the use of climbing boys were under way, including the publication *The Chimney Sweep's Friend and Climbing Boys Album*, edited by the radical writer and poet James Montgomery, which included stories and pictures to raise awareness. It took until 1840 to ban the practice, and even them was more seen in the breach than the observance.

Sarah's other books
Sarah writes predominantly Regency Romances:

The Brandon Scandals Series
- The Hasty Proposal
- The Reprobate's Redemption
- The Advertised Bride
- The Wandering Widow
- The Braithwaite Letters
- Heiress in Hiding

Wild Western Brandon Scandals
- Colonel Brandon's Quest

The Charity School Series
- Elinor's Endowment
- Ophelia's Opportunity
- Abigail's Adventure
- Marianne's Misanthrope
- Emma's Education/Grace's Gift
- Anne's Achievement
- Daisy's Destiny
- Libby's Luck
- Julia's Journey
- Penelope's Pups

Spinoffs:
The Moorwick Tales
- Fantasia on a House Party

Rookwood series
- The Unwilling Viscount
- The Enterprising Emigrée

The Wynddell Papers
- Lord Wynddell's Bride

The Seven Stepsisters series
Elizabeth
Diana
Minerva[WIP]
Flora [WIP]
Catherine [WIP]
Jane [WIP]
Anne [WIP]

One off Regencies
Vanities and Vexations [Jane Austen sequel]
Cousin Prudence [Jane Austen sequel]
Friends and Fortunes
None so Blind
Belles and Bucks [short stories]

The Georgian Gambles series
The Valiant Viscount [formerly The Pugilist Peer]
Ace of Schemes

Other
William Price and the 'Thrush', naval adventure and Jane Austen tribute
William Price sails North
William Price on land
William Price and the 'Thetis' [wip]

Sarah also writes historical mysteries

Regency period 'Jane, Bow Street Consultant 'series, a Jane Austen tribute
Death of a Fop
Jane and the Bow Street Runner [3 novellas]
Jane and the Opera Dancer
Jane and the Christmas Masquerades [2 novellas]

Jane and the Hidden Hoard
Jane and the Burning Question [short stories]
Jane and the Sins of Society
Jane and the Actresses
Jane and the Careless Corpse

Spinoffs:
The Armitage Chronicles

'Felicia and Robin' series set in the Renaissance

Poison for a Poison Tongue
    The Mary Rose Mystery
    Died True Blue
    Frauds, Fools and Fairies
    The Bishop of Brangling
    The Hazard Chase
    Heretics, Hatreds and Histories
    The Midsummer Mysteries
    The Colour of Murder
    Falsehood most Foul
    The Monkshithe Mysteries
    Toll the Dead Man's bells
    Wells, Wool and Wickedness
    The Missing Hostage
    The Convenient Saint and Other stories
    Sell-sword Summer
    Buried in the past
    The Crail Caper
    Sugar and Spice and all things nasty [coming soon]

Children's stories
Tabitha Tabs the Farm kitten
A School for Ordinary Princesses [sequel to Frances Hodgson Burnett's 'A Little Princess.]

The Royal Draxiers series
    Bess and the Dragons
    Bess and the Queen
    Bess and the Succession
    Bess and the Paying Scholars
    Bess and the Flying Armada [coming soon]
Bess and the Necromancer [wip]

Non-Fiction
    Writing Regency Romances by dice
    The Regency Miss's Survival Guide to Bath
    Names in Europe from the Etruscans to 1600
    The [wannabe] Regency Miss's Survival guide to Real Life
100 years of Cat Days: 365 anecdotes

Fantasy
    Falconburg Divided [book 1 of the Falconburg brothers series]
    Falconburg Rising [book 2 of the Falconburg brothers series]
    Falconburg Ascendant [book 3 of the Falconburg brothers series, WIP]

Scarlet Pimpernel spinoffs
    The Redemption of Chauvelin
    Chauvelin and the League
    Chauvelin and the Lost Children

Other Baroness Orczy spinoffs
    Lady Molly – Married

The Winged Hussar Books

The Last Winged Hussar
Under the Banner of the Raven
Wings of Valour

The Last Winged Hussar, Dance subseries
Dance of Sabres
Dance of Falcons
Dance of Ravens
Dance of Justice
Dance of Law
Dance of Fire
Dance of Conviction
Dance of Nestlings
Dance of Locution [coming soon]
Dance of Redemption [WIP]

Winged Hussar Generations

Secrets of the Raven Banner
Fugue in Prussia for the Ravens

The Sienkiewicz spinoffs, Bohun Redeemed.

Falcon without Bells
The Bells of Jasna Góra and other stories
Ring out the False
Ring in the True

Sienkiewicz Spinoffs, Alternate History

Ironfist and the Falcon [coming soon]

Printed in Great Britain
by Amazon